MESSAGES

For information address Amlin Publishing, 105 Fruit Street, Bangor, ME 04401

Printed in the United States of America through Lightning Source.

Amlin Publishing Paperback edition / July 2011
Amlin Publishing Paperbacks are published by Amlin Publishing Inc. through Lightning Source, a subsidiary of Ingram Industries Inc.

This is a work of fiction.
Seriously. Don't do anything silly.

41223

A silver car streaked down a damp Boston street at five to four in the afternoon. David Chance was painfully aware that he had *maybe* five minutes to get out of the city before hitting rush hour traffic. He had made a promise, and he intended to keep it.

It was raining, but only enough to be annoying. The squeak of the windshield wiper blades normally would have driven him nuts, but today was a particularly good day. Today was the anniversary of the day he had met his wife, Sharon, the love of his life, and mother of his two children. He could picture her now, standing in front of their bedroom mirror wearing the sexy dress she'd promised to pick up, admiring the body she had worked so hard to get back into shape. She was a beautiful woman, inside and out, much nicer than David had expected to win, and he did *not* want to disappoint her.

The light ahead turned amber, and David reluctantly pressed the brake pedal, his eyes darting from the digital readout on the car stereo to the rearview mirror at the line of traffic already beginning to form. A familiar but muffled rendition of *Music Music Music* began to chime. David patted his suit jacket, reached inside, and fished out his cellphone.

Beep. "Hello?"

"Did you make the reservations?" It was Sharon.

"Of course," he replied. "Le Bocage."

"Not bad."

He could detect the smile in her voice. Le Bocage was a nice restaurant, and fairly expensive for an intern. David's recent graduation from the New England School of Communication had helped him get a position with the Channel Seven News Team, but moving back to the Boston area and starting from scratch was proving to be more of a challenge than he had expected.

The light turned green and the little Neon accelerated. "Did everything go well at the mall?" he asked.

"Oh, I think you'll be pleased."

"Oh?"

"Oh yes. I *know* you'll be pleased."

David smiled. "I'm sure I will."

The car sped under an overpass and the phone made a digital gurgle.

"Hey," Sharon said, "by the way, Alex called."

"Yeah?"

"I told him we were going out and asked if you could call him back later tonight, but he said it wasn't important."

"I'm supposed to pick him up at the airport tomorrow. He probably just wanted to remind me."

"Probably."

"I haven't seen him for a month. It'll be good to see him again."

There was a noticeable silence on the other end.

"Sharon?"

"Please promise me you'll keep the late nighters to a minimum. That man's a bad influence on you."

"I know, but that's happening less and less, 'cause we're so busy, and you know-- gettin' old."

"I *just* don't understand why he doesn't get married and settle down. He's always saying he *wants* to-- and he certainly doesn't have any trouble attracting women."

"That's an understatement."

"Yeah. Well, just remember, I married you because I like having you around."

"And I like *being* around. Don't worry. I'll keep it under control."

"Alright. --Are you on schedule?"

"So far."

"Kay, then I'll see you when you get here."

"And I'll see *you* when I get there."

She chuckled. "I love you too, David. --Bye."

He pressed the phone with his thumb, tossed it in the passenger seat, and peered up at the sky through the front window. It didn't look like the rain was going to let up any time soon.

The little car cruised on past strip malls, urban housing, gas stations, construction sites... and his mind drifted. *Should I have told her about this afternoon?* He wasn't even sure if it had really happened. How could he expect her to believe it?

It was a little after 1:30, and it was David's odious job to meet with the lead producer and the on-line editor to work on a story for the 6:00 news block. David's role was minor: write down the time-code marks as dictated by the producer and log what he saw on the screen. It didn't require a whole lot of concentration, so usually he found himself fending off waves of drowsiness. His creative mind was well suited for accomplishing large abstract tasks, but less than adequate at mundane repetition.

The editor cued the tape. The television monitor flickered and rolled, and let off its familiar audio squeal. David logged the starting time-code as the producer began the pre-edit strategy, then he leaned back in his chair, awaiting instructions. He stared at the screen, then heaved a sigh and looked around. *This is SO mind numbingly boring! Maybe I can find something to read.* He scanned the room and a notion struck him. His eyes drifted from a coffee mug which read, "Number *One* Producer" to a sign on the wall, "Be All You *Can* Be" to a monitor displaying the program logo "In The *Know*." From each source he drew a word and constructed a sentence. *One Can Know.* He smiled to himself; he hadn't expected to come up with an actual working sentence.

Still bored, he made a second go. His eyes scanned the room and extracted words from the sea of text around him. *Will* from the Will & Grace poster, *exit* from the exit sign, *needs* from a posted letter to employees, and *tape* from a label indicating Reusable Tape Stock. The sentence solidified in his mind. *Will exit needs tape.*

The producer turned to David, interrupting his game. "Hey, Chance, could you go get me a tape from my desk. It's marked..." He paused. "Know what, never mind. I'll go. There's something else I have to do anyway." The producer stood and exited the booth, leaving David in stunned silence.

"What's wrong with you?" asked the editor.

David offered a weak smile. "Ah-- nothing, just something stupid."

The editor shrugged and turned back to the video gear.

David sat motionless and stared. *Did I just predict that?* The incident replayed in his mind. *I think I did! I predicted the future!*

He shook his head. No. It was only a coincidence. It *had* to be.

David turned the little car down a side street and gunned the engine. Four more blocks and he would be on the

6

Interstate, hopefully just ahead of rush hour traffic. As he drove, the mysterious incident continued to nag at him. He wanted to dismiss the whole thing as nothing more than a fluke, but he just couldn't reconcile the fact that the words had been there for him to string together. His eyes were drawn straight to them. There was no premeditation. He wasn't even *trying* to make a sentence. --Still, it *had* to be a coincidence.

He scanned the sea of words zipping by outside his window. They beckoned to him from road signs, marquees, window signs... There were plenty of potential sources for a test, perhaps he could give it another shot. After all, a couple of bona fide failures would set his mind at ease.

He looked left through the wiggling rivers of water on his window. "Your One *Stop* Shop." And right, at an old barn board. "On Sale *Now!*" His mind pulled out the words *Stop Now!* He hit the brake and the car went into a skid.

The driver in the Mustang behind him laid on the horn, swerved out around, and gunned his engine. David, unable to pull his eyes away, watched the vehicle tear off down the road. As it passed through the green light, an eighteen wheeler ran the red and plowed into the little car from the side. Metal buckled and windows exploded as both vehicles slid left and disappeared behind a row of buildings.

David sat wide eyed, gripping the steering wheel, unable to catch a full breath. His heart pounded in his ears, his thoughts a flurry of panic. With a trembling hand, he pushed the door open and stepped out onto the street. Car horns competed with car alarms. Off in the distance a siren wailed.

But to David, it was all a hollow drone.

Sharon Chance peered through the living room curtains at the empty driveway. Two boys stood across the street, waiting for the city transit, and her next-door neighbor, Frank, was watering a flower pot on his front lawn.

It was getting dark.

"Where's your father? He said he was on schedule."

"Maybe he stopped to pick something up," ten year old Ben spoke loudly over the sounds of machine-gun fire and explosions.

Sharon looked in the mirror, tucked a stray blond curl behind her ear, then walked past her son and daughter into the kitchen. "Those video games are gonna rot your brains!"

"Too late!" Ben shot back. There was nothing more satisfying in his moody prepubescent life than blowing his little sister into a thousand meaty chunks.

Sharon looked at the teenage girl sitting at the kitchen table. "The emergency numbers are on the fridge. If you need anything you can use my cellphone. David's cell is in my contacts list." She slid the phone across the table.

The somber-faced teen caught the phone with her palm, "Bedtime's eight, right?"

"Yes."

A car door closed out front and Sharon's eyes lit up. "Okay. Make sure Emily doesn't have any chocolate before bed, and Ben needs to take care of his school work." She snatched her purse and headed for the door.

"Mo- m!" Emily called. "Ben keeps killing me and I

don't get to *do* anything!"

"Ben! Stop killing your sister!" Sharon turned and kissed her son and daughter on the tops of their heads.

"Mom. She won't listen! *Emily!* Just do what I *told* you then you could get away!"

"Be good for *Maggie*," Sharon sang over her shoulder as she reached the door.

"Yes, Mom," they chimed together.

Sharon flung open the door, stepped out, and stopped cold. Two Marines in dress uniform were making their way up the concrete walkway.

"Evening, ma'am."

Her heartbeat quickened. "Can I help you?"

The muscular black soldier on the right stepped in, removed his hat, and offered an envelope. Sharon reached out and took it. She didn't have to read it; she knew what the letter meant, but she found herself going through the motions anyway. The men watched in stoic silence as she fumbled with the seal and pulled the letter out. *Dear Mrs. Chance.* Her eyes flew over the words. *We deeply regret to inform you that your brother, Sgt. Brandon William Walsh was...* She put her hand to her mouth. *...killed...*

The letter blurred.

She had considered the possibility that this day might come, but the words on the page cut deeper than she had imagined. Her baby brother-- dead? *How?* She wanted to know, but she knew these men could not tell her. She understood all too well the way this worked. She remembered clearly the day her mother had received a similar letter concerning her father.

She stood staring at the men, her hand still over her mouth, tears threatening to overflow. She needed to be strong, for her family, for herself. Her brother would have wanted it that way. She drew the emotion in, removed her hand, and let out a controlled breath. "Thank you, gentlemen."

The two men took a step back and snapped to attention with a salute, a salute of respect, a thank you to the family of the fallen, whose burden was considered no less than that of the soldiers themselves. It lasted only a few seconds, but they were the most excruciating seconds of Sharon's life.

They released the salute and the second man spoke gently. "Ma'am, I'm the base chaplain. Would you like me to stay awhile?"

She wiped her face with the back of her hand. "No. Thank you. We'll be fine."

"Alright. But if you have any questions or need anything, please don't hesitate to call."

She nodded stiffly.

The men turned and headed down the walkway under the cover of darkening clouds. From the back, the chaplain actually looked like Brandon, broad shoulders, medium build-- even the swagger in his step. She stood frozen in the doorway; something inside her determined on remembering this moment for the rest of her life.

The men reached the car, opened the doors, and disappeared inside. Sharon looked down at the letter with the official seal emblazoned on the top. It all felt surreal, somehow artificial.

"Mom? Who was that?"

She turned and looked down at her son. "They're from the military," she said softly.

He saw the conflict of emotion on her face and his expression turned to concern. "Did something-- bad happen?"

The innocent question opened a guarded place in her

heart. It bore deep inside and confirmed what she had not allowed herself to fully accept. "Yes." Her voice cracked. "Something bad has happened."

"Is it-- Uncle Brandon?"

She watched as the car pulled away from the curb and rolled slowly down the street. "--Yes, honey. Uncle Brandon was..." She looked down at Ben with his chest puffed out and his lips pursed. He was trying to be strong for her. She again brought her hand to her mouth, and the tears began to flow. He reached his arms around her waist as Emily appeared in the doorway. Sharon crouched down and drew them in. "Your uncle is dead," she whispered. "He died in the war."

3

When David arrived home, the lights in the living room were dim and the room was empty, but there was activity in the kitchen beyond. Sharon was talking with her brother Jerry, no doubt; his car was parked out front.

David entered the kitchen and found his wife in jeans and a comfortable shirt sitting at the table with her brother. Wadded balls of tissue were scattered around the address book on the table.

David took a hesitant step in. "Wh- what's going on?"

Sharon's chin wrinkled as she spoke. "Brandon isn't coming home, David."

He crouched in front of her. "Oh, honey-- I am so sorry."

She gripped his arm but turned away, then leaned in and placed her cheek on his shoulder. "I can't believe it," she whispered. "He's never coming home."

David held her gently and let her cry. There were no words to relieve her pain; her loss was too great. Apart from David and the kids, Jerry and Brandon were the only family Sharon had left, and although she would never say this to Jerry, she had always loved Brandon the most. He was the one who'd always made time for her when she needed him, like after their mother died. He had spent many long nights sitting with her, helping her get through.

He was a compassionate man, and it was this compassion that had driven him to join the military to serve overseas. He had been moved by the events of 9/11. After seeing so many innocent people die at the hands of the terrorists, he had felt compelled to take action. While others rung their hands and did nothing, Brandon's course had been clear.

"I called you," Sharon whispered, "but you didn't answer."

"There was an accident."

She pulled back and looked at him.

"It wasn't me. I got out to see if I could help, and I must have left my phone in the car."

"Was anyone hurt?"

"Yeah. It was pretty bad."

She put her cheek back on his shoulder. "I'm glad it wasn't you."

"Yeah-- me too."

David looked over at Jerry sitting silently with his brows scrunched and his jaw tight. He was clearly angry, David suspected he knew why. It was no secret that Jerry *hated* the war, and hated the current administration for dragging the country into it. He hated, even more, that his brother, whom he loved, had chosen to go and fight in that war. Now his brother was gone-- and that gave him even more reason to hate.

David lifted Karen's head and wiped her tears. "Are the kids upstairs?"

She nodded.

"How are they taking this?"

"As good as can be expected."

"Have you called everyone?"

"Who?" Jerry spoke loudly. "Who's left to call?"

Sharon gave her brother a cold glance. "Please, Jerry."

"Sorry." He pursed his lips, "It's just so..." There was a mixture of emotion on his face. "I loved him too you know."

13

"I know."

"We didn't agree on much-- but I loved him!" He chewed nervously on his thumbnail, his face taking on a desperate look. David didn't know if he was going to cry, or turn the table over.

"Look." David spoke gently. "Why don't you go take a walk, maybe it will clear..."

"Yeah. I'll do that." Jerry stood up. "Maybe a drive or something." He looked at his sister. "I'll call you tomorrow. Okay?"

"Don't do anything crazy. You're all I've got."

Jerry gave a heavy nod, left out of the kitchen, and out the door with a thump.

David pulled out a chair and sat down. "I hope he doesn't do anything stupid."   Sharon stared blankly at the tissues scattered across the table. "If he was going to hurt himself he would have done it a long time ago." She brushed the hair out of her face. "I must look a *mess.*"

David leaned in. "You're more beautiful than the day we met."

"How can you *say* that?"

"Because I didn't know then the depths of beauty I have been blessed to uncover all these many years."

Her eyes watered as her hands began awkwardly tidying up the mess in front of her. "Alright, you don't have to sleep on the couch tonight."

He let out a small laugh. One of the things he loved most about his wife was her sense of humor. Even now, in this dark moment, she was able to find reason to joke.

"Want me to run to the store for some comfort food? Rub your back? Anything?"

"Thanks, honey, but I think I'll just go to bed."

"Alright. I'll be here if you need me."

14

She deposited the tissues in the trash, gave him a kiss on the forehead, and left him sitting alone in the kitchen.

41232

David picked up the phone and tapped in a number. After a few short rings a voice answered. "Hello?"

"Alex. You called?"

"David! Buddy! I can't wait to see you, man. It's been weeks!"

"Yeah, I know. --It'll be great."

"You okay? You sound exhausted."

David drew in a breath. "Yeah. It's been one of those days."

"Wife on your case?"

"I'd take wife troubles over this any day."

"I've had days like that."

"Oh I *guarantee*, you haven't had a day like *this*," David said, thinking back to what had happened earlier. He paused.

"O-*kay*. Want to fill me in?"

Did he? No matter how he told it he was going to end up sounding like a nut job. But this was *Alex,* his best friend since grade school. If he couldn't tell him, who could he tell?

"*Hello?*"

"Sorry, Alex."

"Well?"

"Well, it's just-- really weird."

"You've always been weird. What else is new?"

"Thanks, Alex. Now I really don't want to tell you."

"Come on, David, spill it."

David thought for a second. "Do you believe in ESP?"

"What?"

"You know, ESP, extrasensory perception."

"I *know* what ESP is, but what are you talking about?"

"Well, this afternoon when I was in an edit session with a couple of guys at work I uh, think I experienced it."

"ESP?"

"Yeah."

"You wanna explain?"

"Well," he took a deep breath. "I was scanning the room for something to read, because, you know, I was bored, and my eyes started going from one word to another and... You sure you want to know this, it's really stupid."

"Yeah, go on."

"Well, my eyes were drawn to a bunch of words that made a sentence. It said, 'Will exit needs tape.'" David paused again.

"So-- what's so stupid about that?"

"Nothing. Until it *happened.* The producer got up and went out because he needed a tape!"

"Oh. That *is* weird."

"I know, right?"

The line was silent for a moment. "These words you're talking about-- they were from stuff in the room? You didn't pull them from your head?"

"No. It was a poster, a coffee cup, that sort of thing, from wherever my eyes landed."

"And your eyes went right to them, you didn't guide them?"

"No. Yes. I mean, it was like-- like something *else* was drawing my attention to them. It's hard to explain." He thought for a moment. "It was, like being in a river current. *I* wasn't controlling *it* was controlling *me.* "

"O-*kay.*"

"I know it sounds insane, but that's what it felt like."

"Did you try it again?"

"*Yes.* Get this. When I was driving home, I was thinking about what happened and I thought I'd give it another shot, you know, so I could prove it wrong. But as soon as I started looking, my eyes went right to the words *stop* and *now*. I *knew* it was real and I..."

"You stopped."

"Yeah! I slammed on my brakes!"

"And?"

The guy behind me swerved around and kept going and got plowed over by a Mack Truck!"

"You're joking."

"No! The paramedics said the man *died* on impact!"

"Wow!"

"That could have been *me,* Alex. If I hadn't listened to that message, I'd be *dead* right now."

Several seconds passed. Then Alex spoke. "So you saw *stop* and *now* and you stopped. Just like that."

"Yes."

"Why?"

"Because it was-- it was. It wasn't so much the *message* that made me slam on my brakes, it was the *feeling* I got when it came to me, like a confirmation, like I already *knew* the message, but the words were confirming it somehow. Something deep inside me understood that what I was looking at was not just *real,* but *truth,* something so pure it could not be doubted."

There was no response on the other end of the line.

"Anyway. I *knew* if I didn't stop something terrible was going to happen, so I slammed on the brakes."

"--Wow. David, I gotta say. That's... That's..."

"Crazy! I know it's crazy! Do you think it's possible for it to be some kind of weird coincidence?"

"One heck of a coincidence don't ya think?"

"Alex, I appreciate you not thinking I'm a head case."

"Oh you're nuts, certifiably insane."

David shook his head. "I knew I should have kept my big mouth shut."

Alex laughed. "I'm joking. I know you're for real. You've never lied in your whole life. If you said it happened, then it happened."

David was quiet.

"Have you told Sharon about it?"

"No. I didn't want to upset her any more."

"Why, what's going on?"

David paused. He knew Alex really liked Brandon.

"What's going on, David?"

"It's Brandon, Alex." He lowered his voice. "He was killed in the war."

"Aw, man, you're *kidding* me."

"She got the news today."

"David. I'm *so* sorry. Sharon must be devastated. That's *horrible!*"

"Yeah, we're all struggling with it."

"Brandon was such a great guy. Remember the time I got my car stuck in the mud and he came with his truck..." As Alex talked, David's eyes shifted to the kitchen counter and rested on a can of beans and franks. The word *frank* popped out at him.

David's breathing became shallow.

In front of him, his eyes peeled the word *needs* from the cover of a Good Housekeeping magazine, and from a Valentine's card on the fridge, the word *you* stood out. The message constructed itself in David's mind. *Frank needs you.*

"David? You still there?" The voice coming from the phone sounded distant.

David's heart throbbed in his chest. The room swam around him. He took in a difficult breath. "It just happened again."

"What? The words? Are you seeing the words?"

"I have to go."

"David. Hello? *David!*"

Bleep. The phone went quiet. He placed it on the table. *Frank needs me?* Was he in trouble? Was he in danger? The chair squelched as David stood. His hands were shaking. *This is crazy.* Was he supposed to rush into some unknown and possibly dangerous situation just because some random words came together and made a sentence?

He made his way to the front door. Under the coat rack, in a bag, was Ben's baseball gear. David pulled out an aluminum bat. It was small, but better than nothing. He gripped the front doorknob with a sweaty hand, paused, then forcefully pulled the door open and stepped out into the night. Looking toward his neighbor's house, David saw that Frank's car in his driveway. There were no lights on in the house, but this was normal, he was the gym teacher at the local school and most days he had to be up early. David jumped down into his neighbor's driveway from the stone wall divider and climbed the concrete stairs to his friend's front door. It was open a few inches. A pensive wind sucked it in and out slightly, as if the house were breathing. Shadows moved in the cracks around the door frame. David angled himself to see into Frank's living room, but the darkness was complete. If anyone was inside, the contrast created by the streetlight made it impossible to see.

Now what? Was he supposed to just barge into his

neighbor's house with a bat? He gripped the bat in response to the thought. His adrenaline spiked. *This is nuts! This is what crazy people do! Hear voices, sneak into their neighbor's house with a bat, and end up on the Jerry Springer show-- after a couple of years in prison.* No. He was not crazy. He decided to knock. Sane people knock.

A loud clatter and a desperate moan came from inside. Riding on pure adrenaline, David burst through the door. The room was pitch black except for a path lit by the streetlight outside. Sounds of thrashing came from the kitchen. David crouched low and moved toward the sound. He ran his hand along the wall to find the light switch. His heart was on fire, his senses working overtime. More movement. It sounded like a struggle. He rounded the corner and his fingers found what they were searching for. He gripped the bat, flicked the switch, and stiffened to defend against an attack.

But none came.

On the floor, surrounded by canned food, Frank lay gripping his chest. David dropped the bat and ran to him. "Are you okay?"

Frank struggled to speak. "My- h- heart."

"I'll call 911."

"Get-- pills."

"Where?" David looked around frantically. "Where are they, Frank?"

"I don't kn..." Frank did *not* look well.

David opened cabinet after cabinet, nothing but cups and plates. He slid open several drawers, still nothing. He could hear Frank gasping for breath behind him. He scanned the counter. "What does it look like, Frank?" His voice sounded desperate in his own ears. He needed to calm down. He remembered taking CPR in high school. *Always stay*

21

calm, no matter what. He took a deep breath, and refocused. There was an orange bottle behind the sink. He scooped it up. *Nitroglycerin.* "Found it!" He dropped to his knees, popped the cap, and shook out a pill. Frank eagerly took it under his tongue.

"That's it, buddy. Relax. You're okay. You're okay. I found the pills. Everything's gonna be okay." He leaned back against the cabinet door and looked down at Frank, then jumped back up and left the room.

"Wh- where..."

"I'll be right back. I'm getting you a pillow."

He re-entered and crouched down. Gently he lifted Frank's head and put the pillow in place. "You rest. I'm calling 911."

He stood and grabbed the phone. "Yes. I think my neighbor's had a heart attack. Yes. 103 Birchwood. I gave him a Nitroglycerin. Okay. Thank you." He looked down at Frank and gave a reassuring smile. "They're on their way."

Frank lifted a thumb.

"You scared me half to death you know."

Frank smiled weakly.

David crouched back down and leaned against the sink cabinet. He stared quietly at the recovering man.

Amazing!

Again the words had spoken the *truth.* Frank *did* need him. He might have died if David hadn't shown up. *What is going ON here?* Something-- or some*one* was sending him messages. It had to be. David couldn't *possibly* have known his neighbor was in trouble.

In the distance an ambulance shrieked; the fire station wasn't far. The color was returning to Frank's face. He reached out and gripped David by the wrist. "You know something?"

22

"What's that, Frank?"

"God sent you to me."

David's heart skipped a beat. "What? What do you mean?"

"I prayed that God would send someone, and you came."

A cynical smile creased David's lips. "You must've hit your head when you fell."

Frank looked serious. "I prayed, and *you* showed up just in time."

David hesitated. "Ah, o*kay.* "

"Why did you come, David? I didn't yell. I could barely breathe. But you came."

David didn't say anything. He just sat there, crouched against the cabinet, staring at Frank.

"You *knew.* I can see it on your face. *How* did you know?"

"You wouldn't believe me if I told you."

"Why do you say that?"

"I don't even believe me!" David snapped.

Frank recoiled slightly.

"I'm sorry, Frank. I'm just a little freaked out right now."

Frank's eyes widened. "It's *true!* God did speak to you, didn't he?"

"Not exactly." David put his head in his hands.

"What do you mean?"

"If," said David, poking a finger at Frank, "*if* it was God who spoke to me, and I'm not saying it was, but if it was-- he did it with written words. It was a message."

"A message? Did he write it on the wall with his finger, like in the book of Daniel-- or in stone like with Moses and the ten commandments?"

David put his palm on his face. He wasn't really going to tell him he got the message from a can of beans, a magazine, and a Valentine's card. Was he?

The ambulance siren cut off; it was outside.

"You okay, Dave?"

David let his hand slide down. "Yeah. I'm okay. Look. I'll stop by tomorrow to check on you, but I need some time to process, you know, before I start blabbing to the whole world that *God* is in communication with me."

Frank chuckled. "I imagine it's a lot to swallow, talking to God and all, but I want you to know something." Frank turned his head and fixed his eyes on David's. "If you do decide to come back and tell me about the writing, I promise I won't think you're crazy."

David shook his head. "Well then-- that will make one of us."

1225

David splashed water on his face and looked at his reflection in the bathroom mirror. Was he crazy? If he was, would he know it? Who knows they're crazy? Crazy people think everyone else is crazy. Right?

He splashed his face again, but no amount of washing was going to remove the bags from under his eyes. The glistening water only made his eyes appear more hollow. He toweled off, ran his fingers through his curly brown hair, and adjusted his tie. Again he looked in the mirror. All he wanted to do was crawl back into bed, pull up his blanky force field, and make it all go away. Like it wasn't hard enough being an intern competing for limited full-time positions at one of the largest television stations in Boston, he had to go and add a family crisis, *and* a paranormal psychosis for good measure. He squeezed his eyes shut. "-- Just shoot me. Shoot me right now. In the face. With big bullets."

He turned to replace the towel on the rack and noticed a new piece of artwork taped on the wall. Obviously drawn by his daughter, it was a crude picture of a flower looking miserable underneath an umbrella. Rain was shooting down from big black clouds. In purple crayon were the words, "The flowr is sad becuz he dusnt undrstand that the rane will help him grow." David stood and stared at it.

There was a tiny knock on the door.

"Dad? It's time for breakfast."

David opened the door. It was Ben, still in his pajamas.

"I take it you're not going to school." He reached out and ruffled his matted blond hair.

"Mom said we're staying home."

"And what do you think about that?"

Ben gave a lackluster smile and squeezed into the bathroom.

Poor little guy. He had the day off from school but couldn't even enjoy it. Ben loved his Uncle. They both loved sports. They used to spend hours naming off baseball stats, even rare ones, like what player, in 1946 walked in the third inning, winning the game for the Dolphins. --David wasn't even sure if the Dolphins were a baseball team.

In the kitchen the aroma of eggs and sausages filled David's nostrils. Sharon was at the stove. Emily, with her curly brown hair shooting out in all directions, sat staring vacantly into her bowl of Froot Loops. She was not a morning person, and this morning weighed especially heavy on her little heart.

David picked up the coffee pot. "How are you holding up?" he asked his wife.

Sharon's eyes stayed fixed on the stove. "Fine, I guess."

"We had quite a day yesterday."

No response.

He sipped his coffee and examined her intently, maybe a little too intently.

"I'm fine," she said, evenly. "You don't need to stare."

"Ben says you're staying home."

"Yes. I need to see about funeral arrangements. I guess the Marines want to be involved. There are a lot of details to comb through. I'm not just taking the day off to sulk."

"I never said you were. And I wasn't staring, I was thinking. I was trying to decide if I should tell you something. Judging by your reaction, I guess it can wait."

She slid the contents of the pan onto a plate and set the pan back on the stove. With a heavy sigh she turned and faced her husband. "What is it? Something about work?"

"No. Not really. It's about why I was late last night. I wanted to tell you when I got home, but for obvious reasons, I decided to wait."

"You mean the accident?"

"Yes. Well, not the accident specifically."

"Well then *what?*"

David paused. "You know, I really don't need to tell you right now. It's not that important."

"David. You have my attention. *Tell* me."

"Okay." He took in a deep breath. "Something really weird happened before the accident-- and last night at Frank's. --Here. Let's sit down and I'll explain everything."

By the time he was done, his entire family sat at the kitchen table, staring at him, wide-eyed and open-mouthed.

"Can you do it anytime you want?" Ben asked.

"I don't know."

"Try it right now," he said excitedly.

Sharon interrupted. "Am I the only one who thinks this is creepy? I don't know how I feel about all this, David. It makes my skin crawl."

"How do you think *I* feel?"

"Are you a *super*hero?" That was Emily.

Sharon slid her plate away. "What strikes me is, you started getting these, these-- messages the same day Brandon died."

David felt a chill run down his back. He hadn't thought of that-- and he wished Sharon hadn't either. The thought of a dead relative watching his every move made him uncomfortable, to say the least.

"Do you feel anything when you see the words? Do you hear the words out loud?" Ben asked.

"No. It's not a voice, it's a sense, like déjà vu." His brows furrowed. "It's probably just some latent mental ability or..." He looked up at the wall clock. "Oh! I have to *go.* They're expecting me down at the courthouse." He took the last gulp off his coffee. "I can't believe how fast this morning flew by."

"Are you sure you should go in? Don't you think you should try to figure out what's going on first?" Sharon stared at her husband.

"Competition is fierce for those full-time positions at the station." David stood and set his cup in the sink. "I need to stay on top of things. Besides, It's only half a day, and I need to be downtown anyway to get Alex. I'll call you if anything happens. Okay?"

Sharon sat with her lips pursed.

David looked at the kids. "Be good for Mom, alright?"

"Okay, Dad."

"Yes, Daddy." Emily pushed her chair out. "I'm going to go look for words in my room. Maybe that's *my* superpower too."

David watched her shuffle out of the kitchen in her rumpled pjs and tangled hair, then turned to his wife. "Call me if you get overwhelmed." He bent down and kissed her on the forehead. "I'll come home if you need me."

"Okay." Her hand gripped his wrist. "Call *me* if anything happens. I know how guarded you can be when you're struggling with something.

"I will, honey. I promise."

By the time David arrived at the courthouse it was already mobbed. Police barricades blocked off traffic to the street in front, a barrier was set up to hold back the crowd of spectators that was forming, and reporters milled around at a calculated distance from the doors-- like piranha waiting for a feeding.

On the blocked off street were several news trucks, including the one for Channel Seven. David pulled up to a police checkpoint and flashed his press pass. The officer squinted at it then waved him through. David rolled in carefully and double parked next to the big white truck.

There were quite a few pedestrians on the street for such a cold autumn morning. David stuck close to the car and worked his way to the truck. He found the thin metal door and rapped his knuckles on it. A head poked out from the dimly glowing guts of the news truck. It was the notorious switch operator and technician, Jeffery Nord, nicknamed Nerd by his coworkers. He was six feet and lanky, with green eyes and tousled orange hair that, quite frankly, made him look like a troll pencil. Anyone else would have found the title *Nerd* demeaning, but not Nord. *He* wore it like a badge of honor.

Nerd hovered in the tiny doorway, waving a thick pencil in front of David, like a security wand. "--Boop."

David raised his eyebrows. "Um. Hey there, Nerd."

"Boop."

David craned his neck over Nerd's shoulder. "You the

only one here?"

Nerd ignored the question and continued on as though his pencil joke was going well. "Bleep. Bleep. Bleep. No flesh eating viruses detected." He laughed a breathy laugh.

David gave a half smile.

Nerd pulled back into the truck and took a seat in the switcher's chair, which he perceived as the captain's chair of his little rolling Enterprise. "Brad and John are in front of the courthouse waiting for the Senator to come out." Nerd pointed to a television monitor at Brad Knight, Channel Seven's premier field reporter who was going over notes on his PDA.

"What do they want me to do?" said David.

"I guess they want you to shadow me, kinda see how things work behind the curtain."

Oh how fortunate, David thought, *to learn at the feet of The Great and Powerful Oz!* He sat down at the only other seat in the truck. It was beside the device that put words and graphics on the screen. "What's this thing called?" he said, pointing.

"*That* is a character generator."

"Oh." David looked around at the mass of video electronics, rows of flashing lights, and plastic push buttons. His eyes came to rest on a box of donuts, and he suddenly became aware that he had never eaten his breakfast. His belly gurgled. *I wonder if there are any glazed left?* He tipped the cover and peeked inside. *Yes!* One left. Things were beginning to look up! He reached into the box, but his hand froze. An orange sticky-note hung just above the lid. Scribbled in pencil were the words, "Good and Working." Two letters stood out, *G* and *o.*

Oh no! Not AGAIN! Go? Where? Out of the truck? NOW? His pulse quickened. This was *nuts.* He couldn't just drop what he was doing every time a message came. Yet, he couldn't ignore it. Maybe something horrible was about to happen to the truck! Again his pulse spiked. Nerd, thoroughly engrossed in his preparations for the broadcast, tapped at his keys and examined the readouts. David's eyes dropped to a hammer on the console. On it was a metal label with the words in/out. The word *out* screamed at him.

He sprang to his feet. "I have to step out for a second." The sentence was rushed, but Nerd didn't seem to notice.

"Don't take too long. It could start then you'll miss everything." Nerd continued to study his equipment.

"Yeah. Okay." David fumbled with the latch and opened the door. Light bit into his eyes as he stepped back out onto the sidewalk. He took a look around. There didn't appear to be any danger. More spectators had joined the throng in front of the courthouse, all waiting for a chance to see the Senator whose name had been topping the headlines for the last three weeks. Dread boiled in David's chest at a single troubling thought. *Is something going to happen to the Senator?*

Several doors opened. A delegation poured from the building, and the sea of waiting reporters surged forward like a tide, encircling the emerging group. David felt helpless, transfixed on the scene as he waited in horror for the next instruction to come.

A young man with white cords protruding from his ears brushed past, causing David to step back. He glanced briefly at the man and immediately his eyes were drawn to the back of his red tee-shirt. "Follow me as I *follow* Him." David had no idea what the cryptic message meant, but it didn't matter. The word *follow* soaked into his mind.

Perspiration chilled on David's forehead as he moved through the crisp morning air. Short, nervous breaths shot

31

out in thin white puffs. To his right, reporters fired off questions like hungry wolves chewing on a carcass. The man in the red shirt paid no attention, maneuvering along the sidewalk, dodging back and forth, lost in his own private concert.

David followed, stealing glances to his right, but quickly returning his focus to the man in the red shirt. A woman with a dog cut him off, but he compensated and passed between two men on the left, pushed past another man in a business suit, and caught up.

The man skirted the outside edge of the crowd, stepping in time to his own rhythm, weaving in and out of the gathered onlookers. David trailed him with pensive intensity, afraid to continue, but more afraid to stop. He pressed on past the crowd, away from the Senator. *This doesn't make sense! Why is he moving away?* He stopped and looked around in a panic. Had he missed something? There were words everywhere, but nothing spoke to him. He twisted back toward the truck. Nothing but silence. Was he supposed to continue following this man? Was the Senator *not* the target?

Brandon, if this is you, buddy, throw me a bone here.

He turned back and saw the man a considerable distance away. He broke into a sprint, pushed his way past a group of boys, and sidestepped around a woman with a stroller. The man was now at a crosswalk. David kept his eyes trained on the red shirt. The man crossed the street then turned and disappeared into a coffee shop. David dashed to the entrance and almost plowed into a couple trying to exit. He gave them a look of apology, and squeezed past.

The coffee shop was small and quaint, and unexpectedly quiet in contrast to the throng of activity outside. At one table a little wrinkled man read a newspaper while chewing on a bagel. Three people were standing in line, the last being the man in the red shirt. David stepped in behind him, sweaty, and out of breath. *Now what?* He felt horribly conspicuous. No one knew his reason for being there, but he felt like it was painted across his forehead. *I'm only here to follow this guy because his shirt told me to!*

The line grew smaller and David had no plan. He scanned the room, letting his eyes bounce off words, but only a string of nonsense appeared. *Great! I'm stuck in a stupid coffee shop while right next door a famous Senator is creating a media frenzy! HELLO!* The line reduced again. The man in the red shirt was at the counter now, and David was next. He snatched up a menu and bounced his eyes back and forth. Nothing. *I followed the man in the shirt! Where are you? What am I supposed to do?*

The man clutched the top of his to-go bag and brushed past. David did not make eye contact. He stepped forward and looked up at the menu. His eyes were drawn to a big yellow *3* in a blue circle on top of the kids' section.

"May I help you, sir?" said the young gum-chewing blond behind the counter.

"Yes, I'll take three, ah, coffees." He stole a glance behind him to see the man still standing in the entrance. He was looking at business cards on the cork board. He looked back at the blond.

"That will be five dollars and thirty-five cents," she said with a couple of quick chews.

David pulled out a ten and slid it across the counter, then glanced back over his shoulder. He was gone! He pushed away from the counter and looked out the windows. *Where'd he GO?* David burst through the door and looked back toward the courthouse, then ran around the other side of the coffee shop.

The man was gone.

David wiped his face with his hands. *How* could he lose him? *I only turned away for a second!* He stood in the crosswalk, turned left, then right, then left again. It was no use. The crosswalk sign changed, it said, "WALK." Another message? He crossed the street and stopped in front of a large glass window. On it, written in yellow paint, were the words *IT* Consultant, and Come In, We're *Open.*

His mind grabbed the words *Open* and *IT* and pulled them together.

He stood and stared. *Open what?*

He turned his head and spotted a heavily bearded man playing guitar with fingerless gloves. Next to him, his guitar case sat open with a few wadded bills in its belly. The case was already open. That wasn't it. He turned around. And around again. *Open WHAT!* Behind him was a bench. Shoved between the slats was a magazine. David walked forward, snatched it, and opened it. He scanned up and down the first two pages. Nothing. He turned to the back. Nothing there either.

What now?

He sat down and turned to the center of the magazine. There was nothing special about the glossy pages, and nothing stood out. *Am I doing something wrong? Why do I keep losing the trail? Is there some kind of method I'm missing?*

Maybe I'm just trying too hard.

He closed his eyes, took a deep breath, then refocused on the magazine. "Two Killed with Car Bomb," said one headline. "The President to Stop in Turkey to Meet With Makhim Alad Rheen," said another.

He tried to relax, and allowed his eyes to scan. Two words popped out. *The. President.*

Okay-- now we're getting somewhere.

He continued to scan... *will... die.*

David shoved the magazine from his lap and stood. "I don't want to *know* this!"

An old lady passing by gave him a stern look, but he hardly noticed her.

I don't want to know this! This is NOT happening. I don't WANT to know! He paced back and forth next to the clump of magazine. *Why? Why me? Why did you choose me? I'm nobody!* David hovered over the magazine. His mind was on fire. *If I DO this. If I DO this. If I read this message, can I turn back? Can I walk away?* A sense of futility washed over him. Clearly, he had no control over the messages. It didn't matter what he did, they would find him. And if he did try to stick his head in the sand, he might end up dead. Or worse.

He groaned, crouched down, and snatched the magazine off the sidewalk. Whatever they were, they had saved his life and the life of his neighbor. For all he knew, death was waiting around the corner, even now, in any one of the many varieties found in the big city. Being in the good graces of the author of the messages was certainly better than the alternative. He sat back down and opened the magazine. *Okay, David. Relax. Just relax.* His eyes fell on the word *in*, the number *2*, and finally on the word *days.* The words tumbled in his mind, rearranged themselves to form a new sentence.

In 2 days the President will die.

His eyes flitted to the byline, and grabbed three more words in quick succession. *Stop. The. Killer.*

That was the whole of the message. David stared in stunned disbelief. *Save the President? Of the United states?* Saving his next-door neighbor was one thing, but he couldn't

even *begin* to wrap his brain around this one. *I'm no hero.*
I'm an intern ... I'm not even a fully functioning member of
the workforce! How am I supposed to save the President of
the United States?

He laid the magazine down, and rubbed his temples.
This is not happening. This is not happening. This is NOT
happening... There must have been a clerical mistake
somewhere. He was so obviously *not* the guy for the job!
And what was he going to tell Sharon? "Um. honey, I have
to go to Washington for a few days. The President's gonna
die and I'm supposed to save him. --Oh, and I'll be charging
it to our VISA. You're okay with that, right? Honey ... what
are you going to do with that knife?" Yup. That was how it
was going to go down. She'd think he was crazy, and he was
going to have to agree with her.

He stood and threw the magazine into a nearby trash
can. There was no plan, no next step, just a directive. That
wasn't enough for David. Until the messages chose to give
him more, he decided he was going to sit on the information;
his present situation was going to be hard enough to deal
with. After all, he had just walked off his job site to chase
supernatural messages. How was he going to explain *that*
one?

David headed back across the street and toward the
truck, playing through all the scenarios in his head. In each
one he ended up looking like a nut case, no matter how he
spun it. Mental dysfunction was definitely *not* the way to
endear oneself to a potential employer. *It would be infinitely*
easier if I could just lie. But he would not do that. He'd seen
the destruction lying had wrought in his father's life, and he'd
promised himself long ago that he would *not* repeat the
mistakes of his father.

The coffee! He stopped in his tracks. *Maybe I'm*

supposed to get coffee. What had appeared as a trivial detour now made perfect sense. He turned, bolted back to the coffee shop, and strolled in through the door. He gave a smile to the blond behind the counter.

"Thought you took off," she chewed.

"Sorry about that."

She grabbed the tray and slid it across, then handed him his change.

"Thanks."

She gave a robotic smile. "Don't mention it."

David exited the shop and headed back toward the truck. As he neared, he held the coffees strategically out in front of him. The three men standing there didn't notice him at first, until he was right up on them.

"Chance. Where ya been?" said John.

"Coffee?" said David.

Nerd scrunched his face. "You *completely* missed the broadcast. We went live and Brad got an interview with the Senator. I was feeding video, running the switch *and* punching up Chyron all at the same time."

"I wasn't gone long." He held the coffee tray out. Each of them grabbed a cup.

Brad smiled. "The urge to fetch coffee was just too strong for ya, huh?"

"I am your humble intern." David returned the smile.

"Well," said Brad, "we're heading out to film a piece for the art show, then we'll head back to the station to go over the afternoon game plan. You going to meet us at the show?"

"If you need me, but I'm only on for half a day, right? I have to pick up a friend at Logan."

"Oh, yeah, that's right. Hey, this is turning out to be a busy day and you'd probably find yourself shoved in a corner anyway. Look. Why don't you just take off? We'll pick up on Monday when things have died down a bit."

"You sure? I can..."

"Yeah. You've been busting your hump the past couple of weeks. You deserve it. So go before I change my mind."

"Alright. Thanks, Brad. I owe you one. See you guys Monday." David set the cardboard tray in a nearby trash can and went around to his car. He had two hours until he had to pick up Alex. *What am I going to do for two hours?*

One thing was certain, he did *NOT* want to look at any more words!

11227

David stabbed the elevator button and stepped back. The ring around the button glowed yellow. An arrow on the wall indicated a downward moving elevator. He didn't know which one, so he placed himself strategically in front of the three doors and waited.

A heavy-set man rounded the corner, stood for a second, then reached forward and hit the already glowing button. David gave the man a cordial smile, although privately, he wondered what made people do that. Did it come from an overwhelming desire to appear busy in the presence of strangers, or was it a lack of trust between the individual and the glowing button?

Ding. The middle elevator opened. Four people stood inside. One of them David recognized, an Arabic man who lived around the corner from him. He was of average height, had a muscular build, and rich bronze skin. Seeing the man caused a pit in David's gut. Although he would never admit it, the man made him uneasy-- and his suspicion wasn't completely unfounded. He lived on the low traffic intersection at the end of David's Street. Often, when David waited at the intersection, he found himself not ten feet from the man, who frequently sat on his steps. With all the hysteria about Muslims and terrorism, David had made a conscious effort to smile at the man. It was his way of saying, I don't believe all Arabs are the same, and I trust that you don't want to blow me up. But for all the times he had made the effort, the man had never smiled back. Maybe

David was making more of it than it was, but whether he liked it or not, the man made him nervous. He scanned David briefly with his dark mysterious eyes, and if he recognized him, he made no indication. The people exited one by one. The Arab passed with downcast eyes and headed off down the corridor.

David stepped in, turned, and pressed button number eight. When he stepped out again he saw a sign reading Cardiac Ward with an arrow pointing to the right. During his long walk down the corridor, he resisted the impulse to look through any open doors. He didn't want to invade anyone's privacy, and he especially didn't want to invite the sullen stare of some poor powerless soul who would have closed the door, if they could.

"Excuse me," said David to a nurse typing into a computer behind the counter. "I'm looking for Frank Johnston."

She looked up. "You know what room he's in, hon?"

"817."

She pulled the pencil from behind her ear, held it loosely by the eraser, and pointed over the counter and up the hall. "That way, hon. Last door on the right."

"Thank you."

He left the nurses' station, went up the hall, and peered into the room. A curtain prevented him from seeing the bed nearest the door, but in the far bed by the window, was Frank.

"Dave!" Frank opened his arms wide. Thin rubber tubes dangled.

"Hey there, Frank. Just stopped by to see if you're still breathing."

"I'm in*vincible*-- right up to the moment God decides to take me."

"That's one way of looking at it, I guess." David rounded the bed and took a look out the window. "Nice view."

"Like a five-star hotel."

David tapped the breakfast tray on the rolling table next to the bed. "Food's better in a five-star."

"I don't know why people hate hospital food so much. I think it's *great!*" Frank reached over and grabbed an English Muffin topped with grape jelly. "People would probably like it more if they didn't have to eat it in the hospital."

"Probably," said David.

Frank took a bite and rolled his eyes in ecstasy.

"I don't know about you, Frank."

Frank gave a jelly smeared grin.

David took a seat in a padded chair next to the bed. "I said I'd come check on you today, so here I am."

"Thanks, man. I really appreciate it."

"Do you have anyone to take care of stuff at your house while you're in the hospital? I mean, I'm right next door, if you need anything done."

"Yeah. I have a friend checking in on the cats and watering the plants. That's pretty much all there is, but thanks for asking. You're a good neighbor."

"Well, I just want to make sure you're being taken care of." It was only a half truth. David's real reason for visiting was to hear more of Frank's ideas about the messages, how he had connected them to God and all. He had serious doubts about Frank's God theory-- but what if it was true? What if it actually *was* God? He sighed and gripped his knees. If he wanted answers, he was going to have to tell Frank everything.

"You okay, Dave? You seem pensive."

"I'm just, well, this whole thing is crazy."

"We're not talking about my cats anymore, are we."

David looked out the window. "They started yesterday, the messages. They come from words around me, telling me what's going to happen before it happens." He paused, wondering if he should continue. He squeezed his eyes, shook his head, and went on. "The first time it was something trivial. A producer needed a tape. The second time they rescued me from a fatal car accident. And the third time was when I came and rescued you." David looked up at his friend.

Frank sat, squinting at David, his hand hanging in mid-air, holding the half-eaten English Muffin.

"I told you you wouldn't believe me."

"No. Um- I *believe* you. I'm just trying to understand what you're *saying.* You say these messages come from *words* around you?"

"Yes."

"Can you give me more detail?"

David furrowed his brows. "Okay. My eyes are drawn to certain words and they come together to make a sentence."

"And they tell you, the *future?"*

David looked Frank in the eye. *I might as well spill my guts,* he thought. *What have I got to lose?* "Yes, Frank. They tell me the future, *or* to *do* something. Like last night. I was talking on the phone when my eyes were drawn to a can of Beans and Franks. The word *Frank* stood out. Then I saw the word *needs* and then *you--* and that's why I came over."

"You came over because you saw some words that told you to?"

"It's *more* than that. When I see the words-- it's hard to explain. When I see the words, they stand out, but there's also a kind of *feeling,* somehow I *know* what they're saying

42

is true."

"Fascinating. And they saved you from a car accident?"

David stood up. "Okay. Let me start from the beginning so I don't miss anything. It started yesterday when I was at work..." David went on to explain in full detail the events of the previous day. But he chose to leave out what had happened that morning, the message about the president, he wasn't sure he would *ever* share that one.

When David finished, Frank's eyes were wide. "Wow, David. That's quite a gift."

"Gift? Is that what you would call it?"

Frank didn't respond.

"I wish it were a gift, I'd *return* it, not that I'm sorry I saved *you,* but I don't want *this...* whatever it is. I'm no hero! I'm an intern at a television station." He shook his head and stared at Frank. "Why me? If it *is* God, why'd he choose *me?* I'm just an ordinary guy."

"Less than ordinary," Frank said chuckling.

"Hey."

"What I mean is, God uses less than ordinary people to carry out his plans. God says in the Bible that he uses the *foolish* things of this world to confound the wise. He uses weak people, so that he can show him*self* strong."

That was an intriguing thought. Frank had an unconventional way of looking at the world. It was one of the things David liked most about him. He was always provoking him to think in unpredictable ways, and that was something he desperately needed right now. "Using weak people to do important things seems kind of backwards don't you think?"

"The ways of the Lord are not our ways," Frank said, reaching for his napkin. "His ways are higher than our ways."

43

"But why make me see messages in words around me? Why not talk to me directly?"

"Because then maybe you would ask questions, and if he told you everything he is planning to put you through, you'd probably give up."

"That's encouraging."

Frank smiled sympathetically. "God loves you and wants you to be a success, so he's only giving you small bites, building your faith until you're ready for the big stuff."

David gave a wry smile and shook his head. *Big* stuff? You mean like, I don't know, saving the President of the United States from *assassination?* Does that constitute *BIG?* Call me crazy, but it sure feels like I'm being thrown into the deep end on this one."

At first, the look on Frank's face gave David a feeling of satisfaction. He had won the point. Frank didn't have a leg to stand on. But the longer Frank's face remained in the position of stunned disbelief, the more unsettled David became.

"The messages told you this?"

"Yes." David looked at him intently. "It said in two days the President is going to be killed, and *I'm* supposed to stop it."

Frank's eyebrows rose as he nodded and considered the thought. "Tell me more. Where were you when you got this message?"

David explained the morning in detail, then looked Frank in the eye. "You still think God is only giving me what I can *handle?*"

"Well-- so far you've handled what he's given you, right?"

"I guess, but I feel so completely, I don't know, disoriented? Out of control?"

44

"You can't trust your feelings. They'll always betray you."

David furrowed his brow. "Well then what *can* I trust? Does God expect me to forge ahead in blind faith?"

"Just trust what you *know*. Trust the *facts*. It's amazing how many people make decisions based on what they *feel*. The truth could be staring them right in the face but they choose the wrong direction because they *feel* like it. Feelings are just guesses based on emotional impulses. Stick to what you *know*."

"Well all I *know* is, I'm in *WAY* over my head."

"You think that because you're no longer in your comfort zone, but just because you aren't tucked in nice and cozy in your comfortable little life, doesn't mean that God has viciously tossed you in over your head."

"But what if I don't want to do what the messages say? What then?"

"You have a free will. You can choose not to do what God is telling you. People do it all the time."

David looked out the window again. "What if it's *not* God telling me to do these things?"

"Who else could it be?"

"Who? What if it's not even a *who?*" David studied Frank's face. Apparently in Frank's mind, it *had* to be God, he seemed to believe this with unwavering conviction. David envied him. *Wouldn't it be wonderful to simply walk through life believing with blind faith? To have that sense of contentment that everything was always going to be just hunky-dory no matter what?* He shook his head. "I wish I could believe like you, Frank, but I need *evidence*. Scientific *proof*. As far as I can tell, whether or not there even *is* a God is unknowable.

"Oh there's a God."

"Well it seems more likely to me that this phenomenon isn't a *who* at all, but a psychic ability of some kind, a dormant gene in my brain maybe which has become active through some form of evolutionary leap or something."

"You think your *brain* is doing this?"

"It's possible."

Frank raised one eyebrow. "I think you're missing something."

"How so?"

"You're only thinking of the moment when the messages happen. You're missing the bigger picture. If the words weren't *there* to begin with, you wouldn't be able to find them. Someone had to put that can of beans on the counter so you could grab the word. Did your brain do that?"

"Of course not. If there were different items in the room, my mind would have made a different message, like 'Go next door.' or 'Help your neighbor.'"

"Hmm. Good point. Well, the most important thing is to look at the evidence. Every time this has happened, it's come true, right?"

"So far."

"Well in the Bible, if a prophet is wrong even one time, then he is not of God. So it stands to reason, if he *is* always correct, then he *is* from God. So logically, if the messages continue to be right, then they must be from God."

David stared blankly at Frank.

"Okay," said Frank. "Obviously, I can't even begin to understand what you're going through, but what keeps sticking out to me is the complexity of it. I just don't see how you can think it's your *brain* doing these things. There are simply too many details that have to come together, and you couldn't *possibly* make that happen on your own."

"*Why not?* There are people who can move stuff with

their minds, others who can read people's thoughts."

Frank shook his head. "Look, take me for instance. How could you *possibly* have known that I needed help?"

"Maybe my mind could see you, like through some kind of remote viewing ability. I saw a documentary one time on remote viewing. They scientifically proved that people could draw pictures of things in other places in the world without going there. The test subjects were given coordinates and told to draw what they saw. The results were pretty darn close!"

"Okay. Let's just say all that hocus-pocus is real."

"Hocus-pocus? It's a lot more scientific than just *assuming God* did it!

"You still can't account for the fact that you saw the words *exactly* when I needed you. And how could your brain *possibly* know that someone is planning to *kill* the President?"

Although Frank remained calm, David's agitation was increasing. "I don't *know*, maybe..." David paused. He really had no good answer, but he couldn't let Frank win. "Maybe somehow I could see it, like on a piece of paper. Maybe the killer wrote it down, and my mind viewed it remotely."

"You're brain reached out, subconsciously, and saw a killer, possibly hundreds of miles away, as he was writing down, *I'm gonna kill the President.*"

David rolled his eyes. "This isn't productive."

"I'm just trying to show you how *crazy* it sounds."

"Like God sending me messages doesn't sound crazy?"

"Well, God has been sending messages since the beginning of time. I don't see how this is any different."

"Sending messages? What *messages* has God sent?"

"The entire *Bible* is a message from God, written by people who were moved by His Spirit."

"Allegedly."

"I could show you proof, but that would put us on a rather long rabbit trail, and I don't think that's what you came here for."

David was relieved to hear that. The last thing he wanted was another sermon about how the Bible is written by God even though men wrote it.

Frank's expression took on a gentle intensity. "You wanted to know if God can speak to people, and I would simply tell you this, when you look at a word, even a single word by itself, and you sense a confirmation-- I believe that sensation is God's Spirit. He's been doing stuff like that since the foundation of the earth. I don't see any reason why this kind of manifestation would be out of the realm of possibility for him."

David wiped his hand down his face. "I just don't know. It all seems so *mystical.* I'm a nuts and bolts kind of guy. I need to see to believe."

"Perhaps you need to believe to see."

David was tired of riddles. "Believe to see. Gotcha. I'll have to think on that one." David looked up at the clock on the wall. "Sorry to cut this short, Frank, but I have to go. I have to pick up a friend at Logan. I appreciate you trying to help me."

"I don't know if I helped at all, but I do hope you find your answers."

"I'm sure I will, buddy. Thanks."

"If there's anything else I can do, let me know."

David rose. "Will do. You get better, okay?"

Frank looked at him sympathetically. "Alright. Thanks again for dropping in. I'll be praying for ya."

David smiled. "Sure, Frank."

He left the room and headed down the hall, unsure

whether he was any better off for having visited. As far as David was concerned, if the messages *were* coming from God, that just opened up a whole bunch of new questions. And if his past experience with God was any gauge, he didn't think God was interested in answering any of them.

74482

Ben stopped his bike, shoved the envelopes into the mailbox near the corner at the end of his street, and looked longingly at the worn path on the opposite side of the road. It led to the park where new playground equipment had just been added. He wanted to go check it out, but his mom had said to come right home. They were going to the funeral parlor to talk about arrangements for Uncle Brandon's funeral. That was the *last* thing he wanted to do. *Why can't I just stay home?* At ten, he thought he was old enough. Again, he looked toward the path, then heaved a sigh. He *really* didn't want to go sit at a funeral parlor and think about the death of his uncle all day. He really didn't want to think about anything.

A pressing darkness enveloped his heart as he pushed down on the pedal. The bike wobbled forward. As he made his way down the sidewalk, a dark blue van pulled into a driveway a few houses up; the tail end stuck out onto the sidewalk. Ben eyed the gap as he pedaled toward it. A dark skinned man jumped down from the passenger side and made his way around to the back. A similar looking man came around from the driver's side. They opened the back doors, and Ben decreased his speed. There was no way he could get around without riding in the street. Which would be worse, riding in the street, or getting too close to a couple of strange men standing at the back of an open van?

He pivoted on his seat and looked over his shoulder at the traffic. *I'll just cross now and ride on the other...*

Violently the handlebars twisted as the bike came to a sudden stop. He was launched over the handlebars. The world went into a spin, his elbows dug into the tar as he landed. He flipped over onto his back. His skin was on fire. He fought back tears and turned his head to see his bike lying next to him, and the deep pothole in the sidewalk beyond. *Stupid hole...*

"You there, boy." Ben's body stiffened. "Are you okay?" The voice had a strong accent.

"Y- yes." He rolled over onto his belly and began pushing himself up.

"Here let me help you." The man reached down and gripped Ben by the arm. His grip was strong, much stronger than Ben could get away from. Panic burned in his chest, but he forced himself to stay calm.

"You're bleeding." The man said examining his arm. "Do you live far from here?"

Ben carefully pulled his arm away. *Do I live far? Does he want to know if anyone is watching so he can kidnap me?* "Ah-- no. I live, just over there." He motioned to a white house across the street, a few houses down.

The man wore a leather coat, and as he turned to look across the street, Ben glimpsed a gun tucked into his pants. The boy's heart pounded harder, but he forced his eyes away and pretended he hadn't seen it.

"Let me help you with your bike." The man leaned over. "It looks okay. Here." He handed it to Ben. "You need to be more careful."

Ben didn't like the way the man spoke. He was saying nice things, but there was no kindness, no *anything* in his voice; it was cold and dark.

"I- I will, sir. Thank you." Ben pushed the bike along the sidewalk, hoping to get away. But the man kept pace with him.

Is he waiting for just the right moment? Ben fought to control his breathing as he carefully looked at the man sideways. He was scanning the neighborhood, looking up and down the street. *Is he going to grab me? Why doesn't he just leave me alone!* Ben's elbows throbbed, and his hip ached so that he could barely hide his limp. He looked over his shoulder at the traffic again and shifted his direction toward the street. The man kept pace with him, eyes still scanning.

Silently they approached the edge of the road. There was an opening in the traffic so Ben stepped down and quickly began pushing his bike across. The dark man continued to walk beside him, silently scanning the neighborhood with his black eyes.

When they reached the other side, Ben turned and looked up at the man. "Thank you, sir. I'm okay now." His gaze shifted to the open van across the street. There were two metal boxes inside, one of them had words printed on it. *Hazardous Mat...* The man at the van quickly stepped in front of the opening. His face had a scary, mean look on it. Ben blinked, turned around, and started walking again.

Fear seeped into his soul like oil coating his insides. At any moment the dark eyed man would grab him with his strong hands, and he wouldn't be able to get away. His chin began to tremble. A few more steps, he told himself. He kept his head down to conceal his fear.

"Boy, look at me."

Ben turned slowly, his entire body quaking now.

The man probed him with a deep bone chilling intensity. "Smart boys know what is best to keep secret." He spoke in a cold even tone. "Are you a smart boy?"

Ben shuddered. He unclenched his teeth, and fought

back the shivers. "Y- yes, s- sir."

The man narrowed his eyes. "I believe you are a smart boy. Make sure it stays that way."

With every ounce of courage, Ben managed a nod. He gripped the handlebars, jumped on the seat, and tore off down the sidewalk. The frame creaked as he bore down on the pedals in quick succession. His mind screamed at the bike, *don't even THINK about breaking down on me!* His legs moved up and down like two oiled pistons. The beat of his throbbing heart encompassed him.

He came to the white house he had told the man he lived in, rode up the driveway and around to the backyard. Hopefully that was enough to fool the man with the gun. Ben hoped so. With all his heart, he hoped so.

David sat in his car, staring at the water stains on the cement wall of the hospital parking garage, his eyes slightly out of focus, his mind completely out of focus. Staring at the dark patterns. Staring. Brain switched-- off.

No questions about God.

No messages.

Nothing but the hollow buzz-- of his own-- numb...

A sound filled the interior of the car, David's heart surged. He reached in his pocket and pulled out his phone. "Yeah?"

"Hey, buddy."

"Hey."

"You don't have to pick me up. My flight got bumped. I arrived earlier and I knew you'd be working so I took a cab home."

"Oh, okay."

"I want to see you though. Can you meet me at your house in an hour? I want to know more about what's going on."

"Yeah. That makes two of us."

"Are you okay? Are you going to *hang* up on me again? Punk."

David laughed. "Yeah, about that..."

"Don't worry about it, man. I know you're dealing with some crazy stuff."

"It's gotten worse."

"*Really?* What do you think is causing it?"

David rested his forehead in his hand. "Well-- Sharon thinks it might be Brandon talking to me from the grave, my next door neighbor thinks it's God, I'm leaning toward psychic ability, and based on this morning's conversation with my daughter, she thinks I'm a superhero."

"What? No extraterrestrials?"

David laughed. "Yeah. Or maybe it's my *future self* contacting me from another *dimension.*"

"Okay. Now you're being foolish."

"Oh, and the extraterrestrials thing wasn't foolish?"

Alex laughed. "Hey, everyone knows ETs have been visiting our planet for centuries. That means they've been flying through space at the speed of light since we were pounding rocks to make fire. With that kind of technology they could totally mess with your brain."

"Point taken."

"But I prefer the superhero theory." Alex loved Emily as if she were his own. He'd held her the day she was born, and he had made it a point to make it to her every birthday. His job required him to travel a lot, and he had not yet settled down with a family of his own.

To Emily he was Uncle Alex. To Alex, she was the sunshine itself.

"You know what she did last week at the drug store?" David said.

"What?"

"We were standing behind a rather large woman, and Emily looked up at me and said really loud, 'Daddy. That lady's *fat.*'"

Alex burst out laughing. "She didn't!"

"Yeah. She did. So I crouched down and gave her the father daughter talk. You know the one. I said, 'Honey, if you don't have anything nice to say about somebody, you shouldn't say anything at all.'"

"What'd she say to that?"

"Well she was quiet for a minute. Then she looked up and said, 'Daddy. That *fat* lady has nice shoes.'"

They both burst out laughing.

"And oh," David said, still laughing, "Sharon told me this one. A couple of weeks ago, she was messing around with her and biting on Emily's ear, you know, just nibbling. Emily was laughing her head off. But then when Sharon stopped and said, 'I love you,' guess what the girl said back?"

"What?"

"She looked Sharon right in the face and said..." David started chuckling.

"Come on, what did she say?"

"She said, 'Bite me!'"

There was a pause, then they both burst out laughing.

"That Emily is an endless treasure trove of accidental humor," said Alex, his affection for the girl clear in his voice.

"I know. I should write these things down so I can read them on her wedding day."

"I'm sure she would appreciate that."

David looked at his watch. "Hey. Let's talk face to face at the house, okay?"

"Okay. Sounds like a plan."

"I'll see you there."

"Alright."

David hung up and set the phone back in his pocket. It was going to be good to see his best friend again. It had been far too long.

David pulled into the decaying parking lot of a convenience store, and slipped into the last open space out front. To the right, a couple fought over the pay phone, to the left, a homeless man approached a teenager getting ice. The sign in the window indicated a sale on twelve-packs of Coke. Big surprise there. David just wanted a quick bite to ease the grumbling in his belly. After all, he never did get to eat that donut.

He walked to the doors and made way for a woman coming out. She passed without so much as a glance. That was the way of the city. Making eye contact was risky business, and most avoided it for fear of being caught up in someone else's drama.

Four people stood at the cash register, several more browsed. David went straight to the aisle with the sweets. A couple of Ring Dings would fill the need, and he could finish them before he got home. Sharon didn't eat sweets; processed sugar was poison! Well-- maybe it was, but David couldn't bare the thought of a life without the sweet delectable substance. It didn't matter that Sharon rarely got sick, and he caught every germ within a five mile radius-- he didn't care. He would rather live a short happy life and die of a Ring Ding overdose, than live under the bondage of tofu burgers and carrot juice.

He slapped the package on the counter and looked up past the cashier's head. Above eight rows of scratch-off tickets was a lottery sign with a Saint Patrick's Day theme.

Clovers danced with dollar signs, singing their promises of luck and wealth to all who dared enough to dream. The title of the game was, Take Two. His eyes stopped on the word *Take* and the familiar feeling washed over him, confirming the word, and urging him to bounce to the next. David refused, remaining frozen on the word.

He would *not* mindlessly follow the messages like a soulless puppet every time they came to whisper. But did he have a say in the matter? He recognized the irritation. It was the same irritation he'd felt when talking with Frank. The conversation in the hospital had planted a seed. Were the messages from God? This thought produced an overwhelming frustration in the deep routed sections of his heart, sections where he had decided to not only give up trying to find answers, but where God was hated for making it so difficult. To David, the messages were just one more example of how God hid himself behind riddles.

"Will that be all?" the burly Mexican behind the counter asked mechanically.

David snapped his eyes to the man. "No. Actually."

The cashier raised his eyebrows.

David slid the Ring Dings off the counter and stepped away. "I-- need something else."

"Y'okay, man?"

"Yeah." David shook the dazed expression from his face, "Yeah. Of course. I'm fine."

The Mexican eyed him over pudgy cheeks. He was used to dealing with odd behavior, and was studying David for signs of trouble. David forced a smile, and drifted toward the ice cream cooler. He was going to have to settle this conflict with God, or whatever it was. Either trust the messages and obey, or *ignore* them and get back to his life. He couldn't spaz out every time it happened. He looked around. People were beginning to stare, so he retreated into the movie racks.

Okay. Just breathe. It's probably some stupid message like, take a pack of gum or something. Besides, I don't HAVE to do it. Whatever it is. He peered through the movie racks at the Mexican, he was ringing up the next customer. David relaxed slightly and took a step back. His eyes shifted focus and rested on a movie. *The Sixth Sense. The* and *Sixth* stood out. Was this more of the same message? *Did my brain anticipate my withdrawal into the movie racks, or am I picking up a different message?*

He did *not* want to deal with this right now.

David exited the racks, picked up a pack of Tic Tacs, and stood in line again. *This is NOT God. It's just my mind reaching out, searching for words to communicate with me.* But what were the chances his mind could pick up several words from all over the store to spell out the same message? Wouldn't his moving about cause his mind to seek out a new message from the new location? Or was his subconscious somehow moving him to where the words were? He searched for the word sixth from his place in line. If he had been standing at the counter, would he have found the word sixth? He didn't see it. --He shook his head. It didn't matter. What would it prove?

David put the two items next to the cash register and looked at the Mexican.

"Will that be all?"

He looked past the man and grabbed the words *Lottery* and *Ticket*, from an advertisement on the back wall. The words came together and solidified in his mind. *Take the sixth lottery ticket.*

His eyes snapped back to the Mexican. "No," he said, a little too fast, "I'll take a lottery ticket."

59

The cashier gave an annoyed look and turned to the tickets. "Which one?"

"The sixth one."

"Black Jack?"

"Ah-- yeah. Yes. Black Jack."

"You sure?"

"Yes."

The Mexican tore the ticket and slapped it on the counter. His stout fingers poked the register, and the price appeared on the readout. David slid him a five dollar bill, grabbed his items, and waited for his change.

"Have a nice day," the cashier said, handing him his change.

David did not respond, but turned quickly and exited the store. He jumped into his car, threw the Ring Dings and Tic Tacs in the passenger seat, then fished a quarter out of his pocket. The rules were simple: Beat the dealer's hand and win the amount shown. He scratched the silver rubber coating. The dealer had a twenty. Slowly he worked his way down the card. Loser. Loser. Loser, all the way down to the next to the last slot. No winners. Every set was lower than sixteen. With one slot left, he took a breath, positioned the coin, and scratched. The cards added up to twenty-one. *A winner!* He scratched off the prize with eager anticipation. He couldn't remember ever winning *anything.* Well, nothing but a stupid Hanson CD, and that had come with a price. Someone flung it off the stage at a high school dance and it hit him right in the eye. Some prize-- and he didn't even like Mmm Bop.

He wiped the dust from the face of the card and looked to see what he had won. *Five dollars! What the...?*

He stopped himself.

There had to be a reason, something he would find out

later-- like the coffee shop. He got out, went back into the store, and laid the ticket on the counter.

"A winner?"

"Yes. *Five* dollars."

The cashier ran the ticket through the machine, and a mechanical voice announced, "You are a winner." He opened the register and pulled out a five dollar bill. "Will that be all?"

David looked at the wall of scratch offs. Was he missing something? The message said to take the sixth lottery ticket. Was he supposed to take the sixth ticket *in?* If that was the message, which of the eight slots should he have chosen? He looked down at the five dollar bill lying on the counter and up at the sixth machine.

"I'll take five more."

The Mexican turned and sighed. "Which ones?"

"Black Jack, all Black Jack."

The burly man drew five tickets out of the container, ripped them off, and slapped them on the counter.

David picked up the fifth ticket, which would have been the sixth one in, and handed it to the cashier. "Would you check this for me?"

"Don't you want to scratch it?"

"No. Please, just check it."

He plucked the ticket from David's fingertips and ran it through the machine. "You are a winner," the machine said.

David leaned over the counter. "How much?"

The Mexican looked astonished. "Four-hundred bucks!" He looked at David. "How'd you know?"

"I... It just came to me."

"Congratulations," said the woman behind him in line.

"Yeah. Congratulations," said the man behind her.

David looked back at them. The woman was petite and

pretty, the man, large with a bushy white mustache. "Thanks."

The cashier turned the card over and slid it to David. "You have to fill out the back and sign it."

David took a pen from the container next to the register, filled in the information, and signed his name.

"I'll be right back," said the cashier. "I have to get the manager to sign off on it."

"Has anything like this ever happened to you before?" asked the woman.

"No. I never win anything."

"Wish I had that kind of luck," said the man behind her. His bushy mustache spread wide as he smiled.

David returned the man's smile, pleased with his new found ability-- for the first time.

"You're all set, Mr. Chance," said the cashier coming out of the back room. He punched the ticket code into the cash register, swiped it through, and issued David his prize. "There you go, four-hundred dollars."

David stacked the fifties, folded them, and tucked them in his front pocket.

"Don't spend it all in one place." The man in line smiled at him again.

David smiled at everyone as he headed for the door. But then a newspaper caught his eye. "Senate Passes Bill." He stopped and scanned the cover. His eyes grabbed two words from the article and put them together with the word *Bill*.

The message was, *Give to Bill.*

--Bill? What bill? Oh MAN! Am I supposed to pay some stupid bill with this? How fair is that? It's like the Hanson CD all over again! Was it too much for the messages to give him *eight* hundred, four for the *bill* and

four for him? He let out a deep sigh. Just *once,* he wanted to win something good without having to *suffer* in the process.

He turned and gripped the door handle. *Just when I think something good is going to come from this stupid curse...* A crude flier on the front door caught his attention. The words *in* and *line* screamed at him. *In line? In? Line?* Slowly he turned and looked back at the man in line. *OH! So now I can't even pay a BILL with the money!*

He approached the man and cleared his throat. "Um. Here's a crazy question."

The man turned and looked at him.

"Is your name *Bill?"*

The man's eyebrows rose. "Yes--?"

The woman turned and looked at them quizzically.

David forced himself forward. "Look. I don't want a bunch of questions, okay?" He pulled the money out of his pocket and thrust it toward the man. "Apparently this belongs to you."

The man looked at him sideways. "I- don't understand."

"Neither do I." David was unable to hide his irritation.

The man stood frozen.

David's face grew intense. "This is the part where you *take* it, no strings attached, and say *thank you."*

A nervous hand shot forward. David placed the folded bills in it.

"Thank you," said the man.

David pushed the words to his lips. "Don't mention it."

11234

By the time David reached his neighborhood, he had *almost* managed to put the whole convenience store incident behind him. He kept telling himself that the look on Bill's face had made it all worthwhile.

David pulled onto his street and rolled toward his house. He saw that Jerry and Alex were inside already. Alex's cherry red Mustang convertible sat against the curb. Jerry's Toyota Prius was parked behind it. David shook his head and muttered to himself, "You'd think a professor at the prestigious Harvard University could do better than a *Prius.*"

Everyone was in the living room when David entered. All eyes turned. Alex stood to greet him with a hug. "I missed you, man."

David squeezed him firmly, ignoring the sensation of stubble on his neck and the smell of after shave. This was his closest confidant, his childhood friend. It was not a body he was hugging, but the soul within. He stepped back. "How was your trip?"

"Egypt is beautiful this time of year." His eyes widened. "Oh, before I forget. I got the kids something." He went to his bag and pulled out an ornamental wooden dagger and an Egyptian doll. "What do you think?"

"I think you spoil my kids."

"Well until I settle down and get a few of my own, yours are all I have." He smiled. "I have to spoil somebody."

David looked at Sharon sitting on the couch next to her

brother. "Speaking of the kids, where are they?"

"I sent them up to their rooms to play quietly. They're both having a really rough day."

"I bet."

"Ben's exhausted, and he had an accident on his bike."

"Poor kid."

She nodded and turned her eyes down.

David set the items on the end table and turned to Alex. "I'll give these to them later. They're probably better off in their rooms right now."

"Your head must be spinning," said Alex.

"What do you mean?"

"Losing Brandon and having those weird messages start all at the same time."

David let out an ironic laugh.

"Have you had any more?"

"Only all morning."

"Really? As intense as the first ones?"

"Well-- this morning I read a message that said the President is going to be killed in two days, and I need to stop him. Is that *intense* enough for you?"

"Shut *up.* " He examined his friend's face. "You're kidding, right?"

"Wish I was."

"The *President?*"

David nodded.

Everyone stared in stunned disbelief. Seeing their reactions gave even more reality to the message. It was scary, and dangerous, and bigger than he could handle.

Alex shook his head. "If anyone else said it, I would have called 'em a liar to their face. But not you, David. If you say it happened, it happened."

Sharon stood abruptly. "I don't like this, David. This is

in*sanity.* " Her voice shook. "You're not trained to deal with something like this, and I won't sit by while you go getting yourself killed. I've lost too much this week already." She put her hand to her mouth.

David looked around the room. "I haven't decided on anything yet."

"But Sharon's right," Alex said, sitting on the arm of a recliner. "You have a family to think about. Don't go getting yourself killed."

Jerry cleared his throat. "This will probably be an unpopular statement, but would it be such a bad thing if he did? I mean-- die?"

They all turned a stunned look at Jerry.

"Not *David!* The President!"

The room filled with disgust.

Sharon's eyes narrowed. "I can't *believe* you just said that."

"It bears mentioning," said Jerry. "He's running for a second term, and the war on terror is *out of control!*"

"We're talking about the *President* of the United States!" David snapped. "Whether I *agree* with his *policies* or not, he is still the leader of the free world. We should honor that office." He turned to Alex. "Help me out here."

Alex put his hands up. "I got out of politics a long time ago."

"It doesn't matter," said Sharon. "You're *not* doing it. Tell me you're *not* doing it."

"I don't even know what *it* is."

"Do you know who the killer is?" asked Alex.

"Nope."

Alex grabbed a magazine from the recliner. "Find out right now. Ask the messages to tell you, then tell Homeland Security. You don't need to be involved in this. Turn it over to someone who's trained to handle this stuff."

David stared at the magazine. "I've never tried asking the messages. I don't even know if it would work."

Alex stood. "Try. If it doesn't work, you're no worse for trying."

David looked around; He could see they weren't going to take no for an answer. He grunted, grabbed the magazine, and opened to the first page. "Okay. *Messages,* or whatever you are, what, is the name, of the assassin?" He looked at the page and bounced his eyes around. The sentences were gibberish. No words stood out. The second page was the same. He continued on, page after page.

"Anything?" asked Alex.

"No. Nothing. --Hold on. Wait a second." His eyes fell on the word *flash* and he felt the familiar confirmation. He allowed his eyes to bounce around. *Flash, one, two, three, drop.* It was a message, he was sure of it. But it didn't make any sense.

"What do you have?"

What *did* he have? "I don't know. Just gibberish."

Jerry leaned over the magazine. "Maybe the name's not in there. Ask a more generic question."

David shrugged. "Okay. *Where* is the killer?" Immediately his eyes stuck on one word. *Near.*

His blood ran cold.

"Do you see something?" asked Sharon.

David looked up from the page. "It says *near.* The killer is *near."*

"Are you sure?" Sharon's eyes were wide.

"Positive."

They looked at each other with blank stares. Alex moved to the window and pushed the curtain aside. "Nothing out of the ordinary on the street." He looked at David.

"Maybe the message means in Boston."

Jerry got up and peered into the kitchen nervously. "The definition of *near* is a short distance. I would hardly call Boston a *short* distance." He wiped the sweat from his brow. "I don't like this one bit."

Sharon moved next to David and put her hand on his arm. "Ask another question. Ask what the killer looks like."

He looked down at the page and bounced his eyes around. The message he got shocked him.

"What is it?" said Alex.

He looked up with a stunned look on his face.

"David. What is it? *Tell us.*" Sharon squeezed his arm.

"It says," David spoke slowly. *'Won't tell you, ever.'*"

"What?"

David looked at Sharon. "Apparently it doesn't play by our rules."

She stepped back. "Then you don't play at all! How can you stop a killer if you don't even know who it *is?*

David put his head in his hand and hovered over the page. What was he supposed to tell her? The messages came on their own terms. His eyes focused on the open magazine. "Wait a second. There's more."

They all moved in closer.

"It says, *'too dangerous.'*" He looked up. "It won't tell me because it's too dangerous." David paused. "To protect us maybe?"

"Protect us from *who?* That's hardly reassuring," said Sharon.

"Yes, but it's *already* protected me." He looked her in the eye. "It saved me from a fatal car accident. It rescued Frank from a heart attack. It hasn't lead me wrong yet."

Unbelievable. He was *defending* the messages.

Alex grimaced. "I don't see how keeping the *identity* of

the killer from you could *protect* you. It only leaves you vulnerable. He could walk right up to you and you wouldn't even know it."

Sharon started backing up. "I'm getting the kids. We're not staying here."

David took her wrist. "Hold on. There's no need to get rash."

"If that killer is *'near,'* I want to be as far away from *here* as possible."

"Just because he's near doesn't mean he knows we *know.* It only means he's close. That's probably why the messages chose *me,* because of proximity. Maybe I'm in a position to stop him."

Jerry spoke up. "Putting aside the concept of a TV intern chasing a killer being a ludicrous idea, you're putting everyone you know in danger. And for *what,* for some war mongering crusader who's dragged the country into a ridiculous holy war *against* the will of its people?"

"Now it's a holy war? I thought it was about greed and oil."

"It's *both.* Don't you read the news? They *hate* us over there! Every second we stay, we bolster their *hatred* for us and unify them in their aspirations of global Jihad! This President is stirring up a snake pit!"

David shook his head. "These extremists already aspire to dominate the world with their religion. Nothing *we* do is going to change that. What we have the ability to do, and what I believe this President *is* doing, is rooting them out of the crevices they're hiding in."

"Afghanistan! Not Iraq! *Why* are we in Iraq?"

"What would happen if the terrorists got their hands on nuclear weapons? Huh? What then?"

"Iraq didn't *have* any weapons of mass destruction."

Sharon got between them. "This isn't *helping* anything!"

"It's helping quite a bit." David sneered. He looked past her at Jerry. "I'm learning who I can *trust.*"

Jerry whipped his jacket off the side of the couch. "If you pursue this," he said, pointing his finger, "you are inviting *horrible* consequences, and *I* don't want to be anywhere *near* you!" He looked at Sharon. "You and the kids should come with me. If you stay here, you're likely to get yourself killed."

Sharon turned to David with pleading eyes.

The anger on his face melted. "If you would feel safer there, I'll understand," he told her.

"Do you believe we're safe here? Do you, David?"

He looked at her. "Yes, for the moment. Somehow I feel sure."

She narrowed her eyes at him-- then sighed. "I'll wait, I trust your judgment."

"I'll leave the house key for you," Jerry said, putting his coat on. "You know where it is."

"Thanks, Jerry. Sorry about all this."

"For what its worth," he said, "I don't want to see *anyone* hurt. I just want peace. And I don't think we're heading in that direction." He turned and walked out the door.

"Wow," said Alex. "Check that magazine again and see if the killer is still *near.*"

David gave a small chuckle and pointed at him. "That's not funny."

Alex opened his eyes wide. "Maybe he's the killer and just doesn't *know* it yet."

Sharon folded her arms. "Stop it, this is serious."

A smile creased Alex's lips. "I know he wouldn't harm

a fly, Sharon. I'm just teasing."

"Dad?"

All three turned to see Ben perched on the stairs.

David walked over to the banister. "What is it, son?"

"I heard you guys talking, and I- I know something."

"What do you mean?"

"I saw something this morning down the street, at the house on the corner."

"Which one."

"The one with that guy who never smiles at you."

"Oh? The Arab man?"

"Yeah."

When you fell off your bike?" asked Sharon.

"Yeah. I didn't want to tell you because I didn't want you to lock me up in the house."

She shook her head. "I knew something hap..."

David held his hand up. "What did you see, Ben?"

"The man had a gun in his pants, and I saw two boxes in the back of his van. One said Hazardous M-a- t-something. It was all metal. It looked like something important."

"Hazardous Materials," said Alex.

"You saw this in the back of his van?" The Arab made David nervous, but he never would have imagined *this*.

"Yep. The other man stepped in front of it so I couldn't see. What does it mean?"

"Well, we don't know..."

Sharon gripped his arm. "Call the police. Let them check it out. This is big stuff, David."

"Wow," said Alex, "a terrorist, right down the street. That's going to drop the property values."

David put his hand on Sharon's. "I don't think calling the police is the right move. They might not believe it as a credible lead and just call a car in. Terrorists would at least have a scanner, and more likely something greater. No. We should call the FBI, or Homeland Security."

"What if they have moles in the government?" said Alex. "If they're organized enough to be able to take out a President, they most likely have connections in high places."

David threw up his hands. "This is all conjecture. We have no idea who these people *are,* or how deep their organization runs, *if* there is an organization at all!"

"And," said Alex, looking out the window again, "we don't know how they'll react if they find out you're involved."

"We need to make sure they *don't* find out."

"How do you do that, when you don't have any idea what they're *doing?* Every call you make could lead them to your doorstep."

David paced. "We have to find out more."

"Daddy, what's going on?" That was Emily's voice. She stood on the stairs with her eyes wide, peering at all the concerned adults.

David opened his arms, and she came down and gave him a hug. "It's okay, honey. We're trying to figure something out. Big people stuff."

"Oh." She pulled away and turned to Alex. "Hi, Uncle Alex."

He went down on one knee and she walked into his embrace. "How's my favorite girl?"

"Are you sure you want us to stay here?" asked Sharon.

"I'm going down to the station to see if Nerd can call up any information on this guy. At least there I won't have to worry about any terrorist moles. You'll be safe here, no one knows anything about this. Just keep working out the funeral arrangements, and don't tell anyone about what's going on."

Her eyes pleaded with him.

He didn't want to leave her any more than she wanted to stay, but he had to get some answers, and he believed it would be safer for her and the children to stay put.

"I can stay with them awhile," said Alex. "I have to meet with a new client at six, but I could stay until then."

"Would you?"

"Sure."

David was relieved. His family would be safe with Alex. Alex was a precious cargo courier, and the job required him to have a concealed weapons permit and a hand gun, which he was quite adept at using. He had bested David at the firing range on more than one occasion.

David gave Sharon a kiss. "I won't be long. I promise."

The sign on the door said, CLOSED. The television station was *never* closed. Especially on a Friday. David peered through the glass. There was activity deep inside, but they would never hear him pounding. He turned and looked down the long brick face of the building and remembered the service entrance out back. He made his way around the building and found the black box hanging next to a gray metal door. In the open-faced wooden box was a phone, and a sign reading: For Emergencies: Press 0. For the Receptionist: Press 2. For News: Press 3. David picked up the receiver, pressed 3, and looked up at the tiny black camera lens.

"Hi, David," said the voice on the phone.

"Hi, Janet. Let me in."

"Make sure no one else goes through. Only you, okay?"

David looked around. He was alone, except for a handful of news cars parked under the overhang. "I'm alone."

"Okay." *Buzz. Click.* The door unlocked.

He put the phone back in the cradle and entered.

To his right, beyond glass and girders, was the newsroom where stories were processed and teleprompter script was written. The nerve center of the station; here field reporters contacted leads, filed reports, and cataloged finished pieces. David could tell by the flurry of activity that something *big* was going on. He could almost feel the tension through the glass. Another intern, a woman named Jenny, emerged from the newsroom carrying a handful of papers. David leaned in her path. "Has Brad returned with the crew yet?"

She looked at him like he had globs of Jello on his face. "Nerd's in the newsroom." She turned and walked away. "Where've *you* been?"

David shrugged off the comment and entered the newsroom. Nerd sat beside a desk. Crouched in front of him, gently sponging a nasty cut on his forehead, was Cindy Coulter, the six o'clock co-anchor.

David began making his way toward them, but something caught his eye, a poster for a new television show titled Worth the Wait. His eyes rested on *Wait.* He came to a stop. He looked down at a pile of papers on the desk nearest him. One paper dangling from the side stood out from the rest. He reached down and grabbed it. It was nothing special, a hard copy of a story that ran a week ago. *Is there something you want me to know?* He bounced his eyes from top to bottom, side to side-- and his mind formed a sentence. *Write page forty-nine on Post-it.*

David squinted at the page. --*What?* He looked down. On the far corner of the desk was a bright pink square of Post-its, alone and conspicuous. He set the page down and rounded the desk. He wanted to believe it was a fluke, but he recognized the familiar sense, a sense he was beginning to trust, if only slightly. He glanced around. Was anyone going to care if he used one Post-it? Quickly he grabbed a pen and wrote "*page 49*" on the little pink sheet and peeled it off. *Okay. Now what am I supposed to do with it?*

"David, is that you?" It was Cindy.

He peeled the note from his finger and stuck it to a Federal Express envelope sitting on the desk.

"I thought you had the day off."

David walked toward her. She was still crouching in front of Nerd. "Yeah. I came in to check on a couple things. Is everything okay?"

She looked at Nerd as if to say, 'Does everything *look* okay?'

"You alright, Nerd? You look pretty banged up. What happened?"

The red-headed man, looking whiter than usual, brought his gaze up to meet David's. The familiar flamboyant cockiness was missing from his expression. "They..." His voice broke and he looked away. "They shot him, David," he said in a low voice. "They shot him in cold blood."

The words traveled down his spine in twisting currents. "What? *Who?* Who shot who?"

"John. They shot John-- and they took Brad."

David slumped down on the edge of the desk in shock. *What?* His mind tried to wrap itself around the words. A wave of nausea washed over him. *"Who?"*

"Terrorists," said Nerd. "They broke into the truck and shot him." He swallowed hard. "Twice. In the chest."

David struggled to let the information sink in. *"Why?"* He shook his head. "And what happened to you? Did they hit you?"

Nerd nodded and wiped his eyes. "They gave me a message." He looked up at David. "The only reason I'm alive is because they gave me a message."

Cindy put the first-aid kit down and stood up. "They hit him over the head and left him in the truck. When we couldn't reach the team, we called the police. They found Nerd in the truck with John. Brad was gone."

David looked at Cindy, then back to Nerd. "Wh- what

was the message?"

"They said in two days, Allah is going to give a gift to the people of the United States, and that their demands would soon follow."

Two days? David's head felt light. It was happening. It was really happening. There *was* a plot to kill the President, and *terrorists* were involved. Was it connected to the hazardous material? Were they going to make a bomb? He swallowed. "I don't suppose they said what the gift *was?*"

"No," said Cindy. "But we're guessing they'll want to use the station to broadcast their threats and propaganda."

"Have you called Homeland Security?"

"I can't say."

David squinted at her. "Oh. Okay. I get it. You know, it was *my* team that got hit. I feel like I'm part of this."

"We'll tell you what we can. But for now, just hold tight." She gave him a pat on the arm and walked over to another desk.

David crouched in front of Nerd. "Wow, this is totally crazy. Have you ever been involved in anything like this?"

"Truck operators don't go to dangerous sites. They send reporters and cameramen to do stupid stuff. Smart people don't do stupid stuff."

"Where were you?"

"They hit us right before the art show. I was going to run switch for the art piece, not fight terrorists. And John..."

David had never seen Nerd so pitiful. Every word caused his lips to exaggerate. The incident had completely shattered his normal outgoing persona, exposing a vulnerability everyone knew he possessed. It was, after all, why everyone put up with his normally flippant personality.

"They had silencers, but the shots were still so loud. It was *horrible.* I thought I was dead." His lip trembled. "They

77

grabbed my hair and whispered in my ear. Real close. Then one of them hit me with his gun. That's all I remember."

David stood and carefully considered his words. "Nerd, I know you've been through a lot this morning, and I completely understand if you say no. But do you think you could help me look up some information about the terrorists?"

Nerd looked at him blankly. "How would I do that? We don't know who they are."

"My son saw something this morning, and..." David stopped. "Can I tell you in private?"

Nerd looked to either side. "I guess." He looked down at the wad of bloody bandages in the trash can, then said, "Let's go down to my office."

13

Nerd's office was the wire room in the basement. Every Ethernet cable in the building coiled down to its multiple main frames in less than fashionable green aluminum caging. Boxes of electronics filled every corner. In the middle of the room five monitors sat atop a black work table, competing for space among a clutter of components and partially dissected gizmos.

Nerd opened a silver box and flicked some switches. "It's safe down here," he said, looking up. "We can talk freely. What were you saying about your son?"

"There's an Arab guy who lives down the street from us." David stepped into the caged area. "I've always been a little wary of him because he never responds when I smile and wave at him. But I gave him the benefit of the doubt, thinking maybe he was just an unfriendly guy, which is not a good trait for someone of Middle Eastern decent, what with all the hysteria about terrorism going on. Anyway, I just brushed it off. But this morning Ben said the guy had a handgun in the waist of his pants and two boxes of hazardous materials in the back of his van."

Nerd's eyes widened. "Whoa. Right down the street from you?"

David produced a wry expression and gave a nod.

"You must be freaking. I mean totally *freaking.*"

"I'm certainly not happy about it."

"Where is this house?"

"At the end of my road."

79

"Let's take a look at the map." Nerd switched on his monitor. "I know your town, what's your address?"

"105 Birchwood."

He typed in David's address, zoomed in on his street, and tracked down to the Arab's house.

David pointed. "That's the one."

Nerd called up the address, switched to another program, and entered the data. A record for the house popped up on the screen.

"Hamid Abdul-Jilal. Owner of the house for two years." He cracked his fingers and called up another program. "Let's see who this Hamid guy is."

The name of the program was *People Tracker*. Nerd typed in the name and address. With a click, the screen loaded up a profile. In the upper left corner was the face of the Arab. The rest of the page contained information: schools attended, licenses acquired, history of residences.

"That is amazing. I have to say, Nerd, I'm impressed."

"You should be, it took me two years to earn the credits to get this off a hacker buddy of mine." He stopped and pointed his finger at David. "This is *top secret* stuff. You tell *anyone* and I swear I'll erase your social security number."

It was probably an empty threat, but David lifted his palms. "You have my word."

Nerd tapped the keys in rapid succession. "This is a hacker resource that combines four government trackers into one WYSIWYG interface."

"Wuzywig?"

"What you see is what you get."

David furrowed his brow. His knowledge of computers could fit inside a package of chewing gum, with space left for ten sticks.

"You can find everything there is to know about

someone: police reports, medical records, national security threat assessment, everything but personally protected records like financials and password protected web access."

Do I have a page like this? David wondered. Could any hacker in the world dig up vital information about him? "Does everyone have one of these?"

"What? A record?"

"A page like this."

"Yup. Everyone has a page. The more mistakes you make, the bigger your page." He tabbed over to another copy of the program and clicked a bookmark. Nerd's name appeared at the top of the screen, but there was no picture, and the information was limited to common knowledge: name, address, job... "Everything you do is a matter of record: when you get your tonsils removed, register a car, get a passport. Your entire life is recorded by the government, hospitals, schools, the military. All the personal records that were once kept in filing cabinets are now held in computers so they can be transferred across the Internet from one institution to another. With the right access, you'd be amazed at what you can find. And as you can see here," he pointed, "it *is* possible to hide yourself in the system. But it takes a lot of work."

"What does mine look like?"

Nerd brought up another window, his fingers moving like lightning as he typed. David's picture appeared, and the screen filled with a sea of personal data. David scanned down to an entry for the Boston Public Library which listed a book titled, *The Heart of Fascism.* He pointed. "I don't remember taking that out."

"The government keeps a list of books that fit a certain profile. If you borrow a book on the list, your name is flagged in their database. The more you do it, the more you rise up on their priority list."

"How do you wipe your slate?"

"You want a clean record like mine?" Nerd chuckled. "Every piece of data on the list comes from a different source. The best way to have a clean record is to not get on the list in the first place. Once you get on it's *very* hard to get off. But there are ways."

"What ways?"

"You have to have connections. Some people spend their whole lives exploring the system, looking for loopholes. They're the ones who can do it, the rest of us have to watch our step. The data stream is like Google, it never forgets. If your name ends up on a blog because of something stupid you did or said, it's a matter of record on Google. Everyone who queries your name will get that information, whether you like it or not. And it doesn't matter how old the information is. The most obvious way to get rid of it is to do lots of great things, which will bury the bad search data. The other way is to know someone at Google. In the case of your records, you have to know people."

David's brow furrowed. "Let's get back to the Arab."

With a couple of clicks the Arab was back up on the screen. His record was much smaller than David's. Was someone helping him cover his tracks? The basic information was there: address, phone number, make and model of his car; but more sensitive information like medical records, was missing.

"Why doesn't he have any dental records and stuff like that?"

"Because this is a forgery."

"Really. How do you know?"

"See this date?" Nerd pointed to the screen. "This is the earliest data on the record. That means, as far as the—

computer understands it, this guy didn't exist before that date. And since I'm pretty sure he isn't twelve years old, we have a pretty big red flag. This guy probably acquired a driver's license with a falsified birth certificate, then used it to begin a new identity. That's what I think."

"Is there anything useful here?" David stared at the screen.

"Yep. He used this identity to go to Harvard, and according to this-- he has a degree in chemistry."

"--A terrorist with a degree in chemistry-- that does *not* sound good."

"And-- he's probably a professor there now, look at this."

An intercom on the wall crackled. "Nerd, you down there?"

Nerd ran over and pressed the red button on the white face. "Yep."

"You need to get up here. And if you see Chance, tell him to come too."

He pushed the button again. "Be right up."

14

David squeezed into the conference room and was assaulted by a mixture of cologne and perfume competing with hot breath and furniture polish. The shades were drawn, the track lighting dimmed. A large screen TV sat staring blankly at the far end of the room. David glanced around, there were many faces he recognized. The general manger sat with the news director and assignment editor on either side of him. Various department heads and legal staff stood behind them. The six o'clock news anchors and lead reporters lined one side of the table, but down the other side was a row of suits David didn't recognize. Apparently everyone, who was anyone, had been called into the shade darkened room.

David and Nerd squeezed in behind the news anchors as the general manager brought his hand up. The room fell quiet. Briefly he looked around. "I thank you all for coming. As most of you know, there was an incident with one of our news teams this morning. While reporting on the art show downtown, their truck was overtaken by an unidentified terrorist group."

There was a murmur throughout the room.

"The producer for the team," he spoke louder. "John Luntz was pronounced dead at the scene, and Brad Knight was taken hostage. Now I *know* that many of you were close to John, and I realize this is hard, but we need all of you to stay focused on the tasks at hand. John was a great guy, and the best way we can honor his life at this point, is to do our jobs and get Brad back. And speaking of getting Brad back," he indicated to the group on the right side of the table, "these men and woman are from the FBI. They will be setting up a command center on site to monitor events as they develop. They're doing everything they can to find Brad. Work with them."

He paused and looked pointedly around the room. "As you should already know, the station has been *sealed.* Anyone who does *not* work here, or who does *not* appear on this list," he tapped a clipboard with his finger, "will *not* be allowed in. Got it? He put the board down and picked up a remote. "Now a few minutes ago, we received a video from a man who *said* he was given money to drop it on our doorstep. The label has computer generated Arabic writing."

Another murmur filtered through the room.

"Naturally, we believe it is from the terrorists." He motioned with his hand for quiet. "No one has viewed this tape. It could be anything. So if you're squeamish, now is the time to step out." He looked around the room. "Alright." He pointed the remote at the TV, and someone flicked the lights off.

A knot developed in David's throat. *Please don't let it be dismemberment. Anything but dismemberment!*

Brad Knight in an orange jumpsuit appeared on the screen, a low gasp came from the assembled group. Brad was sitting in a chair in front of a black curtain. Duct tape covered his mouth and circled his ankles. They had all seen images of similarly clad news reporters in Iraq. They were aware of the beheadings, they'd seen the news clips. But it had never been this personal, never this close to home.

The shot had a surveillance quality to it. The camera was fixed.

Somewhere in the room a door opened and closed.

Brad's eyes looked left. A figure came around him and crouched down. Dark eyes peered through a red and white patterned head covering. "You are now wondering, are you not, Kafirs?" He spoke in a milky baritone with an Arab accent. "You are wondering if terror has come to your streets? And what this will mean to your precious freedoms? Will you stay in your homes for fear of the judgment, or will you go spend your money and meet the wrath of Allah where you purchase your sins? Be not deceived. The Great Satan *is* being judged. Those who respect earthly ties and comforts, profits and pleasures, more than Allah and his prophet, will be cut down by his sword. There is no safety from the wrath of Allah. No corner where you can hide, you lovers of the Zionists. You *will* know fear."

He shifted his weight. "I address you at News Channel Seven. I want the message you just heard put on your six o'clock news program. If you fail to broadcast it, we will execute your reporter." He paused and his dark eyes bore into the camera lens. "There will be no negotiation. We will give you three messages. This is the first. If you air them, your reporter will live." He stood and disappeared behind the camera. There was a shudder in the image, and the screen went black. The impression of Brad's pleading eyes burned into David's memory.

The lights came up to show everyone in stunned silence.

The general manager spoke. "I know that was hard to watch. It isn't easy seeing someone you care about in a life threatening position, but you need to focus on the tasks at hand. This day is going to be tough on all of us, but this is the business we're in. It's our job to get close to the action, and sometimes we pay a high price for being so close. So now is your opportunity to prove you have what it takes to make it in network news. I'm not telling you to go out and get yourselves killed. I'm saying turn over some rocks, get on the phones, follow up some leads. --But leave the ground investigation to law enforcement. Your job is to report the story. Their job is to nail these Cretins. Got it?"

He looked over at Karen Watson, an attractive dark-haired Spanish woman. Next to Brad, she was the best field reporter at the station. "Karen, I want you to go through Brad's files and see what you can come up with. He was working on an Arab money laundering piece."

"Mosques and Money," she said.

"Yes. Find out if there's a connection. There's more to this story than a mere kidnapping. Something big is brewing." He stabbed a finger at her. "And pass everything on to the FBI. Remember, this is a team effort."

She scribbled on her yellow pad. "Yes, sir."

"I want this clip run in the first block of the six o'clock newscast. Dawn, call Brad's family and let them know ahead of time. I don't want the broadcast being the first they hear about this."

"Will do."

He turned to the news director. "Any thoughts, Jim?"

"We need to make the story more than just a hostage piece," Jim responded. "People are going to want to know how this ties into national security and the border." He looked at Cindy Coulter. "When you write the copy, add in room for some street interviews. We'll get a crew downtown to grab some live reactions."

She nodded.

The general manager gave a glance to the news director. "Thank you, Jim." He looked around the room. "I'm now going to turn the meeting over to Agent Paul Cooper of the FBI."

The man's jet black hair was tight on the sides, and his strong tan features held an unmistakable confidence. "First," he said in a deep gravelly voice, "I want you all to know that we have been following this terrorist cell for some time. We believe this group is responsible for a recent theft of radioactive material, and we have strong evidence to conclude that they are planning to detonate a dirty bomb in a major city. Our sources say it will be New York, but new leads indicate that it very well may be Boston."

The room filled with a low murmur.

The agent held up his hand. "I understand your nervousness, but I assure you, we have a strong trail. We're not going to let this bomb go off. As we speak, agents are positioned all over the city. We are covering every possible site, including this one." He paused. "And that brings me to my second point. In reference to the lock down, while you're in the station, don't go anywhere without your security badges. Our men will be patrolling the halls. They don't know who you are or how important your job is. All they know is they have standing orders to apprehend anyone who does not have a security badge. Please be patient if you are taken into custody." He finished and looked to the general manager.

"Thank you, Agent Cooper." He again looked at the faces around him. "The FBI has been given complete authority for the safety of this facility and its staff. Cooperate with them. Are there any questions?" He probed the room. "Okay. Get to work."

The room filled with conversation as the staff slowly filtered out. Through the exiting bodies, David found himself staring at the face of Agent Cooper. He knew he had to tell him about the boxes in the Arab's van, but he needed to do it privately. Assuming Mr. Cooper kept the information confidential, David would have time to get home and get his family somewhere safe.

He pushed his way around the table and behind the five agents, who were now standing with the general manager and the news director, discussing the location of the command center.

As David waited to interject, his pocket started to vibrate. He pulled out his phone and flipped it open. A text message came up on the screen. *"Do you think I don't know what you are doing, Kafir?"* He almost dropped the phone. *Kafir*-- the Arabic word for unbeliever, the Arab on the video had used it! David's mind raced. *Who did this message come from? The terrorists? But how would they KNOW?* His eyes came up and met those of Agent Cooper. David's heart panicked.

"You okay?" The man's tone was probing.

What could he say? He couldn't tell him what the message said-- yet his panicked look demanded an explanation.

Agent Cooper waited expectantly.

The best lies were the ones that contained an element of truth; he had learned that tidbit from his father. "Ah- I just, got a troubling text message I have to deal with immediately." He closed his phone and slipped it in his pocket. "Can I come talk with you later?"

Cooper examined him with an intense stare, then nodded. "Of course." He turned back to the other men.

David lowered his eyes and made his way around the table. Every nerve in his body was on fire. He had to get out of the room before anyone asked him any questions; he had to think things through. How could the terrorists track him down? How did they know about him? It didn't make any sense!

The phone vibrated again. David walked briskly down the hall and into an empty sales office. He pushed a sweaty hand into his pocket and brought the phone out. *"I didn't think your son would stay quiet. I hope you have the good sense to set a better example. Think of your family."*

My family! David thumbed a reply. "I haven't said anything, and I won't." He clicked send, flipped the phone shut, and sank down into a visitor's chair near the sales desk.

What a *nightmare!* He had to warn his family. *Could* he warn them? Would that set the terrorists off? Were they watching his house? They must have been; how else could they have known the conversation he'd had with his son? The phone vibrated again and David's heart jumped.

He put his hand in his pocket and felt the phone, but his mind refused to send the signal to draw it out. What else would they say? Would there be demands? Would there be threats? *I don't want to know! I don't want to do this! I don't want to do this! I DON'T want to do this!* He yanked the phone out and flipped it open. A message came up. *"Error 6629 number unknown."* The text message he'd sent could not find a number to send to. Apparently, his communication with the Arab was only one way.

A voice startled him. "Tough meeting, huh?" He whipped around to see Karen Watson standing in the doorway. "You okay? You're as white as a sheet of paper."

He took in a breath. "Personal problems at home."

"Anything I can help with?"

"My son's in trouble. I may need to go."

"What kind of trouble?" She didn't wait for an answer. "I don't mean to sound heartless, but can it wait?"

He held his composure and looked up. "Why? What do you need?"

"Jim and I want to talk with you for a second, to pick

your brain, find out what you know about Brad's current projects."

"Ah-- Yeah. Sure." He looked around. "Ah, just give me a second to make one more call, okay?"

"Meet us in Jim's office in five minutes."

"Okay."

She moved down the hall, and David brought the phone up again. He had to warn Alex. He only hoped he wasn't too late.

He punched in the number and the phone began a gurgled ring. "Come on. Come on! Pick *up!*"

Click. "Hello?" It was Alex.

"Oh thank *God,* Alex. Is everything okay?"

"Why do I get the sense I should be worried? Where are you? At the station?"

"Yes. Where's my family? Are they all right?"

"Safe and sound. Why? What's going on?"

How much could he say? If the phones were tapped... *How could the phones be tapped?* That was *madness!* The Arab wouldn't have had time to tap the phones! "Look. I don't know how, but the Arabs followed Ben home and somehow heard our conversation about the boxes."

"What? You're kidding me?"

"No. They just sent me a text message. I know it was from them. They talked about Ben and they know I know about the boxes."

Alex dropped his voice. "How could they..."

"We are talking about a group who has secured radioactive material, probably to make dirty bombs."

"Okay. Point taken." Alex paused. "You know, I saw a device on a movie once that could eavesdrop on a room from several hundred yards away by using a laser beam. The laser detected the vibration of sound on a window and relayed the sound back. Does that technology really exist?"

"I think so. I think I've heard of something like that. If you're right you need to get somewhere where there are no windows. --I know, take the family down to the basement. Then we can talk freely."

"Good idea. Hold on."

David listened. There was movement and whispers. The wait was excruciating. Finally he heard the familiar creak of his cellar stairs, and the shutting of a door.

"Okay. We're in the cellar. What else do you know? Did your friend find out anything about your Arab neighbor?"

"Nothing very useful. But Nerd thinks the name is an alias. There wasn't a whole lot I could find out, but other things have developed. When I got here I walked right into a hostage crisis. One of our field reporters was taken this morning after a cameraman was shot dead in the news truck. They think it was terrorists. The FBI has taken over the station."

"Oh my word! What have you gotten yourself into?"

"I know!"

"This is *crazy,* David. You need to get your family out of here. Get as far away as you can. You don't need to be a part of this."

"I'm trapped at the station."

"Trapped?"

"At least for the moment. One of the field reporters wants to meet with me. If I try to ditch and go home, they'll start asking questions."

"So lie."

"You know I can't *lie."*

David could see Alex shaking his head in disbelief. "If this isn't the time to lie, I don't know what *is.* You need to put your little *hang up* aside and lie your butt out of there."

"My dad was a liar. You know the devastation it..."

"David! We're talking about *terrorists!* Hazardous materials! Assassination plots! I think this warrants a couple of well place *lies*, don't you think? Besides, you wouldn't be lying like your dad did, you'd be lying for a *good* reason, to protect your family and friends. You're nothing like your dad!"

"I'll find a way to get home."

Alex let out an exasperated breath. "You'd better."

"I will. You know I will. Just stay put."

"We'll stay for now, but if I sense any danger, we're outta here. Got it?"

"Okay, Alex. Calm down. Just keep your phone on you."

"Get here." The line went dead.

He did not like leaving things on a bad note with Alex. They had been through a lot together, but this was by far the greatest test of their friendship yet. He knew though, despite their differences of opinion, that Alex meant well. If the situation had not been so dire, Alex never would have asked him to compromise his principles.

Part of David wished he could have given in a little, but if he had, where would it stop? Once he crossed the line and decided to lie... No. He would not cross the line. Ever. *I will never be like my father.*

15

It took a moment for Karen Watson to realize she was staring at the wall. She squeezed her long eyelashes together, and attempted to recompose. Her college foray into psychology reminded her that she was now in the fourth stage of grief, otherwise known as depression. When she first saw Brad on the screen, helpless, and in mortal danger, her mind responded with the first stage, shock and denial. But those had quickly been replaced by the second stage, anger. Anger-- *at Brad! He should have been more careful! He owes me that much.* She had given her heart to Brad Knight, she had never given her heart to anyone before. *How could he do this to me!*

Karen stood by the water cooler holding back the tide of emotions threatening to overwhelm her. She wanted to cry, she wanted to scream, but she did neither. She would *not* allow a hint of remorse to creep in and ruin the reputation she had worked *years* to establish. Reporters are *objective.* They watch from the *outside.* They do *not* let the emotion of what they report show outside their guarded walls.

But this is Brad! BRAD!

She snapped out of her introspection and pulled a cup from the dispenser. A bubble rumbled to the top of the blue plastic jug, and she brought the cup to her lips. The water was cold, but not wet enough to cure the dryness in her mouth.

Laughter came from the break room. She refilled her

cup and took a step to the side. There were four in there. Most of the laughter was coming out of Larry Turner, the burly Texan who was always bragging about his huge gut. He was Brad's first string cameraman, and for the hundredth time, Karen wondered *why* Brad had chosen *him.* He was obnoxious, opinionated, and generally vulgar. But Brad said Larry had a steady hand and a total lack of fear, which she had admitted at the time were indispensable qualities for a camera operator. However, the thought of spending four minutes in a news truck with *Larry* brought to mind visions of her stabbing him with a pencil. In a soft fleshy spot. Repeatedly.

A man sitting at one of the break tables took a *verbal* stab at the Texan. "There's a fabulous new invention, it's called the treadmill. You should look into it."

Larry rolled his eyes. "Everyone's always talkin' like, *'Hey look at these abs,'* or *'Check out this six pack'.* All I got to say is, *check out this ONE pack!"* He rubbed his belly. "You don't get ab like this from eatin' salad!"

The room filled with laughter again as the man at the break table balled up a napkin and threw it at Larry.

Larry held his belly and bounced. "This here's a *chicken graveyard!"*

Karen stepped into the room, hoping to stop him before he let out one of his signature hoots. "Feeling better I see."

He turned and acknowledged her. "Hey there, Karen."

"I thought you broke an ankle?"

"Rolled." He corrected. "Rolled an ankle, darlin'. It's amazin' how these things get blowed out of proportion." He pulled up his right pant leg to expose a brown brace just above his sneaker. "This little baby's s'posed to keep it in place."

"I assume you know about this morning."

95

He dropped the pant leg and swaggered to a stand. "Yeah, I heard."

She chose her words carefully, not wanting to come right out and ask him if he was relieved it was John that died this morning and not him. "How are you holding up?"

He shrugged. "You know me, sugar plumb. Even though I'm thicker 'n a bucket o' honey, ain't much sticks to me."

That was the truth. As long as she had known him, she had never seen anyone get the better of him. His confidence was immovable. And he was equipped with a boundless trove of pithy colloquialisms. But Karen was in even less of a mood for them than usual. "Are you going to the meeting?"

"The one Jim called?"

"Yes, he wants to talk with Brad's team."

"That's why I'm here, sweetheart, and not on my La-Z-Boy watchin' reruns of *Baywatch.*" He turned to the others and held up his palms. "Hey, what can I say? I love a good beach drama."

The chuckles were subdued this time.

How could he *joke* at a time like this? Didn't it bother him at *all* that Brad was being held by terrorists? Didn't he *care* that one of his team was *shot dead? He's completely clueless! A clueless idiot meathead!* Karen thought as she crushed her cup and tossed it into the garbage. She fluttered her eyelashes at Larry. "I think I speak for everyone," she stated pertly, "when I say we are *fortunate* that you are here." The sarcasm fairly dripped off her words. "I don't know what we would have *done* without such a *crucial* and *intelligent* member of the team." She turned and walked out.

From the break room she caught his barely audible reply. "'Bout time someone noticed. Hope the recognition comes with a *raise.*"

16

David knocked just below the nameplate that read, Jim Coldfield: *News Director.* A muffled response came from within. He opened the door to see Jim sitting behind his mahogany desk studying his computer screen. He gave David a brief glance.

Karen turned and looked up from one of the guest chairs in front of the desk, exposing her nylon legs and the yellow note pad she frequently cradled in her lap. Her subdued countenance spoke volumes. It was common knowledge that she and Brad had become close, common that is, to everyone but Karen. She refused to believe that anyone knew.

Behind her, leaning against a glass cabinet filled with various awards, stood Nerd, looking, if it were possible, an even lighter shade of pale. And to the left, so far behind the door David almost missed him, was Larry Turner, holding a to-go bag. Larry squished a powdered donut under his powdered mustache, and offered a powdered wave. In all of Boston, there was no one quite like Larry.

Jim swiveled and looked up. "Have a seat, David."

David squeezed in between the chairs in front of the desk, and sat down.

"I'll make this brief. Karen is following up on Brad's notes, and she may need to call on the rest of you to fill in the blanks. --I know what you're thinking, Brad keeps his lips pretty tight, but if there is *anything,* make sure you pass it along to Karen. And Karen, treat this as a news piece. I know it's personal, but you're not a detective. Keep your distance from the action."

Karen gave an, *I don't know what you're talking about,* expression.

"Everyone knows you and Brad are seeing each other. You can drop the façade."

She straightened in her chair. "I'm a professional, Jim."

"I know. Just stay objective, okay?" She signaled compliance, and Jim turned his examining gaze to David. "I want you to take a look at something." He motioned toward the flat screen. David got up and moved around the desk. "Do you recognize this document?" asked Jim.

David moved in over Jim's shoulder and examined it closely. "It's a bill for liquid fertilizer purchased by a milk farm upstate."

"Did Brad show you this?" asked Jim.

"Yes. He asked for three copies. Why?"

"Do you know what terrorists prefer to make bombs out of?"

"I thought dynamite."

Jim's countenance caused David's blood to chill.

"Do you remember the Oklahoma bombing?"

"Sure. Everyone knows..."

"The bomb consisted of several tanks filled with liquid fertilizer and diesel fuel."

Karen shifted toward the table. "You're saying Brad *knew* about the bomb?"

"Bombs, plural," said Jim. "Remember the FBI said they're tracking two cases of nuclear material. That means they're probably making several bombs. And this document links a milk farm with ties to the mosque money trail and the purchase of large quantities of fertilizer, by one Afif Al-Qadir."

David couldn't help but notice the tension forming on Nerd's face, he looked like he was about to explode. He knew what David knew, and it was obvious he thought David should speak up.

He returned Nerd's intense expression and shook his head subtly. He couldn't tell anyone about the cases. Not yet. Not while his family was in danger. Nerd's eyes flared slightly, but David pressed his lips, and shook his head again. Nerd's eyes darted to Larry, then back to David.

Karen could hardly contain herself. "Do you want me to go to the farm and ask questions?"

"No. I want you to leave the investigation to the authorities."

"But..."

"I know. You want to find out who's holding Brad, but that's not your job. Find all the angles on the story, figure out how it all connects together, so when it breaks we're on top of it. Can I count on you?"

She looked disappointed, but nodded her ascent.

"You let the FBI confront the terrorists, they'll do everything they can to find Brad. I'm only telling you about the fertilizer because we might have an incident out at the farm tonight and I want you prepared to cover it. Follow up on the leads in Brad's computer and find out how the offshore accounts and the Saudi underground fit into the puzzle. And take Larry with you."

Karen looked somewhat baffled, and completely disgusted. *"Why?* I *have* a camera operator." She looked back at Larry.

He gave her a chocolate covered grin.

"You're stepping into some serious waters, Karen. You need someone strong to back you up."

"You're talking about a man who can hardly climb a

set of *stairs* without getting winded! *And* he has an ankle brace for crying out loud."

"S'cuse me," said Larry, "in the room here."

She snapped a threatening glare at him.

Jim slapped his hand on the desk. "Enough. This is *not* up for discussion. You're assigned to each other. Now get to work."

Karen stood, smoothed her skirt, and exited the room in a poised rage, nearly smashing Larry in the face with the door.

The Texan wiped the chocolate frosting from his mustache and peered out into the newsroom. "I gotta give it to her, that gal's got *class*. She can even storm out of a room with style.

David interjected. "Do you need anything more from me? I have a crisis at home I need to deal with."

Jim looked at him. "No. You're all set, David. I only needed to find out if this document was tied to the Mosque piece. You can go."

"Thank you, sir." David joined Nerd and Larry, and the three filed out of the office.

Larry laughed. "Hoo-eee. Today's gonna be like workin' with the gators."

Nerd snorted. "Or like Kirk in *Star Trek Two: The Wrath of Khan.*" He shook his fists at the ceiling. "KHAN!"

Larry shot David a comical expression and slapped Nerd on the shoulder. "On that note, wish me luck. I'm goin' in!"

David and Nerd watched as Larry strutted off through the desks, amidst the frenzy of activity-- king of the newsroom-- larger than life. With all of his obvious shortcomings, David decided he liked him. Larry was the quintessential alpha male, personable, strong, confident, and besides the gut and a complete absence of buttocks to hold his pants up, not a bad looking guy.

Nerd turned and spoke in a low voice. "What was that all about?"

"He was just having fun with you."

"No. In the office. Why didn't you *tell* them?"

David pulled Nerd over to the large bulletin board which stretched from the news director's door to the six o'clock anchor's room. He glanced over his shoulder. "Look, man, you can't say anything."

"You can't sit on this!" Nerd spoke in a tense whisper. "This is *galactic!* You're withholding evidence from an *official investigation!* You're breaking laws here!"

"I know, I know! I'm going to tell them. But my family is in danger. I need to figure some stuff out first."

"David. John is *dead!* We *have* to..."

"Listen. They *know* I'm here. And they know *I* know about the cases!"

"What are you *talking* about?"

"Someone sent me a text message. They *know* about me. I don't know *how,* but they do. For all I know, they could be watching us right now!"

Nerd's eyes widened.

"My family is in danger. I can't say *anything* until my family is safe, not to anyone."

"But people are going to *die.* The good of the many outweighs the good of the few-- or the one."

"You're quoting Star Trek? Nerd! I need you here in *reality.* This isn't a space opera!" He looked around and brought his voice to a forceful whisper. "I'm dealing with something *real,* and complex, and right now I need you to work with me."

Nerd responded, but David didn't hear.

His eyes fell on a paper above Nerd's shoulder on the cork board. Two words stood out to him. *Read carefully. Oh great!* He looked at the ceiling. *Read WHAT carefully?* He stepped back and focused on the board. Was there a message here?

Nerd's voice crackled in his ear. "Are you listening?"

He brought his hand up and stared intently at the board.

Nerd turned and scanned the wall. "Are you *okay?*"

"Nerd, please!" David touched his fingertips to the board and trolled slowly to the right, his eyes darting randomly from posting to posting with a fierce intensity.

Nerd watched, mouth gaping.

From station memos, to want ads, to posted news clippings, David's eyes bounced and scanned. His mind drew in the message, one, word, at a time. At the end he stopped, and took a step back.

"That was *total* creepsville." Nerd gave a snort.

David turned, as if noticing him for the first time. He brought Nerd's vexed expression into focus.

"Earth to David. Come *in* David."

David blinked. "Sorry. I-- I have to go." He pushed past Nerd and headed for the staircase.

"Where you going?" Nerd said, tagging close behind.

"If I'm right, I know where the bomb is." David pushed through the door and bolted up the stairs.

17

Sharon and Emily sat huddled together on the cold cellar floor, Sharon's back against the hard wall, Emily's back against her mother. Ben was playing with some trucks he'd found in a box under the workbench, and Alex sat on the stairs, looking frustrated.

Sharon hadn't seen Alex like this in years. Since his conversation with David, he'd been in quite a mood. Normally it took a lot more to ruffle Alex's feathers. *Maybe it's Emily,* Sharon thought. He'd always been very attached to Emily. Maybe her being threatened was putting him on edge.

Emily rested her cheek on her mother's arm. "How long are we going to be in the laundry room?"

"Until it's safe, honey."

Alex looked at his watch and scowled. "David better call soon. I have to get to my appointment at six. It's almost five now, I can't just leave you guys here."

Sharon looked shocked. "You're *still* going into the city? With everything that's going *on?"*

"I deal with danger all the time in my work."

"Can't you meet with your client *outside* of Boston?"

"It's complicated." He rubbed his hand through his hair. "If there was any other way, I would. I don't like..."

A distant knock sounded. Emily sat up. Ben stopped playing.

"That's our door, Mom," said Emily, standing up.

Sharon remained still. Listening.

"Aren't we going to answer it?"

Sharon shushed her gently. "We don't know if it's the bad people."

Emily's eyes grew wide. She hadn't thought of that.

There was another knock. This one louder and more urgent. Alex got up from the stairs. "Are you expecting anyone?" Sharon swallowed and shook her head. There was a good chance it was just one of her neighbors checking in on them, but she didn't dare go up and find out.

The doorknob rattled.

Sharon pulled Emily to her. Her little body was shivering. "Mom, I'm scared."

"It'll be okay," Sharon whispered.

Ben came over, crouched down, and put a hand on his sister's shoulder. "It's okay, Em." He made a pretty good pretense of coming over to comfort his sister, but Sharon wasn't fooled. His pensive stare towards the cellar door revealed his real reason for coming. He was scared too, and he needed his mother.

Footsteps creaked in the kitchen. "They must have come in through the back door," Sharon whispered.

Alex put his finger to his lips, he slipped his pistol from his work bag, and motioned for them to get under the stairs. Sharon and the kids moved silently across the floor. The footsteps moved through the living room and up the stairs to the second floor. They waited in silence, barely breathing. The footsteps returned to the stairs, and slowly descended. Very slowly they came back into the kitchen-- then stopped next to the cellar door. The knob twisted. Emily let out a squeak. Sharon clamped a hand on her mouth.

Click. The door opened.

Alex looked back at Sharon with reassurance, the gun gripped tightly in his hands. From the top of the stairs came one slow creak, then another...

Sharon desperately tried to control her anxious breaths. Emily dug her fingers into her mother's arm, making Sharon realize that her daughter couldn't breathe. She loosened her grip, and the little girl panted quietly, frozen in fear.

Another creak, and another. Ben burrowed in next to his mother. Alex brought the pistol up. More creaks. The footsteps reached the bottom. A shadow quivered on the basement wall. Sharon's eyes locked onto it in silent terror. The figure rounded the corner. Alex brought the pistol up.

Sharon looked left and saw his reflection in the mirror on the wall. She sucked in a breath. "ALEX! *NO!*"

Jerry's hands flailed as he screamed and fell back against the cement wall. *"Don't shoot! Don't shoot!"*

Alex jerked the gun up and shook with annoyance. *"Stupid fool!"*

The family scurried out from under the stairs. "You *scared* us half to death! Why didn't you call out and let us know it was you?"

Jerry composed himself. "I saw both of your cars out front, but the door was locked. With all the talk about killers..." He looked from Sharon to Alex. "I thought something bad was going on."

"Were you trying to *sneak* up on the killers?" Sharon said. "We could *hear* you going through every part of the house. Not exactly a *ninja.*"

Jerry glared. "Very funny."

That brought a slight smile to Alex's face.

Jerry surveyed the room. "What are you guys doing down here?"

"Hiding, what does it look like?"

Alex picked up his work bag. "David got a message from the terrorists. They know he's onto them. We think they might have the technology to listen into the house from a distance. Maybe with lasers. We don't know. But none of us are safe here. I've been waiting for David to call back, and this is the only place we know we can talk safely. You know what, it's actually good you showed up. I have to go. Can you take everyone to your house?"

"My house? Wh- what if they see us leave?"

Alex put his hand up. "Don't worry, I have a plan."

Jerry furrowed his brow.

"They won't follow you if you leave by yourself, because they aren't after you." Alex grabbed a notepad out of his bag and moved over to the laundry table. In the light of the fluorescent lamp, amid a pile of socks and folded underwear, he drew a map. "This is the house." He made an X on the paper. "Beyond the back gate is a stone walkway leading through the neighbor's yard to the road. Take your car, Jerry, drive around to the next street and park here." He pointed. "Sharon and the kids can go out the back and meet you. Hopefully they're only watching the front of the house."

"Seems like it might work," said Sharon.

"I'm scared," said Emily, gripping her mother's hand tightly.

"It's okay, honey, we just need to get to Uncle Jerry's car. Then we'll be safe."

Emily's little face was flushed. In her seven years of life the most traumatic event she'd had to deal with so far, was the flu. Ben looked like someone about to leap off a cliff. Sharon reached out and ran her fingers through his hair. "It's okay kids. This will all be over soon."

18000

David ran down the second floor hallway toward a door marked *Computer Lab*. Nerd followed in breathy pursuit. He had given up calling out. Clearly, David wasn't listening. With a twist and a thrust on the door handle David burst into the lab. The eight computer stations were unoccupied. *Good! No one to ask questions.*

Nerd pushed in behind him, gasping for air, rubbing his knees.

David sat down and swiped his access card, the computer monitor came to life.

"Could you- please- tell me..." Nerd panted, "what you're talking about? How do you- know where the bomb is?"

"If I told you you'd think I was crazy."

Nerd snorted and extended his gangly arms. "News flash, David. Already do."

He didn't have time for this, his family was in danger. And now he had to crawl through four weeks of emails, looking for a needle in a haystack.

Nerd folded his arms. "Either you tell me, or I'm telling the FBI what your son saw."

"You wouldn't do that." David's eyes stayed fixed on the screen.

"Of course I would! Thousands of lives could be in danger! I saw one man killed today, I don't want to see any more!"

David's hand slid off the computer mouse; Nerd had

him. There was no way around it. David sighed. "Alright. *Okay*. You want to know? I'll tell you, but you're just going to think I'm nuts."

"Try me."

David looked Nerd in the eye. "I've been seeing messages in words around me. I string random words together and they make sentences. They tell me the future, and they tell me to do stuff. So far they've saved my life and the life of my neighbor. There. You happy?"

Years of addiction to science fiction and fantasy had, no doubt, prepared Nerd for this moment. Immediately he grasped the concept and accepted it as truth. "You saw a message on the bulletin board! Your brain decoded it?"

"Yes. I know how crazy it sounds, so don't bother telling me."

Nerd matted his fluffy red hair with his hands. "This is *awesome!*"

David raised an eyebrow. "You believe me."

"Absolutely! My brother Craig smells stuff, then weeks later he'll go somewhere and the smell is *there!* Wild, huh?"

"Yeah. Can I get back to this?"

Nerd shot his hands straight out. "Wait. Wait. What did the message say?"

"It said..."

Music Music Music filled the computer lab. David shot a startled hand into his pocket, pulled his phone out, and looked at the caller ID. Not the terrorists. Just Alex. He held his hand up toward Nerd. "I have to take this."

Nerd looked around awkwardly, then sat down in one of the computer chairs.

David brought the phone to his ear. "Yeah."

"You're not here yet."

"I know. I'm sorry."

"My appointment's coming up fast and I want to make sure your family is safe. I've come up with a plan."

"Good. What are you thinking?"

"Jerry came back. He's going to take Sharon and the kids to his house."

"No. No. That's not good enough. They should be somewhere unpredictable." A dark thought crept into David's mind. *What if they go after my extended family? Is Mom safe?* He'd have to warn her soon. David shuddered. "No. Have Jerry take them to a friend's, or to a hotel, or somewhere else. Okay? I need to know they're safe."

"Alright. That's fine. I can do that."

"Wait! What if they follow him?"

"It's okay. He's going to leave first, by himself, then Sharon and the kids are going to run out the back and meet him on the other street. That way the terrorists will think he left alone and will keep watching the house."

"Alright. Good plan. Thanks, buddy."

"Sure thing, man. I wish I could stay with them, but I've been working on this meeting for months. I'd miss it if I had to, I mean, you and the family are more important than anything, but if I can make it..."

"I know. You don't have to explain."

Alex let out a subdued laugh. "I also wouldn't be braving a potential nuclear blast if it wasn't so important."

"Do you *have* to go? Is it really worth it?"

"It never is. --Anyway, when it's over, I'll catch up with you. It shouldn't take too long."

David furrowed his brow. "Just be careful, okay?"

"I always am. It's what I do."

"Okay, well I'm going down to the Industrial Park by the bay."

"The Industrial Park? A news assignment, or more

messages?"

"A message. It said, '*Danger at the West Downs Industrial Park.*'"

"You're *kidding* me. You're not *going*. --*Are* you?"

"You think I *want* to go? I know my family needs me. But I'm afraid *not* to do what they say."

"It said, '*danger*' it didn't say *go.*"

"Actually, it did."

Alex let out a long frustrated breath. "I could strangle you! If you get yourself blown up, I'm going to kill you. Got it?"

David's tone was sarcastic. "Got it. Don't get killed or you'll kill me."

"Okay, *mouth.* Man! When did you get so *mouthy?*"

"I'm as frustrated as you are!" snapped David.

"Well at least *wait* for me. I'll get my meeting done and head over to you as fast as I can, then we can go together."

"The message said..."

"The message! The *message!* I'm sick of this! They've got you thinking you're some kind of *secret agent.* You're a television *intern,* with friends and family, and might I add, not a *shred* of combat training. I mean for crying out loud, *Emily* could take you!"

David took in a controlled breath. "Sharon and the kids will be safe. Jerry will take care of them, and I'm... Well, I believe I'm going to be fine too."

Alex's tone relaxed, slightly. "You really believe these messages will protect you?"

"I have no reason not to trust them."

"You don't even know what they *are.*"

"--Okay. Alex, I have to go. Tell Sharon I'll call soon."

Alex sighed. "Do you at least have a firearm, or can

you get your hands on one?"

"Sorry. Not that I can think of."

"I'll get my backup handgun and bring it with me. If you're going to go head-to- head with terrorists, you'll need something."

"Thanks. Okay. I have to go. Call me when your meeting gets over."

"Promise me something."

"Yeah?"

"Don't try to be a hero."

"If I become a hero, it won't be intentional."

"Alright. I love you, man. I'll call you soon." The phone went dead.

Nerd shifted forward in his chair. "Was that a friend of yours?"

"Yeah."

"What's his name?"

David squinted at him. "Alex Blackstone. Why?"

"Oh. Just wondering. You sounded pretty *bugged.*"

"He wants me to leave town but I can't. Not yet anyway."

"What are you gonna do?"

David turned back to the computer. "I know I have to go to the Industrial Park, but I don't know where exactly. The only clue I have is the part of the message that said, *'where the diesel flows.'"*

"Diesel?" Nerd leaned forward. "That's one of the components of the bombs. You have a lead on the diesel?"

David tapped the keys. "More than that, I have a lead on the bombs."

"The *bombs?"*

"Yeah. The message also said, *'Danger at the West Downs Industrial Park.'* I'm pretty sure that means the bombs are there. But first I have to find the place. That's where the diesel clue comes in. Brad sent me an email a little while ago. He wanted me to find out which companies in the West Downs Industrial Park stored diesel. I looked it up and sent him a list. If I can find out which one has a connection to the Arabs, I might have the location."

"The message didn't tell you which place?"

"No. Only the clue."

"Why?"

"I don't know. Maybe the right words weren't on the bulletin board." He paused. "Wait. I think this is it."

The email came up on the screen. Four companies were listed.

Nerd pushed on David shoulder. "Move over. I can do this faster than you."

David got up and Nerd plopped down and began copying and pasting and transferring over to his own login. Within minutes he had the public business records for each company.

David scanned them. "Here, Ace Wrecking and Repair. The owner is Robert Finney, but there's another name, Afif Al-Qadir. He co-signed for the building lease."

Nerd gave David a wide eyed stare. "That's the milkman."

The connection was unmistakable. Brad had stumbled onto more than a money trail, and Al-Qadir was at the center of it all-- he and the Arab down the street, Hamid Abdul-Jilal. One had the diesel and the fertilizer, the other had the nuclear material. And David had all the leads. But was he ready to share those leads with the FBI? He could, once he knew Sharon and the kids were safe. He would give Alex twenty minutes, then tell Agent Cooper everything. After that he could head over to the Industrial Park. The message said go, and he didn't dare disobey.

Sharon gripped Emily by the hand and tucked in tight behind Alex. He turned the cellar door handle, peeked out into the kitchen, then around the door into the living room. It was clear. He motioned it was safe, so Sharon poked her head out. Alex moved across to the front window and pulled the curtain aside.

"Do you see anything?" she whispered.

"There's a car up around the bend with two people in it. Other than that, everything looks like it should."

Jerry came up the stairs, did his own check of the kitchen, and looked at Alex. "Do you think the people in the car are the terrorists?"

"Could be. It's difficult to tell at this distance."

"What if they follow me?"

Alex gave him a firm look. "They won't. You're not the target."

"But what if they *do?*" Jerry questioned everything.

"I don't *know!* Drive to the police station, or the fire station. That's just around the corner."

Sharon didn't know if Jerry scowled at the thought of being chased by terrorists, or because he hadn't thought of going to the police station himself. She thought about her brother. He had never been a thrill seeker. As a boy, he was always the one who would plop down in the snow bank to watch everyone else slide down the big hill. He never liked sliding, it was too dangerous. He preferred to make patterns in the snow-- or just eat it. There was no drive in him for danger, no need for adventure. Bravery simply wasn't in Jerry's character. Brandon had gotten all of that. Yet in her time of need Jerry had come to her rescue. A feeling of gratefulness washed over Sharon. She reached out and rubbed his arm. "You're a good brother. Thank you for coming back for us."

The nervousness melted from his face and was replaced by a hint of valor. "You're the only family I've got," he said, smiling slightly.

She gave him a sympathetic look. She hadn't thought about it before, but without her, Jerry would have no one. At least she had David and the kids, and David's family. If something happened to her, Jerry would be completely alone in the world.

Alex went to the staircase and peeked up. "Alright, Jerry. It's clear."

Jerry squeezed his sister's elbow. "I'll see you in a couple of minutes."

"Be brave," she said, patting his arm.

He smiled. For once in his life she saw him as the brave one. As the Hero. He seemed pleased with the thought. His face beamed, if ever so slightly. He brushed past Alex, quickly looked out the door, then exited with a soft thump.

Sharon ran to the window to see Jerry pause briefly on the stairs. He took his keys from his pocket, then made his way down to his car. She could only imagine what was going through his mind, and a disturbing thought occurred to her. *The car could be rigged with a bomb. A bomb! Why* hadn't she thought of that *before* Jerry went out? She needed to tell him-- but then the terrorists would know she knew. *Oh, Jerry, please check under the car!*

Jerry reached the curb, walked around to the driver's side of the Prius, and stopped. She wanted to run to the door and warn him, but remained fixated on her brother's still contemplation. He looked up at her, then down at the door.

Please, Jerry. Check! Please, God, don't take Jerry!

He gripped the handle. Her heart constricted. The thought of losing two brothers in one week produced an aching stab in her chest. She couldn't bear it, her desperate fingers dug into the curtain.

The car door popped open and Jerry climbed in.

All was quiet.

Sharon let out a controlled breath, then looked back up the street at the parked car. It remained still. Jerry pulled away from the curb, and slowly moved off down the street. She backed away from the curtain and looked over at Alex. "I don't hope to do *that* again anytime soon."

Alex squinted. "Do what?"

"Nothing." She put her hand to her forehead. "My imagination just got the better of me."

Ben spoke from the top of the cellar stairs. "Mom? Emily's crying."

As he said it, Sharon realized that her daughter had been crying for awhile. The faint sobs had not registered because her attention was locked onto the events outside. She descended the cellar stairs and found Emily squeezed between the washer and the wall. Her face was wet, her hair tangled in moist clumps. Sharon pulled her out gently by the wrist.

Emily clutched her mother's waist and buried her face in her belly. "I don't want to go outside, Mama. Please don't make me go outside."

Sharon hugged her tight. "I know you're scared, honey, but we have to leave right now. It's not safe here."

"I don't want to!"

Sharon crouched down and held her daughter by the

shoulders. "Do you remember when we jogged with all those people and earned money to help babies?"

Emily nodded, but didn't look up.

"We are going to go for another jog, but this time, just over to the street out back. Okay?

Emily continued to clutch her mother.

"You alright down there?" Alex called.

"Yes. We're coming." Sharon ran a hand across Emily's cheek. "Come on now. Mama's right here. Everything's going to be fine."

"Will you carry me?" Emily looked up.

Sharon raised her eyebrows. "I'll try but it might be faster if we both run. Okay?"

She pouted and looked at the floor. "Okay."

Sharon stood up and took Emily by the hand. They headed up the stairs. Alex was at the back door, scanning the back yard. "You see anything?" Sharon said, peering past him.

"No. It's quiet."

"Mama, I don't want to..."

"Shhh. Everything is fine." She crouched down and put her arms around Emily, and looked up at Alex. "Do you think Jerry made it to the other street?"

"He wasn't followed. Everything should be okay."

Alex slid behind the three of them and back into the kitchen. "I'll check the car one more time."

"Okay."

Sharon looked out the back window again. For once she was thankful they couldn't afford more lawn furniture. She dreaded the thought of running through the yard enough without dozens of potential hiding spots for the terrorists to jump out from. She looked down at Ben. His eyes were like saucers, but he was holding together pretty well, all things considered.

Quick footfalls sounded through the kitchen and Alex appeared in the doorway. The look on his face said everything. Something was very *wrong.* "We have to go. *Now!"*

"What's..."

"They're coming up the front steps!"

Panic filled her mind as she grabbed the kids and pushed them through the door and across the yard. Alex raced around them, skidded to a stop, and fumbled with the gate, and his pistol. He looked intensely over his shoulder.

"Here!" Sharon pushed forward. "I'll get it!"

Alex trained his eyes on the back door and window as Sharon expertly flipped the latch. It pivoted up with a squeak. She swept Emily up in her arms. *"Go Ben! Go!"* she yelled. They skirted down the path, around the neighbor's lilac bushes, and out to the street.

Jerry's car was there.

Sharon opened the back door and the kids jumped in. She looked back at Alex. "What are you going to do? You can't go *back* there!"

Alex paced, stopped, and slid his hand down his face. "I guess I have to go with you."

There were so many things she wanted to say, but one look at his face told her she'd better save it. She turned and hopped into the back with the kids. Alex climbed in the front.

Jerry had a confused look. "I thought you were..."

"No time for questions!" Alex said, *"DRIVE!"*

20

The conference room on the second floor had been converted into a mobile SIOC, or Strategic Information and Operations Center, as the Feds called it. It consisted of four laptops tied into stacks of mysterious electronic equipment, and a dozen agents with headsets tied into cellphones.

David was stopped by a rather intimidating agent at the entrance of the room. He feigned confidence. "I need to speak with Agent Cooper."

"What do you need." The agent's tone was calculated.

"I have vital information concerning the investigation."

"All information needs to be passed through your chain of command."

Agent Cooper's head came up. His eyes met David's. "Agent Garis, let him in."

The agent moved to the side, his features still cold, his body language still unwelcoming.

Agent Cooper waved David in then started talking into his headset again. "All teams in standard chem gear. Download the SOP to your location." He held a finger up to David. "Yes. And put Charlie Team on the ridge to the left of the silo. Build the team as you see fit. Okay. Out." He pulled his head set off and placed it on the table.

"Hope I'm not interrupting."

"You're the one who came to talk with me earlier."

"Yes."

"Name's Cooper." He offered his hand.

David shook it. "David Chance, sir."

"You looked pretty shaken up in the conference room, like you're sitting on something big. Am I right?"

"How did you..."

"Training, son. I've been in this business a long time. I know a man running scared when I see one."

David squirmed slightly.

"Tell me what you're dealing with, and I'll walk you through it, whatever it is."

"Yes, sir. Well-- this morning my son saw two boxes with 'Hazardous Materials' written on them. They were in a van at a house belonging to a man who lives down the block from us. I believe his name is Hamid Abdul-Jilal."

Agent Cooper's eyebrows rose. He reached over and tapped the woman sitting at the table next to him. "Amy, take this down please." He looked back at David and paraphrased. "You have come in contact with Hamid Abdul-Jilal, and your son saw hazardous materials in the back of his van?"

"Yes. There were two men there this morning, one of them had a gun tucked in his pants."

"Do you have a license plate number for the vehicle?"

"No."

"Give Amy the address, she'll look into it further."

David leaned in and told her the address. Her fingers flew over the laptop keyboard.

"Did your son see anything else suspicious?"

"No. But when I came in today I tracked down some leads and learned a few other things." David handed him a printout. "Brad Knight was working on a story about mosques and terrorism. I think his goal was to find a correlation between the recent increase in the national threat level and terrorist activity in Boston-- specifically finances coming in from the Middle East through local mosques."

121

"Yes. We know. Brad has been sharing information with us for months."

"Oh. Well did he tell you about Afif Al-Qadir."

"We are in the process of following up on that lead."

"Do you know about the diesel?"

The agent's eyes widened slightly. "No."

"Brad was onto more than the milk farm. He had me on task to check out the West Downs Industrial Park. He wanted to know how many businesses in the park had the capacity to store diesel. Of course, I didn't think anything of it at the time, but- ah, something clicked for me today, and I started digging. It turns out, Afif Al-Qadir has his hands in a company called Ace Wrecking and Repair, located in the industrial park.

Agent Cooper read from the paper David had given him. "So Afif Al-Qadir co-signed for the lease on a garage and warehouse in the Industrial Park, a garage with a history of diesel shipping and storage." He handed the paper off to Amy. "Add this to working leads."

"Yes, sir." She snatched the page, swiveled in her chair, and started entering the data.

Cooper turned back to David. "You've had a busy day, Mr. Chance."

David gave a half smile. "Oh you have no idea."

"Anything else we should know about?"

He shook his head. "No. That's about it."

Cooper reached into his pocket and pulled out a business card. "Here, take my card. If you hear or see anything else, give me a call."

David took it. "Thank you."

"No, David. Thank *you*. This information will help a great deal."

Nerd was standing outside with a look of expectancy

on his face. "So what are you going to do now?"

David looked back at the agent guarding the door and starting walking down the hall. "I'm going to the garage," he whispered.

"Are you out of your *mind?* That's where the terrorists are."

"We don't know that."

Nerd leveled his eyes on David.

"All I know is the messages are leading me to the garage. There must be something there I'm supposed to find."

"Yeah! *Terrorists!* "

David stopped. "I wish everyone would stop telling me what I already *know!* " He tried to keep his voice level. "I *know* it's dangerous. I know I'm in way over my head. I understand terrorists kill people. I'm not stupid. *Man!* "

"The FBI is going, why do you need to go?"

"Because *they* don't have *God* talking to them!" As soon as the words slipped through his lips, he wished he could suck them back in.

Nerd looked at him sideways. *"--God?"*

"The *words*. I- I don't know what it is!"

"You just said God."

"Drop it, Nerd!"

"It's just like the Vorlon on *Babylon 5...* "

David turned on him. "I swear, if one more word comes out of your mouth, one more word! You'll be sorry! *Got it?* "

Nerd cowered against the wall.

"I *don't* want to *talk* about it anymore!" David pressed the button for the elevator. The door opened. He stepped on and turned around. "I'm going to the Industrial Park because lives are in danger, and I may be the only one who can do *anything* about it!"

The elevator doors were almost closed when Nerd nuzzled up to the slit. "You're a prophet, David."

David punched the crack where Nerd's mouth had just been.

A *prophet?*

David didn't know *what* he was, but he certainly didn't need Nerd's whacked out sci-fi theories messing up his already confused mind. Sure, he wanted to believe it was God. That's why he had made the statement. He needed to believe the source of the messages was something bigger than himself, a force capable of leading and protecting him. But the possibility of believing it was God was challenged by his past experiences with religion, and religious people. He had seen too many contradictions to allow himself to be sucked into some kind of euphoric safety bubble. If only *God* would just tell him straight out. But *no!* Everything had to be a *riddle. A stupid stinkin' RIDDLE!* David looked toward the elevator ceiling. *"YOU are SO frustrating!"* His phone went off and he ripped it out of his pocket. *"Hello!"*

"You okay?" It was Alex.

"Sorry. Today's been a bit, *trying*, to say the least."

"Well, I just wanted to bring you up to speed."

David forced himself to lighten his tone. "Yes. How is everything?"

"Your family is safe."

"Good."

"Jerry took them to his friend Claire's house, over by Harvard."

"Yeah, I know where that is. We had a picnic there last summer."

"And David. Don't go home. Some men were coming up your front steps as we were leaving out the back. I think it

124

was the terrorists. Apparently they're interested in more than just eavesdropping."

"Great!" The elevator doors opened. "Well, I hadn't planned on going back there anyway. *Man!* I hope they don't break *in."* He stepped off the elevator and headed toward the back door of the station.

"I had to leave my car there. I hope they don't mess with that. If they mess with it, I'm gonna be *ripped."*

"Are you going to miss your meeting?"

"No. Jerry dropped me off at a rental place. I'm all set for the moment. Although, at this point I'm pretty sure I'll be late."

David looked at his watch. "It's quarter to six. Where are you now?"

"On 93, heading into Boston."

David passed by the newsroom, it was still roaring with activity. "Well, call me as soon as your meeting is done."

"Better believe it. I won't let you get killed alone."

David had to smile. *"Yeah.* Thanks for the vote of confidence."

"Stay safe till I get there. See ya."

David flipped the phone shut and held in the button on the side. If Alex was going to call him later and meet up, he wanted to make sure the phone was set to vibrate. It buzzed in his hand-- then buzzed again. The readout said, *"Incoming Text Message."* He flipped it back open and looked at the screen. *"I will kill you, Kafir. Mind your own business."*

David's heart froze.

Did they know he was going to the wrecking company? *How?* Maybe they only knew he had looked up information in the computer and shared it with the FBI. Maybe they didn't know where he was headed. He reached out and

125

steadied himself on the wall. What if they were watching him right now, waiting to kill him? Suddenly, the hall to the back door seemed like the throat of an enormous beast, expanding and contracting, in anticipation of swallowing him whole. He forced himself forward, gripping the wall as he went. The messages had told him to *go* to the industrial park. The author of the messages, whoever it was, had clearly shown a knowledge of future events. If the messages said *go*, then it had to be possible for him to go. Otherwise, why send him?

He reached a shaking hand out, gripped the door handle, and turned it. The door creaked open a crack. Cold air and the smell of oil and tar hit him in the face. There was no one in the carport. He pushed further and peeked out at the hill on the other side of the service road. No movement there either. His muscles loosened, but only slightly; there was still a lot of distance to cover from the station to the garage-- and the terrorists could be anywhere. He rubbed his face with his hands. *This, is going to be, a LONG night.*

21

A low tone came again from somewhere in the distance, far beyond the wall of storage boxes where Brad Knight sat on the floor, hugging a rusted metal pipe. He strained to listen, hoping to decipher its source, but the transient sound drifted away into numbing silence, for the third time.

He rested his groggy head against the pole, allowing his neck a break. One eye opened sluggishly and studied the tiny camera on the tripod five feet in front of him. Its cold lifeless stare scrutinized his every move. They had warned him, any attempt at escape would be punished severely. So he remained still, and waited. The duct tape on his wrists forced his hands into a praying position, and the continual pressure had caused his fingers to turn a dead shade of blue. The feeling had left them, and that concerned him, but he remained calm.

This was not the first time he had faced horrors in his job as a field reporter. Sometimes at night when he closed his eyes to sleep, he still heard the bombs and the wailing of air raid sirens outside his hotel in Baghdad. He saw images of the decay in Somalia, and smelled the blood in the subterranean torture chambers of Uganda. Yes, he had seen his share of horrors. But somehow he felt he would get through this one as well.

A door slammed and a scratchy voice spoke in Arabic on the other side of the wall. Brad listened intently. He had continued studying Arabic even after his time in Iraq, and had become quite adept.

"Get up, we are going," the voice said.

"Are we going to the bomb site?" said the guard.

"Not yet. Now we will move the hostage to the truck and wait."

"Wait? Why can we not go now?"

"Afif says to wait. So for now, we wait. But we will move to the truck. When it is time, we are ready."

"Has the bomb site been secured?"

"Soon. If the arms dealer does his job."

The guard kicked something. "Why do we trust that Kafir?"

"Must I say it again? We only trust him to a point. For now, his goals are our goals, so we will work together. Have you not heard the old saying, 'The enemy of my enemy is my friend?'"

"I don't trust him. He should have killed the American by now."

"He will do what he is paid to do. We are on the brink of our finest hour. Soon, every city in America will be begging for mercy."

"Allahu Akbar, brother."

"Allahu Akbar. Now, let us move the journalist."

A bolt slid and the storage door creaked open. Brad looked up at the outline of the man vibrating in the doorway. The drugs they had shot into his arm made it difficult to concentrate, but he forced himself to focus. The guard had on a black shroud but was otherwise dressed in normal street attire, blue dress shirt, jeans, black shoes. Without the head covering, he could have been any college student.

"Get up. We go," he said in English. He pulled a knife from the sheath on his belt, gripped Brad by the wrist, and cut into the duct tape.

Brad winced as the tape ripped ample sections of hair from his arms. He rubbed his eyes with rubber fingers then attempted to focus on the knife in the man's hand. Under normal circumstances he would have made a move for it, but in his current state, he decided against it; his brain was doing somersaults in his head.

"Get up!" the man said, waving the knife in the air.

Brad rolled onto his hands and knees, pushed himself to a stand, and steadied himself on the pipe. The room dipped and swayed uncomfortably.

"Let's go." The guard gripped him by the shirt at the shoulder and pushed him into the other room. "Kneel and put your hands out." Brad knelt. The guard held him down by the shoulders as the other man peeled off strips of duct tape and re-taped his wrists.

It struck Brad as odd that these men would use duct tape. If these were the same Arabs responsible for the recent theft of nuclear waste from Pilgrim Station on Cape Cod Bay, he would have expected handcuffs. Breaking into a secured depot and making off with two cases of plutonium, he was sure, took a level of professionalism several grades above duct tape. Could this be a different terrorist cell?

He was gripped under the arms and lifted to his feet. He teetered a moment, but when he found his balance, the men led him out of the room and down a short hallway. Brad couldn't tell what kind of facility it was, there were metal doors with glass windows, but the walls had been stripped bare. They turned a corner and went through a door leading out to a large bay containing a mid-sized U-Haul. The back was empty.

"Get in," said the man with the scratchy voice.

Brad walked up the ramp with slow unsteady steps and stole a few last glimpses of the bay. The swimming pools of color kept him from clearly identifying anything. The man climbed up behind him, forced him to a sitting position, and crouched down. "If you are not bound when we again open this door, we will shoot you. Understand?"

Brad gave a heavy nod, though he suspected it was nothing more than an empty threat; they needed him alive. He was their bargaining chip with the television station, assuming the broadcasting of their tapes was still crucial to their plan.

The Arab reached up and grabbed the canvas belt on the sliding door. It rattled all the way to the bottom, and sealed with a clunk-- leaving Brad alone in utter darkness.

The glaring sun was nearing the horizon when David nudged his car up to the chain link fence across the street from Ace Wrecking and Repair. The industrial park was always busy, and today was no exception. There was activity up the street at the GE plant and behind him in the large glassed face of the cable company-- but on the other side of the road, in and around the garage, all was quiet.

To the left of the building sat a silent fleet of tow trucks, not a space empty. The bay doors facing the trucks were closed up tight. David didn't know much about tow truck companies, but he was fairly certain that they didn't close up shop before seven on a Friday night.

Was he late? Had they already moved the bomb? He'd expected at least some kind of activity, something he could observe. The message said, *Danger at the West Downs Industrial Park, where the diesel flows. Go alone.* So, here he was, at the park, against the more prudent course of heeding the terrorist's threat and bugging out of the city. So once again he was *stuck* with no idea what his next move should be, walking around with a big fat target on his chest.

Rage boiled in his veins.

This is RIDICULOUS! I'm putting my LIFE in danger, the least you can do is give me what I need to get the job done! He looked around the interior of the car. There were words, but nothing spoke to him. He reached down and flipped the glovebox open. Inside was a small stack of napkins, an old hide-a-key box, and the manual for the car.

He pulled the manual out and opened it. "Please," he spoke through clenched teeth, "a little more information would be *helpful.*" His eyes bounced around the page, but there was nothing. The next page was the same, and the next, and the next. All the way to the back of the book, *nothing!* Not one usable message in the entire manual. He gripped the book and threw it against the door.

So what are my choices? Stay here-- or go over to the scary looking building and peek in through the windows? Yeah like THAT'S ever going to happen! Maybe I'm supposed to wait. Maybe I'm early. Maybe, maybe, maybe! It'd be nice to actually KNOW what I'm supposed to do next!

He folded his arms and settled in to watch the building-- but as he waited, his imagination began to get the better of him. There were a hundred elaborate and graphic ways the terrorists could sneak up and kill him. His eyes moved continually from the rear view mirror to the side mirrors and back again. Fear rose inside him like a tide, building and building, until he could take it no longer. He jumped out of the car and crouched next to the door.

Behind him, three people walked in the direction of the cable building, to his right a man was getting into his car. Otherwise, the lot was quiet. David straightened, realizing how obvious he would look if he was the only one walking around crouched.

He followed the narrow pathway between the fence and the row of parked cars to the gate. The man inside the ticket booth noticed him and nodded. David gave the man a pressed smile and a robotic wave. A red car came up the road; David tracked it with his eyes. It slowed and pulled into the entrance. A bearded man rolled his window down and grabbed a ticket. Feeling self-conscious, David took a few steps back, to give the car plenty of room. The man stabbed the ticket into his visor and proceeded into the lot.

David looked again at the parking attendant, then back at the lot behind him. *FLASH!* The light from the setting sun reflected off the side mirror of a car and the word *flash* jumped into his mind. The message from that morning suddenly came back loud and clear, reciting itself with rhythmic automation. *Flash, one, two, three, drop.*

DROP!

His legs buckled and his body hit the ground as a bullet ricocheted off the fence behind him. The sound echoed through the parking lot as gravel bit into David's forearms and he scrambled next to a car. Another shot glanced off the hood. His breath came in gasps. His heart pounded in his ears. He put his back to the car and looked up at the window of the ticket booth. The attendant had dropped out of sight. Only a coiled black wire could be seen wavering in the window.

Oh, God! Oh, GOD! What do I do! Panic threatened to overwhelm him. *Do I stay? Where's the shooter? Can he see me? God help me. Please!* His head swam, he felt like he might pass out. *--Okay. Be calm. Be calm. Calm. Think, David. THINK!* He squeezed his eyes shut. The shots couldn't be coming from the cable company; the angle was wrong. They had to be coming from the right corner of the parking lot, from the old shoe plant.

He reached up, wrapped his fingers around the glass of the side mirror and pulled. The mirror snapped from the socket just as the sniper took two more shots, the windshield cracked and the driver's side window exploded. He cupped his arms around his head as glass rained down.

Carefully, he leaned on his elbow and raised the mirror up to see over the hood. Shards of glass fell from his arm. The image in the mirror wobbled erratically. He could not stabilize his trembling hand. He squinted at the shifting reflection of the old shoe building. He had to be there. No other angle made sense. Then something caught his eye, a pinpoint of light glinting from a fourth story window; was it the scope of the shooter? He repositioned and concentrated on the spot; the glimmer was still there.

He brought the mirror down and dug his shaking hand into his pocket for Cooper's business card. Coins and car keys dumped out onto the pavement. As he fished around, a loud noise began to reverberate from the garage across the street. One of the bay doors was opening, and a large diesel engine rumbled inside.

David slid under the car and craned his neck to see out around the tire. A large U-Haul truck was pulling out. Were they moving the bomb? Where would they go? Two men of Arab descent were in the U-Haul. He didn't recognize either one of them. The driver glanced in David's direction as the truck came to a stop. David jerked his head aside, slamming it hard against the tire, a stab of pain shot down his neck. He ignored it and scrambled further under the car. His heart pounded harder. *Do they know? It looked like he saw me. Will they come after me?* He needed to be on the other side of the car. From there he could sprint back along the fence-- and maybe outmaneuver the shooter. It was a slim chance, but it seemed to be his only option. The diesel gunned its engine and again began to move. David froze and waited breathlessly. The gears shifted as it pulled out of the lot then turned and lumbered off down the road.

Why didn't they stop and finish the job? They saw me looking right at them! Were they rushed by an impending raid? Neither had *looked* nervous or rushed. David slid out from under the car and reached back into his pocket. His shaking fingers retrieved the card along with his cellphone.

He had to let Agent Cooper know what he just saw. *The license plate!* "How STUPID am I?" His teeth ground in his mouth as he pushed the numbers with a frustrated finger and put the phone to his ear.

"Cooper here."

"Agent Cooper this is David Chance. I spoke with you a little while ago." The words came out fast and furious.

"Yes, David. What's wrong?"

"I'm at the West Downs Industrial Park..."

"What? What are *you doing* there?"

"--Uh, following a lead."

"A *lead?* You shouldn't be there! We have a team on the..."

"They're too late."

"What? What'd you *do?"*

"I didn't *do anything!* I came to watch the place and saw a U-Haul..."

"What place?"

"Ace Trucking and Repair. A U-Haul truck just left the building with two Arabs in it. I thought you might want to know."

"Did you get the plate?"

David bit his lip. *"No.* --I was, kinda busy being shot at."

"Shot... By who?"

"A sniper. I think he's on the fourth floor of the old shoe factory."

"Why on earth! Hold on." Cooper spoke to someone in the room. "Have West Downs Bravo divert to the old shoe factory. Watch for a sniper exiting the building." He spoke into the phone again, "Where are you now?"

"Hiding behind a car across the street from Ace. There's a parking attendant hiding in the booth next to me."

"Alright. Stay put. The team should be there any minute."

"Thanks." The call dropped and David shut the phone.

Sirens sounded in the distance. The phone buzzed on his chest. David looked at the digital display-- another text message. He gathered his courage, and flipped the phone open.

"Do you feel safe?"

His chest constricted. Had the sniper come closer? He could be anywhere. David rolled onto his belly as a car pulled up to the entrance of the parking lot. He slid his body over and tried to get a look at it. It was a blue mid-sized compact, but he couldn't see the driver. *Alright, David. Just because the car pulled in when the text message came, doesn't mean it's the sniper. Get a grip!*

The car door opened and a set of shoes touched down on the ground; David's optimism flew right out the window. Frantically he started crawling toward the fence. He would stay low and keep moving. Not a great plan, but all he could come up with at the moment. He scrambled to his feet and sprinted full force. If he could just get to his car...

"David!"

It took several frantic steps before he recognized the voice. He dove between two cars. "Alex! *Get down!"*

"What's going on?" Alex shouted.

"There's a sniper in the old shoe factory."

David watched Alex's feet as he ran along the fence. He reached David and crouched down. "What? A *sniper?"*

"He shot at me from the old factory behind you." Alex ducked down more. David crawled closer to him. "How'd you know where to find me?"

"I saw your car."

"You scared me half to death! Why didn't you call?"

"I *did* call!" Alex smacked him.

David rubbed the phone through the fabric of his pants. "I must not have felt it."

A line of black SUVs came down the road and filed into the parking lot of the towing company. One by one they took position. Behind them was a SWAT truck, and behind that, a dozen police cruisers.

Alex smiled. "Looks like the cavalry has *arrived.*"

12390

The navigator in the news car chimed, a digital voice spoke. "Take exit twenty-three." Larry flicked the blinker, looked past Karen into the side mirror, and pulled the news truck into the far right lane. "You're quiet," he said.

Karen continued to stare out the window at the passing trees. She had no interest in making small talk with Larry Turner. Jim could make her suffer the trip, but she didn't have to suffer the conversation.

Larry sighed. "Ya don't have to be a sour puss, darlin'. Everyone's upset about Brad, but we gotta keep on keepin' on. I know you two had a thing and all..."

Have! Not HAD! You dumb oaf. He's not dead! She wanted to *bite* his head off, but she knew better. *Any* response would put her right where he wanted her.

"You gotta keep your head clear, darlin'. Now- I know it looks like *I'm* not upset about Brad..."

Was she going to sit there and listen to a lecture from a man who didn't know the difference between a napkin and his sleeve? She *had* to speak up, she simply couldn't *bear* one more second of listening to Larry wax nostalgic about his years of male bonding with Brad. "Look, Larry, give it a rest, okay?"

His eyebrows rose slowly. "I'm aimin' to give you my two cents, 'cause I think you ought to know. I like the guy. I'm all broken up about it. Brad and I've been through a lot. But us guys don't wear our hearts on our sleeves like you gals do."

Why did men always have to play the sex card? Why did she have to continually prove herself over and over? She was every bit as strong as he was, in some ways stronger. Just because she didn't *feel* like talking about Brad, didn't mean she was fragile and overwhelmed by her femininity. She just didn't want to talk about it! She turned to him, and leaned in. "Larry?"

"Yeah, sugar plumb?"

She painted a helpless look on her face. "Would you do something for me?"

He cocked his head. "I aim to please, darlin'."

"Would you open that little ol' door right there. And throw yourself out onto the rapidly passing pavement?" She batted her long lashes.

There was a momentary pause before he erupted into laughter and ended with one of his repulsive signature hoots. "Girl, you got a tongue like a cactus quill."

She shook her head in disgust. He was so *dense.* She wondered if he even *knew* he had been insulted.

"Like I was sayin', me and Brad been through all kinds of stuff. Why that boy had me bunkin' in a hotel room in New Orleans the night of Hurricane Katrina. I'm like, *'We're sittin' in a bowl here! We're gonna have to swim outta here in the mornin!'"* But he knew right where we needed to be, and we were on the ground reportin' through it all. That boy's got guts is all I'm sayin'. So if you're frettin' your pretty little head about him, don't. If anything, I'd be worried for the terrorists."

An approaching road sign informed Karen of the distance to the Gram Well Milk Farm. Twenty miles. Which meant about twenty minutes. Nineteen minutes and fifty-nine seconds *too long.*

24

David tapped the pad on the laptop and brought up the next set of mug shots. But with each passing page the memory of the two men in the truck grew less distinct in his mind. If he didn't take a break soon, he feared there would be nothing left of the image but the impression of a jumbled collage of eye colors and beard shapes. He put his head in his hands.

"Anyone stick out to you?" asked the FBI agent next to him.

"No. Not yet."

"It may not feel like it, but when one of the faces comes up on the screen, you'll know it. Trust me. I've seen it a hundred times. You think you can't remember, and then *bam,* there it is."

"Do you mind if I take a quick break?" David looked up, bleary eyed.

"Sure. Why don't you go grab a cup of coffee from the break room. Your friend's in there."

David slid the stool back from the table and got up. "Thanks. I'll be right back."

The break room was a little hut in the middle of the bay. Cardboard boxes and black plastic hoses were piled high on its aluminum roof. The inside was much like the rest of the towing company, archaic and covered in a greasy film of dust. The vending machine said the coffee was thirty-five cents, but the taped-on note below said one dollar.

Alex was nursing a cup at the only table. "Any luck

identifying the terrorists?"

"Not so much as you'd notice," David said, punching the hard plastic button on the coffee machine.

"The last eight hours feel surreal," said Alex. "You always expect this kind of thing to happen to someone else, but here it is, in our own backyard."

"I haven't had time to slow down and think about it."

"We've been through some crazy stuff haven't we?"

David nodded. "Yes we have. It's amazing we're still alive."

Alex grinned.

"But, bar none, this takes the cake," David said, grabbing four packs of sugar.

"I still think you're crazy for not leaving the city."

"We're not going to go through *this* again, are we?"

"Look. All I'm saying is, there are terrorists with bombs in the city, and you don't seem to care that you and your family are at risk. Not to mention me-- 'cause I'm just dumb enough to stick by your side."

"You're used to danger."

"That doesn't mean I *invite* it."

"I'm not *inviting* it. I just..." he considered his words carefully. "I *believe* the messages will tell me when it's time to go."

Alex rolled his eyes.

"Come on, Alex. Every one of the messages has been right. You can't call it chance or-- random luck."

"I'm not questioning whether or not they're *right*. I'm questioning whether or not you're *sane* for listening to them. For crying out loud, you don't even know who or *what* is sending them! Sure they're *accurate,* and they saved your life once, but you don't know *anything* about the sender. What if you're being set up? You wouldn't know it until it was too late."

David took a sip of coffee and sat down across from Alex. "Nothing like this has ever happened to me before. For all I know, this has never happened to *anyone.* If this was happening to *you,* wouldn't you want to know what is was? Wouldn't *you* want to follow the messages to the end?"

"Not if it meant my doom."

David let out a deep sigh and rubbed the back of his neck. "You don't understand. If only I could explain the experience, how it *feels* when the messages come."

"Try me."

David thought for a second, then let out a breath. "--It's like I get this *sense* when I put the words together. Something deep inside me confirms the message as true, as if some part of me has the capability of *knowing* what is *truth*, and what is not." He stopped to think, then continued. "I know I'm doing a horrible job of explaining, but it's like a *truth* that is *so true* it could never be doubted. It's immovable-- *unchangeable.* How could the author of such things be anything but truth as well?"

"Sounds like euphoria to me. Like when you jar your brain and you feel a sense of peace wash over you for no reason. The brain is a complex organ, David. When you prod it, you can get all kinds of sensations."

David examined his friend. He was right. The brain was a complex organ with functions and capabilities far beyond human understanding. It received and sent out millions of tactile impulses every minute. Was it unreasonable to think that his subconscious mind was producing the phenomena, and issuing the feelings to confirm the validity of the extrasensory input it was receiving? Would he even know if such a thing was occurring? Did he take notice when his brain told his lungs to draw in a breath, or his heart to pump? Could his desire to have some kind of verifiable communication with God be overshadowing his reasoning? He had longed for proof of God's existence since childhood. Whenever the opportunity arose to speak with someone who claimed a faith in God, he had leapt at the opportunity. Hours upon hours had been spent in debate, but his questions remained, questions which would have easily been answered if only God would *speak!*

His unbelief sat like a weight on his chest.

Immovable.

Unshakable.

He wanted to call Frank again. Talking to Frank had planted a seed in his mind, a seed of trust, a seed which gave him the hope to believe that it *was* God speaking-- and the more he believed, the more his burden lifted. He didn't need to have *all* the answers, if he could just have the faith to *believe*. Frank's unwavering confidence in God had somehow rubbed off on him, but now it was slowly fading, being replaced with the all-too-familiar doubt and cynicism. David rubbed his hands through his hair and stooped over the table.

"You okay?" asked Alex.

"I really wish I knew, but I don't. I just have to see where it takes me."

Alex's voice softened. "Why don't you just go somewhere safe, grab a bunch of books and explore to your heart's content. You don't have to be in the middle of a combat zone to find out what these messages are."

"I think the messages are only coming to me *because* of this crisis. They're warning me so I can stop what's about to happen."

"If you keep pressing this," Alex's voice grew intense again, "those terrorists are going to put a bullet in your head, or worse."

The familiar pit was forming in David's stomach, and was intensified by returning doubts about the source of the messages. "I know, Alex. Can we just drop it? I don't want to talk about it anymore."

"I'm just trying to be a good friend."

"I know. And you are. I just need to think things through on my own."

Alex stared at his friend. "I'm sorry. I'm sorry, David. Just... With everything going on, I guess I'm- a little scared."

David looked up. The comment took him completely by surprise. Alex was a lot of things, but scared was not one of them. This was the guy who broke his arm trying to skateboard down a staircase railing at school, then broke the other arm a week later, doing the same trick, on the same railing. He was an adrenaline junkie. For him, fear was something to overcome. David squinted at him. "When have *you* ever been scared?"

"Scared, worried, whatever you want to call it. All I know is, when I think about Emily being in danger, it makes me crazy inside. These terrorists do ugly things to people, David. It's only a matter of time before they find out where your family is. I've seen what monsters do to innocent children, and my gut burns to think of such things happening to that precious girl of yours."

"I know. Believe me, I *know*."

"You and your family are all I have. My family is a bunch of nut cases."

David suppressed a smile. A truer statement had never been made. As families went, Alex's was the worst.

"Emily is safe," said David. "The terrorists couldn't possibly know where she is."

"They don't have to, all they need is a bomb. And oh

144

yeah! *That's right.* They have one!"

"The terrorists said in *two days* they were going to do their big thing. Until then, we're probably okay. But if it will make you feel better, I'll pack the family up in the morning and send them out of the city."

"You promise? Tomorrow morning you'll get them out of here."

"Yes. I promise."

"Even if you get some message that says to keep them in the city?"

"As unlikely as that would be, yes. I promise, no matter what happens, I'll send them to my cousin's house in Worcester."

"Alright. I'm holding you to it."

David stood up. "I'm going to go back and stare at more criminals."

"Wait."

David stopped.

"Are you going to Claire's tonight?"

"No. I'm gonna stay at a hotel. I don't want to cause any more inconvenience for Claire, and I don't want to lead the terrorists to her doorstep. Tomorrow, I'll make sure I'm not followed, double back around, and pack up the family."

"You planning anymore mischief tonight?"

"I'm going to help the FBI identify these two men, then I'm going to go put my head on a pillow."

"Alright, then I'm going to go get some stuff done. There's not much I can do here." Alex got up from the bench and walked in close to David. "I put a hand gun in your glove box," he said under his breath. "If you get in trouble, use it."

David looked up. "Okay."

"And call me before you go doing anything else stupid.

I don't have any more meetings planned, so my schedule is open. If I don't hear from you, I'll meet you at Claire's tomorrow. How does eight sound?"

David nodded. "Yeah. That's fine."

"Good. Eight it is."

Karen saw the flashing lights of law enforcement long before the run-down wooden sign for the Gram Well Milk Farm. Larry turned the news truck into the farm's dirt driveway and skidded to an abrupt stop. An officer motioned for them to pull onto the grass. Larry acknowledged with a wave, and pulled up next to a car belonging to News Channel Five.

Up the driveway, a barricade of six black SUVs sat, and beyond them, on the other side of the police line, were several cruisers. The area was alive with activity. Flashing beams cut through the dark in erratic sweeps, causing the sparse woods near the driveway to pulse and shift.

Karen's heels sank into the muddy grass as she stepped out of the truck. She walked to the back where Nerd was already standing. "Are you feeling up for this?" she said, placing a gentle hand on his back.

Nerd's fists were shoved firmly in the pockets of his spring jacket, his body rigid against the chill of the night air. "Yeah," he said, his jaw tight. "I like knowing all these officers are around."

"I'll bet." She smiled.

Larry meandered around the truck, and immediately Karen was back in a foul mood. What *was* it about him? Even the way he carried himself rubbed her wrong. *Is it me? I'm not difficult to get along with. Am I? It's got to be him.* Was it the arrogance? Or the smug look of confidence on his dopey face. *Does he take anything seriously? Here we are at the entrance of a terrorist encampment, and he looks like he's going in to film a bar mitzvah.* She glared at him. *Maybe he's emotionally stunted. Maybe he has brain damage or something.* The thought brought a tinge of comfort. Perhaps if she could think of him as mentally disabled, she would feel pity for him, instead of loathing.

"Want me to put some sticks down next to the truck here, dumplin'?"

"Please afford me the professional courtesy of not reducing my name to a redneck term of endearment." She scrunched her nose. "I'd appreciate it." She headed off toward the flashing lights, then stopped and turned. "And, yes, please set up by the truck. I'll be back in five."

Nerd laughed, and Karen didn't want to know what Larry had said. She needed to clear her mind. This story had a direct connection to her heart, and if there was *any* possible way, she was *going* to get into that farm. At the yellow police line she flashed her press badge at one of the officers standing guard. His eyes glanced at her badge briefly, then resumed their scan of the flashing darkness. "Sorry ma'am. No one's allowed past this line except authorized law enforcement. I'm surprised they let you by the exterior perimeter."

Actually, they hadn't. They'd just made it in before the roadblock was set up. But she wasn't going to tell him that. "Can you tell me what you've learned so far? Have you entered the farm yet?"

"No ma'am. We're still setting up a perimeter."

"Do you have a time table for entry?"

"I can't tell you," he said shortly.

"Do you suspect the bomb is inside?"

"If you want information, talk to the POC." That was police jargon for Point of Contact.

148

"Can you direct me to the POC assigned..."

"Ma'am. Please!"

She brought her hands up in surrender and stepped back. She didn't want to risk being put back behind the six-hundred meter perimeter. "Okay. Sorry, officer."

His eyes continued to scan as though she were invisible. This was a new experience for Karen. Most men couldn't keep their eyes off her, which usually worked to her advantage. She looked back towards the truck at Nerd and Larry. Nerd was fumbling with their light kit, but Channel Five had theirs up already, and Karen's counterpart was in front of the camera prepping for her piece.

In the old days she would have considered all the angles, weighing out how long it would take Channel Five to get the recorded tape back to the studio and prep it, compared to her advantage of having the live truck. Even five years ago the scoop was still king, but not now. In these days of twenty-four hour news coverage and lightning speed blogging, it was more about *nuance* and less about getting the scoop. --And at the moment, she had *zero* nuance. She knew nothing about what was taking place up on the hill.

She looked up at the night sky, hoping the news helicopter would arrive soon. There were two choppers hovering near the farmhouse. Their spotlights sliced through the darkness, but they had to be law enforcement. News helicopters would have been ordered to stay back.

"Ma'am?" Karen turned back to the officer behind the line. "You need to move out of the way."

An FBI agent leaped from a black SUV and started waving his arms. "Move the line back! Set the perimeter back behind marker B! And get those reporters out of here! *Now!*"

She snapped back to the officer. "What's going on?"

149

Before the man could answer, the speaker on his shoulder came alive. *"All units 40a, pull back. Repeat. 40a. All units pull back!"*

40a? That was a bomb threat! They found a bomb! She started running. *"Pack it up, guys!"*

Larry and Nerd were quickly loading gear back into the truck. Karen stepped off the road into the grass to let the Bomb Squad truck pass. She pulled her cellphone out of her jacket and flipped it open. "Station!"

"Station." The phone repeated. Karen put the phone to her ear.

"Jim here."

"Jim! They found a bomb. The whole place is going crazy!"

An officer approached her. "GET that truck out of here! Ma'am you need to *get* off that phone and get out of here!"

"Hold on, Jim." She pulled the phone away and leaned in toward the officer. "Is the bomb irradiated?"

"Get in your vehicle NOW!"

"Okay. Okay!" She turned and brought the phone back up. "We're going live in less than a minute."

"We're on it," said Jim.

She flipped the phone closed and walked to the back of the truck. The gear was packed, but she reached in and pulled out a mic from one of the boxes. "On me in twenty, Larry."

Larry smiled. "Now that's what I'm talkin' about!"

She looked over her shoulder as Larry grabbed the camera. The police officer had walked to the other side of the road.

"Nerd. Get the mobile uplink ready. We won't have long before they kick us out."

"It's already warmed up, I just have to switch it back on." He ran along the truck and disappeared into the side.

Larry put the camera on his shoulder. The light came on.

"Ready?" she asked.

"Ready."

"Ready, Nerd?"

"Ready!"

"On me in three, two, one. Hello, I'm Karen Watson at the site of the Gram Well Milk Farm where it appears a bomb has just been found. As you can see behind me, the police line is being moved back. We don't know yet if the building has been secured, but the Bomb Squad is going in. This site is believed to be the location of a terrorist cell operating in the Boston area, which is connected to local area businessmen filtering money in from Saudi Arabia."

Karen jumped as a siren went off beside her. An officer stepped out of the car. "Ma'am! You *need* to evacuate!"

"We will keep you up to date as this story unfolds, I'm Karen Watson at the site of the Gram Well Milk Farm."

The camera light went black.

"I should throw your butt in the back of my cruiser!"

"We're leaving, officer." She backed up awkwardly. "Larry, get in the truck."

Larry had a mischievous grin stretching from ear to ear as he let the camera fall from his shoulder. He replaced the camera in the back and, with a smirk, nearly danced around the corner of the truck.

They had one thing in common, she and Larry, they both loved the thrill of the hunt and the danger of pushing the envelope. When things started to stir up, Karen was in her element, and as it turned out, so was Larry.

For a split second, she almost liked him.

151

--Almost.

26

David tossed the to-go bag in the trash, and the damp towel onto a chair in the corner of the double occupancy room. The hot shower had made him feel a little more human, but it could not even begin to wash away the uneasiness which pressed in on him in waves. He bent a few slats in the front window blind to check the parking lot again. He had driven as wild a pattern as he could and parked in an open lot down the street before sneaking into the motel for the night. But the message from his phone still haunted him.

Do you feel safe?

No. He did not. And there was nowhere he could hide from the fear-- fear that crawled under his skin like a stalking creature. There was no way to push back the encroaching darkness, or remove the feeling of suffocation pressing in on his face and lungs. No matter how deeply he breathed, it didn't relieve the heaviness in his chest. It lingered like a grim cloud, filling every corner. Hiding from terrorists was easy, but how could he hide from his own fear?

The slats snapped back in place, and David checked the door lock for the sixteenth time, before plopping down on one of the beds. He flicked the television on and navigated through the news channels. Every one of them was carrying the story.

On one channel, the newscaster spoke about the increase in homegrown terrorist cells and of the increasing unrest in American Muslims. He bridged to the hostage situation, then returned live to the Gram Well Milk Farm. Finally they flashed back to the raid on the towing garage. Those were the top pieces of the current news block. Every bit of what was going on had made the national news.

Before the hour was over, he knew they would show Brad in his orange jumpsuit and the mob of FBI vehicles outside of Ace Wrecking thirty times over.

He turned the volume down and picked up the phone; he needed to talk to Sharon. The phone rang three times. Claire's husband answered with a hearty, *"Hello?"*

"Hi, Stan, it's David. Can I speak with my wife?"

"David! We're all watching the news. Are you okay?"

"A little frazzled, but none the worse for wear."

"Hold on. Here she is."

Sharon came on. "David? Where *are* you?"

"I checked into a motel."

"A motel? Why?"

"I didn't want to take the chance of leading the terrorists to Claire's house. I figure if I hole up here for the night, it will be safe to circle around to where you are in the morning."

"I've been worried sick."

"About me?"

"Who *else* would I be worried about?"

"Sorry. That didn't come out right. I meant to ask if it was me you were worried about, or the terrorists finding you."

"Oh. No, honey, we're fine." What we're seeing on the news is a bit disconcerting, to say the least. But it looks as though Homeland Security is on top of it."

"Well, they said this morning that they have some strong credible leads, and that they would find the bombs before they get set off in the city. I hope they're right."

"I don't like being so close."

"I really don't believe there is anything to worry about yet. The terrorists said that Allah was going to give a gift to the people of America in two days. We should be safe until at least sometime tomorrow night."

She whispered into the phone. *"Two days?* That's when you said the President is going to be assassinated."

"I know. I think they are going to use the bombs to try to kill the President."

She paused. "But that doesn't make any sense."

"Why? What do you mean?"

"According to the news, the President just canceled a trip to Maine because of the terrorist activity here in Boston."

"Why was he going to Maine?"

"I think he was scheduled to speak at the airbase there."

"So, if they knew he was going to be speaking in Maine, why raise the threat level?"

"Exactly." Sharon whispered. "Something doesn't add up. You're sure one of the terrorists is the assassin?"

"All I know is that someone is going to kill the President in two days, and that the killer was near when we all met at the house."

"And the terrorists are the only suspects you can think of."

"At the moment. But you made a good point, Sharon. If their plan is to kill the President, it doesn't seem like a very good move." He paused. "Unless it's a feint."

"A what?"

"You know, like in boxing, or chess, when you make your opponent believe you are going to go one way, but then you go the other. Let's say the President is the king piece.

On the surface it looks like a bad move, because the king is now safe behind the pawns. But a trained chess player knows that in this position, the king's movement is limited, and it is sometimes easier to put him in check mate."

"I don't know, David. It seems unlikely-- unless they plan on blowing up the White House."

That was a startling thought. Could that be their intended target? Were the bombs en route to Washington? No. That didn't make sense either. All of this activity would have tripled the security at the White House.

A nagging thought entered his mind. The preemptive nature of the hostage situation and the bomb scare weren't the only things peculiar. In all of the turmoil of the day, he hadn't had time to stop and think about this, but now, it seemed obvious. The terrorists had given his son a warning, and later they had given *him* a warning. Granted, they only gave him one before they started trying to kill him, but why give any warning at all? He had never heard of terrorists calling in a bomb threat. It had always been the higher the casualty count the better.

These terrorists apparently had a conscience. Why hadn't they just stormed his house and killed everyone? Why take the chance that he and his son would inform the authorities of the cases? Maybe this was a new breed of terrorist, birthed here in the United States, instilled with a value for human life, but still driven to create fear for the sake of bringing about change.

"David?" Sharon's voice brought him out of his introspection.

"Sorry. I was thinking."

"Well, I should let you go, so you can try to process things. When are you coming tomorrow?"

"First thing."

"Okay. I hope you're not up all night. You've had quite a day."

"Yours wasn't much better."

There was silence on the other end.

"This will pass, honey."

"I know," she said.

"I'll see you all in the morning. Give the kids a kiss for me."

"Yes. I love you, honey. Bye."

David rolled over and put the phone back on the receiver.

Terrorists that didn't act like terrorists. Supernatural prophetic messages. Dirty bombs. It *had* been a crazy day. He clasped his hands behind his head, leaned back on the stack of pillows, and watched numbly as the scene at the towing company played out on the silent television screen. It felt like a distant memory now, even though it had happened only a short while ago.

Amazing. This was perhaps the biggest story in recent history, and he was there, right in the middle of it, a prophet of God sent to save the city from the hands of evil men. He laughed at himself. *Prophet of God-- more like some fruitcake with a bizarre brain mutation-- a poor empty-headed monkey venturing out from the genetic pack.* Was he a prophet, or nature's guinea pig? The question gnawed on his soul with venomous fangs.

Science versus religion, it was the age old debate he had long since given up on. But now it was back, without his consent, demanding an answer. But he had no answer to give it. He could *ask* the messages if they were coming from God, like he'd asked about the assassin. But even if the messages came right out and said, '*Hello David, God here, nice to meet you.*' Would he believe it? No, probably not, because

157

he would just convince himself that it was only his jacked-up mutated mind acting upon his own wishful thinking. Would it kill God to just show himself? Was that too much to ask? He gritted his teeth and drove his head back into the pillows. *Why does it have to be SO complicated?!*

He envied Frank. To believe without proof, how wonderful that would be. To have confidence in one's own destiny and to move toward it with unwavering purpose. *That* was true peace. But David could never fully taste a peace like that. He denied himself what he longed for the most, for fear of wasting his life on a lie. He could not bear the thought of subjecting himself to the strict tenants of a religious belief, only to find out it never really mattered. What a sad pitiful existence it would be, forced into a weekly regimen of door to door evangelizing, only to find out the god you believed in was nothing more than a figment of your imagination. David would only give himself to truth, and as far as he could ascertain, it was not possible to *know* truth. His cynicism had seen to that.

But despite everything, something Frank had said or done had given him a measure of peace. Was it possible he had gained a little faith? There had been moments that day when he had *almost* believed it was God directing him with his divine hand. Yes. There was something infectious about Frank. And whatever that something was, David wanted more. He fished his cellphone out of his pocket and navigated to Frank's number. With his other hand he picked up the hotel phone and dialed.

"Hello?" said Frank.

"Good, you're home. I hope I'm not bothering you."

Frank sounded pleased. "No, not at all, David. I was just thinking about you."

"They let you out, so you must be doing better."

"Yeah. For now. They have me scheduled to go under the knife at the end of the month anyway, so there really wasn't much else they could do now. I'm just supposed to stay close to my nitro until then, that's all."

"Well I'm glad you're okay."

"Yep. Fit as a fiddle. Is that why you called? Just checking up on me?"

"Yes and no. I mean, yes, I wanted to see how you were doing, obviously. But I'm still trying to figure out where these messages are coming from."

"Still getting them, huh?"

"They're drawing me into all this terrorist business. Have you seen the news?"

"Oh, yeah. I'm following it. Everyone is."

"Of course."

"Well, I'll help you any way I can. Although, I'm not sure I helped much last time. You were pretty bugged at the end of your visit."

"Yeah, sorry about that. The topic of God gets me cranky."

"And yet-- you want to talk about him some more?"

"N- No, not really. But yes. I mean. I'm facing terrorists with guns and bombs and I'm feeling a little vulnerable right now. If I make one mistake, I could end up dead. And ah-- I guess I better be as ready as possible, you know-- if I have to meet my maker."

"Makes sense."

"My whole life I've tried to confirm the existence of God, and over and over I come away with the same conclusion: God just doesn't want me to know."

Frank laughed. "Doesn't want you to know? Why would you say that?"

"It doesn't seem like he wants *anyone* to know. He put

us on this earth with all of these writings from people who *claim* they have spoken with him, and it's our job to figure out who he is. Why doesn't God just speak to us directly?"

"He used to. He spoke to the people of Israel from Mount Sinai in the time of Moses, but the people went to Moses and begged him to ask God *not* speak to them any more, because they couldn't bear it. I don't think you understand what you're asking for. The Bible says no one has ever looked upon God and lived. God is perfectly good, and can't be in the presence of evil, even the smallest evil. Without his Son's sacrifice as a covering, we can't be in the presence of God without being destroyed, because his anger would be kindled against us."

"Okay, let's just say that what you're saying is true, why doesn't he give us some kind of supernatural evidence so we know what the right religion is?"

"Like what?"

"I don't know, like, if the Bible is the one true book, then why not make it burn with a fire that can't be put out? Then it would be easy. Follow the instructions in the burning book and go to heaven, follow the instructions in the non-burning books, and go to hell."

Frank laughed again. "Besides the fact that it would be a little difficult reading a *flaming* book, having a supernatural object like that would remove the need for faith."

Here we go. Here come the riddles. "Faith? How does *faith* help *anyone?* Terrorists have faith-- enough faith to drive a plane into the side of a skyscraper. Is that what God wants?"

Frank was silent. David could almost sense him squirming. Finally he spoke. "If you saw a man punch a little girl in the face, would you know that was wrong?"

160

"Of course I would, what does that have to do with faith?"

"If you saw a man strap a bomb to himself and go blow up a café filled with innocent people, would you know that was wrong?"

"Yes."

"If someone told you to put people into ovens and incinerate them, would you know *that* was wrong?"

"Frank. You're changing the subject. The topic is faith. I hope you have a point."

"You *know* what is right, and what is wrong, because God has put it in you to know. But there are many who hear lies, and for whatever reason, be it wealth, sex, power, you name it, they give their ear to the lies. Something inside *chooses* the lie over what they know is truth, and slowly, almost imperceptibly, they begin to allow their heart to be calloused, until they are no longer bothered by the evil, because they have justified it in their own mind."

A calloused heart, that was an interesting idea. Could a person lose the ability to know right from wrong?

"On some sick level, they have *convinced* themselves, or have *been* convinced, that blowing up innocent people is *pleasing* to God. I agree with you, the terrorists have faith. But you have to ask yourself, what is their faith *in?* Someone has told them that Allah wants them to kill, because on the other side of the killing, there will be a reward, and peace. They *know* that peace is good, so they do the evil, so good will result."

"So good will result."

"Yes, but this is not the kind of faith God wants from us. He wants us to put aside our *own* desires, and put our faith in *him,* and *him* alone."

"O-kay."

"See, it's not *faith* itself, but what, or more accurately, *who,* we have faith *in.* Okay, think about this. If a person is going to go bungee jumping, but decides to use a piece of string instead of a bungee cord, do you think the string would hold him if he had enough *faith* in it?*"*

"Of course not."

"See. Faith itself has no power, it's what you put your faith *in.*"

"But how can you know you have faith in the right thing?"

"Because he confirms it, like you told me he is doing with you. When you look at those words, something inside you confirms what you are looking at, and you *know* for sure it's true."

A shadow passed by the blinds of David's room and came to a stop. David whispered into the phone. "Someone just stopped in front of my door."

"Where are you?"

David slid down between the two beds, leaving the phone behind. Outside the door he could hear shoes scuffling. Had the terrorists found him? How *could* they have? He'd covered his tracks with flawless precision. The sound of a key card in the door made him frantically yank open the nightstand drawer and grab the pistol he'd stashed earlier. The handle wiggled, but the door did not open. There was another swipe, and the handle shivered again.

David crawled around the bed and across the carpet to the wall, avoiding the door. He'd seen his share of television cop shows. Thugs always shoot through the door; he wasn't going to fall for that one. Leaning back against the cold wallpaper, the shuffling of shoes was much clearer. It sounded like two sets, but he wasn't sure. He looked down at the gun, it was heavy in his grip. *Who am I kidding? If I get away from this without shooting myself in the leg, I'll be doing well.* He inched himself up, keeping his back to the wall. When he was high enough, he opened the slats with trembling fingers.

Three men stood outside. Their attire was semi casual. All wore spring jackets. He couldn't see their faces but the one closest to him had tight curly black hair under a baseball cap. Possibly Arab, but he couldn't be sure. They were huddled together and their voices were muffled. One turned again with the key card. David shifted his weight and held the pistol toward the floor, his body quaking with terror. The card slid through the slot and the handle wiggled again.

What would they do if they couldn't unlock the door? Kick it in? Go through the window? The pistol had six shots. There wasn't much room for error. He pressed his back to the wall under the curtain blinds and positioned himself in the corner. That way, if they forced entry, he would have the drop on them.

There was a knock at the door.

What the...

The knock came again. "Alright. Very funny. Open up."

Not what he was expecting. The voice had no accent, no hostility. Were these the terrorists?

Knock. Knock. Knock. "Come on. Open up! Our key won't work."

Terrorists don't beg you to open the door so they can kill you. David slid the pistol behind the mini fridge and crawled back to the bed. Once there, he stood and walked to the door. He wiped his hands over his face and opened the door a crack. "Can I help you?"

The men looked surprised. "Oh. Sorry. We must have the wrong room," said the man with the key card. He was

163

clearly inebriated, his voice carrying a distinct slur.

David opened the door wider. "Who are you looking for?"

"Our buddy."

David held out a hand. "Let me see your key." The man handed it over. It said 211B. "You're in the wrong complex guys. You need complex B." He pointed. "It's over there."

The men looked across the parking lot.

"Thanks, dude." The man retrieved his card. "Sorry to bug you." The others joined in the apology and the three set off down the open air corridor.

David retreated back inside the room, closed the door, and let out a long labored breath. Once his pulse returned to something close to normal, he walked over and picked up the phone. "Frank? You still there?"

"Yeah. What was that all about?"

"I thought they were the terrorists, but it was just some guys looking for a friend's room. They had the wrong building."

"Are you okay?"

"Yeah. I overreacted. Look. I'm gonna let you go. I know it's abrupt, but I don't think I can wrap my brain around anything else tonight, okay? Maybe I'll call you later."

"Yeah, anytime. But, David, I just want to say one more thing. You keep asking me questions about God, which I don't mind, but I want you to know that all you really need to do to find answers, is to read the Bible yourself. I know you aren't convinced it's from God, but if you just pray, and read it, and be patient, God *will* answer your questions, and you'll find peace."

"Yeah, I know, Frank. I'll have to do that."

"But don't hesitate to call if you have more questions.

I'll be here."

"Thanks. I appreciate it."

"Alright, well, take care."

David laid the phone back on the receiver. He did have more questions, but the incident at the door had derailed him. He grabbed the remote and aimed it at Brad in his orange jumpsuit flickering on the television screen, like a digital apparition. He pushed the button and the screen went black.

He laid back and fixed his eyes on the stucco ceiling with its brown water stains, the fear still tingling in his forehead and chest. He took in a deep breath and let it out slowly. He wished it would all just *go away*, the messages, the terrorists, the fear, all of it.

He rolled over and his eyes fell on the open drawer of the nightstand. Inside was a dark blue book with gold lettering on the cover. He didn't have to look to know what it was. He took in another deep breath. "--Yes, Frank," he mumbled. "When all this is over, I'll read it. I *will* read it."

Because I want what you have, Frank. I want that peace.

32721

Karen folded her arms and glared out the truck window at the sea of flashing lights. From their new position, she couldn't even *see* the farmhouse. *If I'd wanted a view like this, I would have stayed at the station!* she thought, turning her glare upon Larry. "What are you smirking at?"

His smile broadened. "I know somethin' you don't know."

"What?"

"Andy." He gestured to a man in a Bomb Squad jacket standing by a black Humvee. "*He* just happens to be the Public Relations Officer for the Boston Bomb Squad, and me and him, we was talkin' a couple a weeks ago about him increasing public awareness about the dangers his men face every day."

Karen gave him a stunned look. "And you're still in the truck *why?*"

"Well back home there's a little word we like to call *please.*"

Her eyes narrowed. *Come on, Karen. It's for the sake of the story. --For the sake of Brad. You can do this.* She smiled. "Larry, would you *please* go and see if the nice man will get us into the farm?"

"Well, since you asked all polite like..."

She waited until the door had closed completely before beginning a rapid tirade of Spanish curses, it was the only language she could speak coherently when she was angry. Larry appeared in front of the truck, she ceased abruptly. He

166

looked at her casually. *What is he doing?* A smile caused the Texan's mustache to rise. She reluctantly returned his smile with what could be best described as two parts sarcasm, and one part loathing. The big Texan took in a deep sniff, adjusted his pants, and turned toward the Bomb Squad officer.

Her eyes burned into the back of his red neck with the curse of a thousand painful deaths. The nerve of *him* to ask *her* to say *please. I should have to told him off. I don't need him!* She could have approached the officer herself and worked the situation just fine without *him.*

Larry spoke with the man for a few minutes then returned to the truck. He looked pleased with himself as he climbed back into the driver's seat. "They're making a sweep of the farm to make sure there's no more terrorists"

"*More* terrorists? They found *some?* How many?"

"I think he said four."

"You think?"

"Once they've secured stuff, Andy says he'll let us observe the disarming of the bomb."

Karen's mouth dropped open. "You're kidding."

"Nope. Guess he's been bugging people in high places. They're gonna allow closer coverage of a bomb extraction, for public awareness."

"How close?"

"Right in the barn where the bomb is, darlin'."

Elation and fear surged through her chest. The thought of being so close to a bomb put twists in her stomach, but this kind of coverage could put her on the fast track to a larger market. This kind of story was what *made* the career of a national journalist. But Brad, he was the most important thing. There could be clues here about where he was being held. For all she knew, he could *be* here somewhere.

"Andy says to gear up, then we're gonna have to sign a waiver, you know, case we get vaporized." Larry flipped the latch on the door and stepped back out. Karen followed, and together they walked across the dirt drive to a black van marked Bomb Squad where Andy stood holding a clipboard. "Hey, Andy. This here's Karen."

He held his hand out. "Good to meet you, Karen, I'm Agent Tanner."

She took his hand. "I can't thank you enough for allowing us this opportunity."

"Don't thank me yet," he said, shaking his head. "This bomb has a nuclear component, we don't know the extent of radioactive leakage. And we're not sure we've secured all of the terrorists operating within the facility."

"I appreciate your candor."

"Here." He handed her a clipboard." You need to sign this, in case of-- unforeseeable circumstances."

She read down the page. It was standard legal stuff. The city of Boston could not be held responsible for any injury resulting from access to the site. There was also a clause about severe penalties if she did not obey every instruction given by authorities. She scribbled her signature at the bottom and handed the clipboard to Larry.

Agent Tanner held out a bomb vest. "You have to wear this, though it won't do any good if this thing blows." She gripped the heavy vest, noticing it had the word PRESS written in white across the front. Agent Tanner helped her heft it over her head. The weight of it pressed heavily on her shoulders. "Here, let me get these for you," he said, as he grabbed the tabs and velcroed them to the side of the vest. The fit was snug.

"You ready for this?" Larry gave a dopey grin.

"I have on my vest that won't save me, and I have your

endearing charm. What more could I want?" She blinked at him.

Larry slapped her on the back. "Sounds like you got it all, little missy."

28

The front door of the barn was open. ATF and FBI littered the area, many of them in HAZMAT suits with the letters WMD written in bold on the back. Andy looked into the back seat of the Humvee at Karen and Larry. "You can stand at the entrance to the barn, but don't go in. Understand?"

"Yes," said Karen, adjusting her vest.

"Take footage of the extraction, but stay out of the way."

Karen nodded. "Understood."

The three exited the Humvee and cautiously strode toward the opened doors of the barn. Inside, floodlights glowed around a group of orange barrels. Men in white suits scoured the room with metal paddles.

Larry pointed to the right side of the doors. "Over here, Karen."

She surveyed the spot then gave him the thumbs up. She turned to agent Tanner. "You have time for a couple of questions?"

"I don't know if I'll have answers." He gave a wry grin.

"How many terrorists have been captured?"

"Four."

"What is the radius of this bomb?"

He thought for a moment. "This bomb is about four times the size of the one used at the base of the trade towers, *and* it includes a nuclear component. It isn't capable of a

170

nuclear detonation, but the blast would level this farmhouse, and the radioactive fallout would make," he shook his head, "*quite* a mess."

Karen jotted down notes. *"Wow."*

"Thank God we caught it out here, before they could move it to a populated area."

"How far would the fallout spread?"

He shook his head. "There are many criteria involved in measuring that. FEMA is working up the numbers based on several pre-planned strategic models. At this time, we don't have the figures."

"Will there be an evacuation of this area?" She continued to scribble.

"There's an evacuation going on as we speak."

"When you seized the farm, did you find any connection to the whereabouts of the Channel Seven journalist being held hostage by the terrorists?"

"I can't answer that. Let's stick to the bomb extraction." An agent came up behind Tanner and handed him a cellphone.

Karen grabbed him by the sleeve. *"Please.* Off the record."

He pulled his arm away gently. "Sorry. I have to take this."

Karen stepped back. *Be patient. Don't force things.* She would just have to turn over the rocks one at a time and hope something moved. She turned back toward Larry. The camera was set on the tripod and he was waiting for her. She walked toward him.

"You get the scoop?"

"Not as much as I'd like, but the night is young. Let's go ahead and tape what we have."

"Ready when you are, darlin'"

"On me in three, two, one. --I'm Karen Watson, reporting again from the site of the Gram Well Milk Farm where authorities have apprehended four terrorists and are continuing their search. Behind me, officers from the Boston Bomb Squad, in conjunction with FBI, ATF, and FEMA personnel, are working furiously to dismantle what they believe is a dirty bomb, a bomb which contains nuclear waste as a component. If it detonates, it could pose a major threat to an undetermined radius around the farm. Law enforcement officials are engaged in an evacuation of the surrounding area. As you can see, the situation is tense, but first response units are working hard to bring the threat under control. It's a story of bravery and selfless…" A shot rang out and something bit into Karen's tricep. She yelped and fell to the ground, disoriented. She couldn't tell where the pain was coming from, her whole left side hurt. She rolled onto her side and gripped her arm, something wet leaked between her fingers.

Officers scrambled in a flurry of chaos as a figure appeared over her. His strong arms gripped her gently, pulling her up. Another shot rang out and he drew her legs and head in, shielding her with his crouched body. Her cheek pressed against the front of his flak jacket as the deafening sound of returning fire exploded around them. She looked up at the face above. Was she losing her mind? *Larry Turner* was offering himself as a human shield to protect her!

More shots rang out from the farmhouse, and Larry pulled her closer. As he stood, her head fell back so she could see the broken window. It was tattered from gunfire, and looked empty. Police held their positions.

Her grip on him tightened as Larry carried her down to a parked van. He set her down against a tire and as he did so, her arm brushed against it. Pain shot through her side. Had the bullet pierced the side of the vest? She wasn't ready to know. --All that mattered was the story, and as long as she was able to concentrate, she *would* deliver coverage. She looked back toward the barn. "The camera!"

"You're hurt, Karen."

"Please!" She clasped her fingers on the neck of his vest. *"Get the camera!"*

He looked at the blood soaking her arm. "Honey, both your paddles ain't touchin' the water. You're hurt bad, and you want the camera?"

"Larry. *Please!"*

"Alright. I'll get it. But you *stay* put. Understand?"

She pulled in a labored breath and nodded.

Larry scooted across to the nose of the van and looked up at the farmhouse. Still no activity. He took off in a crouched run, keeping his eyes on the broken window. The scuffing of his own feet and a police radio in the distance were the only sounds to break the silence.

Karen's breath was labored as she watched Larry approach the camera. But when he reached it, he didn't pick it up, something in the barn had his attention. He stood motionless in the middle of the driveway.

What are you DOING, Larry? Just GRAB it and come back!

Finally, his hand clutched the grip on the camera, and he brought it up and aimed it into the barn. Whatever was going on, he was willing to risk his life to get a shot of it.

Karen tried to get up so she could see the window, but the pain in her arm was too much. She closed her eyes, taking in shallow breaths. Quick footsteps approached. It was Larry. He was limping. He slid in behind the van and turned with his back to the edge of the fender.

"What's going on up there?"

"SWAT was forming up. They're gettin' ready to take the farm."

"You got it?"

"The light's pretty bad, but I got a shot." He looked around excitedly.

"Okay. Let's do a piece here and get that tape to Nerd."

"You sure? You got hit pretty bad."

"Are you *kidding?* Some reporters wait their whole *lives* for a story like this." She straightened up, and winced. "On me in three."

He scooted around and brought the camera up. The red light came on. "Your wish is my command, little darlin'."

She looked down at her blood covered left hand. The microphone was still in her grip. It surprised her to see it there. She let go of the wound with her right hand and took the microphone from her left. "Close up on me," she said, "and don't get a shot of my arm or the microphone, we don't want the gore. Okay. On three, two, one. --Continuing our coverage of the terrorist situation at the Gram Well Milk Farm. It's clear there are more terrorists yet to be apprehended. What was already a tense situation has become more volatile as shots have been fired from the farmhouse at the first response units who are working on disarming the bomb. In the barn, SWAT teams have positioned themselves to take the house. As we learn more, we will keep you updated. I'm Karen Watson, reporting from the Gram Well Milk Farm."

The light went dead. Larry let the camera drop from his shoulder. "You're not gonna tell 'em you got shot?"

"They *saw* me get shot! What more is there to say? I report the news. I don't care to *be* the news." She winced again as she lowered the mic.

"I'm just sayin'. People are gonna wanna know."

"It's not a big deal."

His eyes narrowed.

"I'll think about it, okay? We have more important things to worry about, like getting this tape to Nerd. If we send tapes back every ten minutes or so, it'll give the appearance of live coverage. Right now, we're the only ones getting it."

"Right. I'll get the tape to Nerd, but we're not done talkin' about this."

Karen dropped the mic in her lap and gripped her arm again. It was *really* throbbing now.

"I'm gonna get someone to look at that arm before you bleed to death."

She looked down at the pool of blood forming on her left side, soaking into her leg. She *had* lost a lot of blood. Left unchecked, the wound could prevent her from continuing-- and she *had* to continue.

"Stay put," said Larry, moving toward the back of the van. "I'll be right back." He started for the truck in a crouch but slid to the ground as dozens of gunshots went off inside the farmhouse. The noise, like popcorn in a microwave, seemed like it would never end.

Once again, all was quiet.

Larry checked to make sure it was clear before resuming his course to the black Humvee. Karen watched as the vehicle backed down the driveway and disappeared.

He returned with an EMT, and Karen had a hard time focusing on him. She shook her head, trying to clear the cobwebs. The EMT gave a friendly smile and quickly went to work, gently cutting away the cloth of her suit jacket. He examined the wound and her blood soaked clothing, then looked her in the eye. "Young lady," he said gently, "it looks like you've torn an artery. You need a transfusion."

She gazed up at him, trying to focus on his words. "N- No. I can't lea…"

"Yes, you *can.*" He pressed a bandage on the seeping wound. "You have no choice."

There was so much at stake. This was the story of a lifetime-- and her chance to dig for clues. No. She wouldn't leave. She wouldn't let them take her. "N- No. I- I have to… have to…"

They carried her to the ambulance, strapped her onto a gurney, and started an IV. She fought to stay conscious. "Larry." Her mouth felt dry.

"Right here, Karen."

She tried to bring his face into focus. "Larry."

"Yes, darlin'."

"Find the clues. Don't—don't let 'em miss it. – Larry?" She squeezed her eyes tightly. Then opened them again. "Find..." She took a labored breath.

"Yes, Karen."

"Brad."

"I'm on it." He squeezed her hand.

"Our story. --Get it-- for both of us."

"I will. You relax. You've lost a lot of blood."

A sentence formed in her mind, and before she could stop it, it came out. "I was wrong about you." There he had it, her drug induced confession. She tried again to focus on him. Well, he *had* gotten them into the farm, and selflessly protected her from getting shot again. And she had to admit, there weren't many like him who shared the same passion for the job. She smiled up at him through closing eyelids. Sure he was a crude chauvinistic arrogant meathead who liked to listen to his own voice, but now she saw him in a different light. He had something more, a noble quality. He had saved her—even after she'd treated him so badly.

"Well I was right about you." Larry smiled. You're the toughest, classiest gal I ever had the good graces to meet."

She reached over and found his hand and tapped it with her rubbery fingertips. "Jus- when I was- startin' to truly," she took a breath, "*enjoy* hating you."

He laughed. "Girl you could heckle a mountain lion from your death bed."

She let her heavy head lay back on the crinkly gurney pillow. Unconsciousness crept over her like a warm blanket, she had no strength left to fight it. The hum of the ambulance engine mingled with the buzz of electronic medical gear as she drifted away. The last sound she heard was Larry's voice, distant and shallow. "I'll find him darlin'. We'll get him back. I promise.

29

David knocked on Claire's door and checked again up the street. No one could have followed him without him noticing. He'd been careful to take long barren roads, stopping several times to examine his rearview mirror closely.

The door creaked open and Claire's plump concerned face appeared in the crack. "David! Oh, David. Come in. Come in." She stepped aside to let him pass, then quickly shut the door behind him. "We were worried about you."

David looked beyond the doorway to Sharon standing in the middle of the living room, staring at the news on TV. Stan sat on the left side of the room, opposite the couch, in a barcalounger.

Sharon's face welled with emotion as she turned and started toward her husband. She looked like she had been through the ringer. She wrapped her arms around him and buried her face in his neck. "We saw what happened to Karen on the news. Is she okay?"

David hugged his wife close. "I called the station this morning, she's supposed to be released from the hospital a little later."

"Oh thank God."

Stan stood up slowly, his age and weight impeding his mobility. But he was a rugged old man and bore through it. "Can I get you something to drink, David?"

"No thanks, Stan. We've been enough of a burden on you."

Claire scowled. "Oh, you're no burden. It's a blessing to open our house to your family."

"Our casa is your casa," said Stan with a smile.

David looked around. "Where's Jerry?"

Sharon pulled away and wiped her eyes. "He dropped us off yesterday and left right out. We haven't seen him since."

"He's at the University," said Claire.

Sharon gave her a surprised look.

"He called last night. I'm sorry, honey, I forgot to tell you. One of the other professors needed him to help with something. I guess they've been working on it for quite awhile, and there was a breakthrough last night."

"Well, if it keeps his mind off the terrorists that's fine with me. I was expecting a long night of paranoia and political ranting. So, honestly, I'm glad he's found something to keep him occupied."

Stan waved his hand toward the couch. "If you won't let me get you anything, a least come in and have a seat."

David looked out the living room window on his way to the couch. "I suppose I can stay for a moment. But I really want to get the family further away from Boston. You and Claire should go too. It's not safe here."

They all sat in the living room, Sharon and David next to each other on the couch, Claire in a love seat next to Stan's stately barcalounger. Claire was brimming with questions. "Sharon said you believe the terrorists plan to do something on Sunday. I had to rattle her bones to get it out of her."

Sharon gave him a look of apology, as if to say, she was *very* persuasive.

"So they found a bomb at the Gram Well Milk Farm. Do you think that was the bomb they were planning to use

179

on Sunday?" Claire asked.

"I don't know."

"The Bomb Squad said the terrorists didn't have time to finish the bomb. If that's true, wouldn't they have found other bomb material there, if they were making another bomb?"

"Yeah," said David, "that makes sense. Maybe it's all over."

Stan spoke up. "There was an analyst on this morning. He said someone he knows on the Bomb Squad said the bomb was set up as if the terrorists had never planned to put a detonator on it."

David shifted in his chair. "You mean, it was a decoy?"

"All I know is what the analyst said. The bomb wasn't created to be blown up."

"Why would terrorists make a bomb if they weren't going to blow it up?"

"I don't know." Stan put his hand to his chin. "But I'd be willing to bet they have a fully functioning bomb somewhere else, and that the one in the barn was *meant* to be found."

"Detonators don't cost much to install though. Do they? If they wanted the authorities to find the bomb, and feel like they had stopped a *real* threat, why not put a detonator on it? It would add to the realism." He squinted at Stan. "I don't know. It just seems weird."

"Have you heard anything else about Brad Knight?" Claire interrupted. "They haven't said much about him on the news."

"Not yet. He's..." David's pocket buzzed. "Hold on a second, my phone's going off." He reached in, pulled it out, and flipped it open. Immediately his blood ran cold. He twisted around on the couch and scanned the room. Where's

Ben?"

"What?" Sharon's mouth gaped.

"Ben! Where is he?"

"He's playing in the backyard. Why?"

"Is he alone?"

"Yes."

David sprang to his feet and ran toward the back of the house.

"What's wrong, David! What's going on!"

"Ben's in danger!" He reached the sliding glass doors and his heart constricted. *Oh God! No! This isn't happening!* It was true. His son was alone, and the terrorists knew it.

Ben's fragile life was vulnerable to whatever evil the terrorists intended, there was no way David could stop them. The twenty-five yards separating him from his son lying on the merry-go-round felt like a mile. David gripped the handle on the door.

"David?" Sharon said, clutching his arm.

He looked at his wife, his face shivered with emotion. There was so much to say, but no time. "Sharon," he whispered, "if this is the wrong move, I'm sorry. I'm so sorry." He slid the door open and tore free of her urgent fingers.

"David!"

He leaped from the back porch onto the cold crisp ground. He didn't call out. He didn't announce his presence. He just ran as hard as he could. He ran, pushing with every ounce of his strength, bridging the gap between him and his son. *I'm here! Take ME! Take your shot! I'M the one you want!*

But no shot rang out.

Only the sound of crisp thuds on the cold ground, and short fevered breaths.

181

The merry-go-round turned slowly as Ben's head came into view. David struggled to keep his eyes trained on his son. Just as his face came around, something flashed in the darkness below. David slowed, his head tilted. *What the...* The tiny light blinked a slow steady rhythm. With each flash, David's horror increased.

"Dad?" Ben rose to a sitting position.

"Ben! Don't move!" David put his hand up. "Stay! Stay right there!" He slowed to a jog, then to a slow walk.

"What is it?"

"If you've ever listened to me, listen to me *now.* Stay where you are. Don't *move.*" He reached the slowly spinning circle and got down on his hands and knees. Inside the dark opening of a large paper bag, the light blinked steadily. *WHO put this here? How did they know?* He drove his fist into the ground. When was this *nightmare* going to *end?* He crawled in closer and squinted. There was no countdown on the face of the device, which meant there was a remote detonator, or another trigger.

Alex shouted from the porch. "David! What's going on?"

"It's a bomb! Call the police!" Thank God it was Alex. He knew more about this kind of thing than David did.

"Is there a timer?"

"I don't know! I don't think so!"

"I'm coming down there!"

"No! It could go off!" He heard the ground crunching behind him, and for once, was actually grateful that Alex never listened to him. Even as kids, no matter how hard he argued, Alex always managed to talk him into going on some foolish *adventure,* which David never wanted any part in. Mostly because Alex's idea of adventure was always connected to something life threatening, and David liked living.

"Well-- what have we here?" Alex crawled up next to David.

"Something blinking in a bag."

"Dad?"

"Not now, Ben. Just hold tight." Ben didn't look happy. At *all.*

"Here we go," said Alex. "It's pressure sensitive." He poked his head out. "Ben, stay *very* still." He put his mouth close to David's ear. "This thing set itself when he got onto the merry-go-round, it's rigged to blow when the trigger is released."

"Ben, do what Alex says. *Don't move.*" He ran his fingers through his hair in frustration.

"Dad..."

"Just *do it!*"

Ben held his position. "Is it-- a bomb, Dad?"

He looked up at his son. "--Yes, Ben. That's what it looks like. And if you move, it might go off."

"Where are your messages now, David?" said Alex, half under his breath.

David snapped his head around. "Yeah. That's what I need right now."

"Calm down, man." Alex burrowed under the merry-go-round and carefully ripped the bag open.

David looked over his shoulder, scanning the rooftops and windows of the houses on the other side of the fence. The dark feelings from yesterday still lingered in his mind. He could almost feel the crosshairs hovering over him. Watching him. Waiting for the perfect moment to end his life. *Did they follow me here? If so, why not just kill me last night?* Maybe they followed Jerry. No. They couldn't have. *A bug!* Maybe they bugged Jerry's car. But if that were true, they would have used his family against him last night. But they hadn't. David stood up. "Alex?"

"Yeah?"

"What kind of terrorist plants a bomb under a merry-go-round, instead of on the side of the house?"

"What on Earth are you talking about?"

"I don't think the terrorists want to kill me or my family. They just want to scare me."

Alex came out from under the merry-go-round. "I know you're under a lot of stress, David, but snap out of it, your son needs you."

"What kind of terrorist *warns* his victims? No kind I've ever heard of. They just blow things up and let the terror ensue. There's something different about these terrorists. They have a plan, and *I* fit into it somehow."

"David..."

"Alex! If they wanted me *dead,* I'd be *dead!* If they wanted to kill my family, they would have done it already! They don't *want* us dead, they want us *scared!* They could have thrown the bomb through the window and left a hollowed out socket for me to find. But they *didn't.* They threaten me, play games with me!"

Alex looked at him blankly.

The emotion left David's face. "Alex. Go back to the porch."

"What are you..."

"GO BACK TO THE *PORCH!*"

Ben's eyes got wide. "Wh- what are you doing, Dad?"

David turned around and began sitting down on the merry-go-round. "I'm taking your place."

"Dad!" Ben pushed at his father's back.

"You need to get up slowly as I sit down. I am going to replace your weight."

184

Alex took a step back. Then forward. "Have you lost your *mind?"*

David looked at Ben with fierce intensity. "Get up slowly, son. Lean forward and get up slowly."

Ben's body shook as he put more weight on his feet. David watched and applied more weight as his son got off. Ben turned to his father. His whole body was trembling. "Why, Dad? Why did you..."

"Because I love you. Now go.*"*

Ben began to cry. "I love you too, Dad. I don't want you to die."

His heart broke. "I'm not going to die, Ben. I'll be okay."

Sharon came down from the porch. Her face was covered with tears.

"Go to your mom, son. Alex and I will take care of this."

Ben nodded and wiped his eyes with his sleeve, then turned and ran across the lawn to the porch.

Alex shoved a finger at him. "You've got a screw loose!"

"It's only going to get worse." David looked up at his friend with lifeless eyes.

"Please tell me you are not going to test your foolish theory."

"You never listen to me, Alex, but you don't have a choice this time. I'm going to count to twenty, and then I'm going to stand."

Alex began to pace. "You're serious, aren't you? You really believe these terrorists want you *alive?* They *shot* at you last night! They tried to kill you in that parking lot! Have you forgotten?"

"Why a sniper, Alex?"

Alex's face twisted in disbelief. *"What?"*

"Why not drive up and shoot me in my car?"

"I don't *know!* Maybe they didn't want to be seen."

"Why didn't they kill Ben and cover up the cases of hazmat? Why threaten my family? Why not just kill them?"

"I don't *know!"*

"They've had plenty of opportunity, but they've avoided taking it. *Why?* I'll tell you *why.* They *don't want me dead!"*

"You're nuts!"

"One."

"Don't do this, David!"

"Two."

"You're making a big mistake!"

"Three."

Alex fell to the ground and crawled under the merry-go-round as David continued to count.

"Four. Five. Six. Seven. Eight..."

"For the love of all that's holy, at least count slow!"

"Nine."

Alex wiggled like a worm, desperately tinkering with the bomb. David counted. The number climbed slowly, and as it did, David's resolve solidified. He was going to do it. He was going to force their hand, and no one was going to stop him. Not even Alex. He *had* to know the intention of the terrorists. He wasn't going to play their game any longer.

"Seventeen. Eighteen. Nineteen..."

Alex let out a long bold scream, like a warrior racing into battle.

"Twenty." David leaned forward and stood up. The merry-go-round squeaked, and a deafening silence filled the yard. David sucked in a deep breath and let out a stuttered exhalation. His whole body tingled with adrenaline. He turned and started backing away from the merry-go-round. The light was no longer flickering from the darkness below.

Alex crawled out, got to his feet, and brushed himself off. "You are so gonna get a beating."

"I was right. It didn't go off."

"You could have gotten us both killed!"

"You didn't have to stay."

"What was I going to do, let my best friend get splattered all over the yard in front of his wife and children?"

"I knew what I was doing."

Alex came up into David's face. "You were reckless!"

"What *is* it with you? You never *trust* me! You've *never* trusted me! I know what I'm doing! But you don't trust me!"

"This isn't about *trust!* This is about you making some kind of power play, risking your life on a foolish notion!"

"Oh, it's a power play? I question the all knowing Alex, and I'm on some kind of power trip! Call it what you want. You just don't trust me."

Alex scowled. "I trust you."

"You always make the decisions and it burns your butt that I made one for a change. You've never trusted my opinion. You *always* do what *you* want!"

"I don't always *agree* with you, but I *trust* you."

"Then why don't you listen? Why do you bully me into doing things your way?"

Alex's tone changed. "I'm persuasive. You think I'm a bully? You didn't have to go along with me. I never forced you."

"You're my best friend. I had to. Who else would keep you from getting yourself killed?"

Alex looked wounded. "I didn't know."

"Well now you know," David said defiantly. It felt good to stand up to Alex. In all their time growing up, he had always looked up to Alex, but never once had he stood up to him.

Alex reached out and gripped David by the back of the neck. David resisted, but Alex had a strong grip. He pulled David's head in and their foreheads touched. Alex spoke softly. "I'm sorry, David. I should have listened more."

David looked down at the ground, his forehead pressed firmly against his friend's. "Yeah. You should have."

"I'll do better. You're closer to me than family--than blood. I would never do anything to hurt you. If I'd known you felt this way, I wouldn't have pressured you. You know that, right?"

"I know, Alex. I'm sorry. I was frustrated."

They pushed apart.

"You made the right choice today, and if I wasn't such a prideful idiot, I would have listened."

The group from the porch gathered around them. Sharon threw her arms around David.

"Are you okay?"

"Yes. I'm fine."

"I called the police," said Stan. "They're on the way."

As Stan spoke, David realized that sirens were echoing in the distance. They had been there all along. But he hadn't noticed.

30

Karen stepped into the newsroom and was greeted with a standing ovation. She returned their enthusiasm with a humble acknowledgment, although she couldn't have disagreed more with their praise. The story of the milk farm bomb threat had been left unfinished, and she had uncovered nothing about Brad. She felt like a complete failure.

But the staff of Channel Seven thought differently. Karen had stood on a spot no other reporter could get to and covered a story the entire country wanted to hear. Not to mention the fact that she got *shot* while the camera was rolling! Surely she had earned her fifteen minutes of fame.

Fame? What an odd creature. It had a life of its own, choosing when it would come and to whom it would visit. People love the person who can do what they cannot. People love the ones who exude excellence. Karen had displayed excellence simply by being where no other reporter could be. It didn't matter that it was random luck that had placed her on that spot that particular evening. The viewers didn't care. She had displayed courage in the face of danger, and America had seen a beautiful, sophisticated woman willing to take a *bullet* to report on an impending public threat. Excellence. All excellence.

Some crowded in to offer further congratulations on the story, some remarked on her recovery, others passed by with silent looks of camaraderie. Jim Coldfield came up and put a gentle arm around her. "It's good to have you back in one piece."

She smiled graciously. "It's good to be back."

"How's the arm?"

She wiggled it in the sling. "Never better."

"You'd say that if they cut it off."

She scrunched her face.

"If you want to take some time off, I'll understand."

"No. I'm all set." She looked around the room.

"I figured you'd say that," he said, chuckling. "Well, your desk is right where you left it." He gave her a squeeze on the shoulder. "Let me know if you need anything."

"Will do."

Jim left the newsroom and Karen went to her desk. Still messy. No surprise there. She plopped down and slapped the space bar on her keyboard; the computer came to life. She had followed up on some things with her PDA at the hospital (much to the frustration of her doctors) but there was no replacing her desktop, her lifeline to the world of fluctuating information. She slid some newspapers out of the way, and a little pink Post-it caught her eye. It was attached to a Fed-Ex package. It said, *page 49. What's this?* She ripped the package open to find a book inside, a novel by an author she had never heard of. She looked at the address on the package. It didn't ring a bell. Maybe it had ended up on her desk by mistake? She cracked open the book and turned to page forty-nine. It was the first page of a chapter titled *The Tryst*. Her eyes scanned the page. She didn't know what the author of the Post-it wanted her to find. There was nothing noteworthy in the three paragraphs on page forty-nine, besides the mild coincidence that the main character's name happened to be Karen.

In the brief narrative, the woman found herself at eighty-five Chestnut Drive, a stately yellow house with black shutters, the home of her childhood sweetheart. She remembered fondly swinging from the tire swing that hung from the oak tree in the yard, and the love that had been kindled there so many years ago on that little dead end street in rural Massachusetts. She wanted to go up the dirt driveway and knock on the door, but she didn't dare. Instead she did what she and her former sweetheart, who still lived in the house, had agreed on. She beeped her horn three times to let him know she had come. And that was it. End of page.

"You're back," said a voice over her shoulder.

She turned and looked up. "Oh. Hi, Nerd."

"Got shot, huh?"

Right to the obvious as always. Nerd had a gift for speaking the unnecessary.

"Yep. Right in the arm."

"What's that you're reading?"

Reading? The question caught her off guard. The book had made so little an impression, she'd already forgotten it was in her hand. "This?" She looked at the book, then around the office. "I think someone's playing a practical joke on me. They left a Post-it on this Fed-Ex package with a page number on it." She threw the book on her desk. "It's nothing. Maybe someone put it here by mistake."

Nerd picked up the Post-it. Karen gave him a quizzical stare. "Looks like David's writing," he said.

"Chance? The intern? How do you know?"

"David makes his p's weird. See how it looks like the stem comes out of the center of the circle?" He stuck the note in front of her. "He does that when he's rushing."

"Why would David Chance want me to look at some obscure page in a book?" She flicked the Fed-Ex envelope. "And in a Fed-Ex package that hasn't even been opened? And it's not even *from* him.*"

"I don't know. But if David *did* leave you the note, and

I think he did, I would pay close attention."

Was he joking? She examined his expression. Nerd had the worst poker face of anyone she knew. If he was messing around, he couldn't keep it from her. His countenance didn't waver. "Well, sorry, I don't get what he's trying to tell me. He'll have to explain it. I don't have time for games."

"What did the book say?"

"Please, Nerd. Whatever your fascination with this is, can you give it a rest? I have work to do. And as you so aptly mentioned only a few moments ago, I've been shot-- so I'm a *little* irritable."

"Can I read it? I'll bring it back."

"I don't care. Take it. Just leave me alone."

He grabbed the book. "Thanks."

"And, Nerd?"

"Yeah?" He stopped.

"If you do happen to see something you think I missed, send me an email, okay?"

His whole face lit up, and he all but saluted, then rushed off to his office.

Poor Nerd. Karen shook her head. *He probably thinks there really IS some secret message there and that I've given him his BIG chance to be a hero by finding it.* --But in reality, she just wanted to be left alone, and an email would be the easiest thing to ignore.

Karen slid the Fed-Ex package aside and got back to following up on her correspondence. She didn't have the luxury of living in a fantasy world like Nerd, there was far too much work to be done.

David waited in the study while the police finished questioning Alex. They had interrogated everyone, even Emily. David had never seen anything like it. Every law enforcement agency in the city had descended on the retired Harvard professor's home with every piece of counter terrorism gear available. Each and every corner of the home was being scanned thoroughly. Marked and unmarked cruisers blocked both ends of the street.

Sharon was upstairs with the kids, giving them a break from all the excitement. Claire and Stan were roaming the house, hoping to prevent any accidental damage caused by overzealous investigators. Alone in the study, David went over the events of the day. He was right about the terrorists, they were purposely trying to scare him-- but he couldn't imagine *why*. There was nothing unique or special about him. It wasn't like he had access to anything a terrorist would consider of value. And other than his new found ability, which they had no way of knowing about, he was nothing more than an ordinary guy.

When David told the police about the strange behavior of the terrorists, they had concurred, there *was* something suspicious about the way they were acting. They had been far too merciful with David and his family. One officer had eluded to a greater significance, beyond the treatment of David's family, but what he said didn't make sense. These were clearly *not* pacifists. Pacifists don't *shoot* reporters. They killed John and wounded Karen. Clearly these men were dangerous. Furthermore, the officer pointed out that it wasn't so much that the detonator was *missing,* but that it looked as though it was constructed with no intention of *ever* having a detonator. David couldn't imagine why they would go through all the trouble of creating a bomb if they never intended to use it!

He reached out and pulled a book from the old oak bookcase next to his chair. *Gulliver's Travels.* He smiled. He had read the book as a young boy, he remembered losing himself in its pages. How strange he should find himself living a story nearly as fantastic. But Gulliver was fortunate enough to have had only himself to worry about. He cracked the book open, closed his eyes, and formed a question in his mind. *Who are you?* His eyes flickered open and landed on the words *I am. Okay, that didn't get me anywhere. You are WHAT?* He turned the page and rested his eyes on the word *that.* His fingers grasped the corner of the page, but before he could turn it, his eyes bounced to another word. *Still. I am that still?* He turned the page and continued his journey, picking up words until he was sure the message had ended. What he found was confusing. *I am that still small voice. Fear not the distant horn sounds signal run left bullet stairs she waits.*

O-*kay*

It *was* a message, David was sure of it. But what he was supposed to gather from it, he had *no* idea. *Fear not the distant horn sounds?* What could be frightening about a distant horn? He grabbed a pen from a nearby table and looked around for something to write on. Finding nothing, he carefully wrote the message on the back of his arm, then pulled his sleeve down over it. Gently he slid the volume back into its slot then picked up a newspaper lying on the end table. Before he could think, his eyes began to bounce again. A new message formed. *Tell what son do what it says.*

David rubbed his face. What on *earth* did *that* mean? Was it talking about his son? Tell him to do what *what* says? David's phone went off, and he jumped. It was *Music Music Music*, not a buzz, which meant it was a phone call, not a text message. He relaxed, a *little,* pulled the phone out, and looked at the name on the caller ID. Karen Watson. His mind whispered, *what son.* He stared at the name. *Tell Watson, do what it says.*

Am I supposed to say that? --Hey, Karen. --Do what it says. And what would he say prompted him to tell her such a bizarre and inexplicable directive? The phone rang again. Beep. "--Hello?"

"Hi, David. This is Karen over at the station."

"I know. How are you doing? I heard about last night, found some excitement, huh?"

"I guess you could call it that. Hey, listen. I was going to wait until I saw you, but I keep looking at this note on my desk, and I have to say, it's bugging me. So if you're playing a joke, you got me."

David was quiet a moment. "Ah. I don't know what you're talking about.

"It's a Post-it, with a page number on it. Did you leave it?"

Was that *her* desk he'd left the Post-it on? It seemed so long ago. *Oh great, now I have to try to explain two things.* He sat, unable to find the right words.

"David?"

"--Uh. Yeah, I left the note." If only his phone would go dead. He looked at the five bars in the upper corner of the display. A perfect signal. *Great! Thank you AT&T!*

"Were you referring to the book in the Fed-Ex

package? Cause I went to the page and I read it. But I have no idea what you're trying to show me."

"All I can tell you is, you're suppose to do what it says."

"It doesn't say to do anything. It's a novel."

"It must say to do *something*. What does it say?"

"What do you mean, what does it *say?* You're the one who put it on my desk. You don't know what it *says?"*

"No."

"Then *why* did you put it on my desk?"

"You wouldn't believe me if I told you. All I can say is, whatever it says, do it."

"You're as bad as Nerd. *Fine.* Whatever game you're playing, leave me out of it, okay? I can't afford the distraction."

"It's not a game, Karen."

"If you've got something to *say* to me, David, *say it.* Don't leave cryptic Post-it messages and Fed-Ex packages on my desk. Okay?"

David understood her frustration more than she could possibly imagine. He was *living* it. But unlike her, he now understood the importance of heeding the messages. "Karen. I know it doesn't make sense right now, but sometime in the near future, you're going to have a moment of clarity, and when you do, remember that I told you to do what the book says."

"Are you for real?"

He didn't know what to say.

"Okay. I'm hanging up now. When you're done playing your little *game,* you have my number." The phone went dead.

He didn't blame her for hanging up on him. He could only imagine what she was thinking right now. Some intern she hardly knew was telling her to act out the pages of a novel. At least he had managed to avoid telling her what prompted him to leave the note in the first place. Even still, she obviously thought he was a nut job-- and he wasn't so sure she was wrong.

32

Okay. She was going to put *that* completely out of her mind. Why did she think for a second that David Chance would give her a straight answer after the mysterious way Nerd was acting?

Jim poked his head into the newsroom. "Look alive, folks, we have our second terrorist tape. Meeting in the conference room in two minutes."

It must be the first set of demands-- and still no leads on Brad. Karen's belly twisted. She was *not* ready for this. There was only so much a person could process, and she was nervously approaching her limit. She slid her desk drawer open, took three painkillers out of a white bottle and swallowed them dry. *Get it together, Karen. You're a professional.*

People were filtering down the hall and into the darkened conference room. Karen grabbed a yellow pad from her desk and followed. The same players from the previous meeting were around the table. Karen's chair was waiting. She set her yellow pad down and took a seat next to Cindy Coulter.

Cindy gave a cordial smile. "Hi, Karen. How you feeling?"

"I'd rather take a bullet in my other arm than watch this tape."

"I'm sure Brad's fine."

Karen didn't respond.

The general manager quieted the room and aimed the

remote at the television. A picture of the Arab flickered onto the screen. He was wearing the same headdress and outfit as before, but this time, Brad was not in the room.

"You have been busy, have you not?" he said in his deep baritone. "Do you feel safe now that you have found our bomb?" He got up close to the camera. "Are you curious? Does it not make you wonder? You say to yourself, I am safe. My country will protect me. They have found the bomb and captured the terrorists. But then there are questions. Questions you cannot answer, and the fear continues to eat at your belly. Why was there no detonator? Why do they make a bomb that will not explode? I will share with you the secret, but you will not like it."

He pulled back and held a red ball before the camera. His other hand came down in front of the ball. With a simple gesture, the ball vanished. "When one hand moves, the other is invisible. You ask, where is the ball? I ask you, where is the bomb? How predictable you are, Kafir. You had your eyes on the wrong hand. While you were capturing a harmless bomb, we planted the real one, in the *heart,* of your city."

Several people started talking, the general manager held his hand up. *"Quiet!"*

"You ask yourself, am I safe? Can my country protect me from the judgement of Allah? Can what happens in this city happen in others? Allow me to answer this question for you." He came in close again. "Allah is merciful. You have until 7:00 p.m. to leave the city. All who remain will be judged." He stood and gripped the camera. With a stutter, it twisted and Brad came into view. Karen's heart sank. He looked sallow. His feet were taped to the chair as before, his hands were bound behind his back. "To the managers of Channel Seven. You have until 11:00 a.m. to air this warning. If you do not, the next tape you receive will contain the execution of your journalist. Do not test our resolve." He reached out and the camera went dead.

The lights came up. The general manager addressed the stunned room. "Well-- it doesn't get any clearer than that. We have an evacuation on our hands. As of right now, all station staff are free to go." He looked at his secretary. "Dawn, announce it over the intercom."

"Yes, sir."

"Alright. If you're not seated at this table, clear the room. We have some logistics to go over. Are there any questions?"

The room was quiet.

"No? Okay. Thank you. Stay safe."

The room slowly cleared. Agent Cooper leaned over and spoke quietly with the general manager. Karen couldn't hear what they were saying, but judging by the GMs face, it wasn't good. Karen fidgeted with her yellow pad.

"I'm going to give the floor to Agent Cooper," said the general manager, straightening up.

"Let me be up front with you. I wish you hadn't seen this tape because it makes what I am about to say that much more difficult. It was my recommendation to division that the tape be seized as evidence, but they did not agree. In the spirit of the patriot act, they felt that full disclosure would unify our efforts with yours. I hope they were right-- because now I have the displeasure of telling you that this tape cannot be aired."

The room exploded with questions.

"Please. *Please!*" said Cooper. "I'll answer your questions *after* I've explained our position." He looked around. "I understand your friendship and obligation to Mr. Knight, but there is a greater responsibility, and that is to the citizens of Boston. The kind of uncontrolled evacuation that would result from the broadcasting of this message would cause an untold number of deaths. We cannot allow that to happen. Not with..."

Cindy spoke up, "There's a *bomb* in the city! How many deaths will *that* cause?"

"Allow me to finish, Mrs. Coulter. I assure you, this bomb will not go off. We are close to wrapping up this investigation. It is our analysis that a mass evacuation will give the terrorists *exactly* what they want. Chaos. Under those conditions, our resources will be stretched too thin. Our leads are strong, we have people on the ground..."

"What about Brad?" Karen fought to keep her voice even.

"We have the situation under control."

"You know where he is?"

"Once we have secured the bomb we will extract Mr. Knight."

"You *do* know where he is!"

"That information is classified."

She looked at the general manager. "*Unbelievable!* You have his location, and you're going to let him *sit* there?"

"What we know, or do not know about the location of Mr. Knight is irrelevant. Finding this bomb is our primary mission."

Karen fought back her emotion. "*Irrelevant?* So he's nothing but a pawn? Collateral damage? How easy it is for you to sacrifice the life of someone you hardly know..."

"That's enough, Karen," Jim interrupted.

She threw her pen down.

"We cannot concern ourselves with the life of one man," said Cooper. "We have an entire city to protect, we believe the best way to do that is to keep this tape from airing, and follow up on our active leads. If any of you interfere with this investigation, I assure you, you will be prosecuted to the fullest extent of the law." He stood, the other agents joined him. The man on the end took the mini DV tape from the tape player and placed it in a plastic bag, and the team filed out of the room.

There was no protest from the assembled news team, only silent acceptance. The agent had made it clear. They had leads and they were doing everything in their power to follow up on those leads. There were tough choices to be made, and if it came right down to it, Brad would have to be sacrificed for the greater good. There was no reason to debate the topic. The agent was clearly running by a playbook, and it was not up for discussion.

Karen had her own decision to make. Was she going to leave Brad's life in the hands of law enforcement who saw him as a strategic decision, or risk imprisonment for interfering with an official investigation? --Of course she was going to interfere. It was in her very nature to interfere. She wasn't going to let the life of someone she cared for be determined by an unconcerned third party.

The conference room door closed, and everyone started talking at once. Everyone, that is, except Karen. She had made up her mind. Whining about how unfair it was for the FBI to take the tape, or debating what the station's official on-air response should be, was of no interest to her. The politics and emergency procedures were meaningless. Time was running out, she needed to move. "May I be excused?" She spoke loudly above the other voices. The general manager gave her an annoyed nod and turned his attention back to Cindy, who was protesting the most.

Karen slipped out of the room and stood in the hallway. Her mind was in a tailspin, her emotions circling close behind. She had lost her friend John, had come face to face with a bomb, had taken a bullet in a major artery-- and the love of her life was being held by terrorists, with a looming death sentence.

She took in a deep breath.

Down the hall three agents talked quietly. Up the hall two station employees stood waiting for the elevator. Karen corrected her posture, walked across the hall to the supply closet, stepped in, and locked the door behind her. Time was short, there was no time for self pity. Brad needed her to be strong. The thought of giving in to her fear and frustration caused a fury to boil. She clenched her fists. *Do NOT give in to your emotion!* There had been a time when all that mattered to her was her career, but that was before Brad stole her heart. No, not stolen, earned. She had made it exceedingly difficult for him, but he had waited patiently for all of her walls to come down. He understood her. He was like her. He shared her love for adventure and her aspirations to one day anchor on a major network. He shared her passion and obligation to report the news, to be a part of history as it unfolds. She was a woman of intense principle and conscience, and no man had ever measured up-- until Brad. His integrity, his kindness, his smile, his smell. How could she ever fill the hole his absence would rip in her heart?

She forced the emotion back with all her will, but tears began to stream down her defiant cheeks anyway. She hadn't realized how much she loved him, how much she needed him, how empty her life would be without him. Her knees weakened and she sank to the floor, sobbing uncontrollably.

33

Alex entered the study. He looked annoyed.

"You alright?"

"Yeah. I just get bugged by the way police do things. Everything has to be official and by the book. I had to spend thirty minutes explaining what I could have shown them in one, if they had just let me near the bomb, but that would break protocol, and we can't have that."

"Watch yourself. You might get yourself thrown in the clink."

"*Clink?* What are you, from some sixties detective series? Who says clink?"

"I do."

"--Maybe they'll throw me in the *sah-lammah.*"

They both laughed.

"So what are you going to do now?" Alex sank into a chair.

"Good question. I might go through some more of these books to see if I can get any information."

"Still following the messages?"

"I have to, but I gotta tell you, this bomb thing has put me on edge. What if the terrorists decide that my family is worth more to them dead? They've proven they can find them. The only time I've felt they were safe was when I left them with you..." He looked at his friend, his eyes lit up. "Hey! You could take them! Take them somewhere even *I* don't know about. You, Sharon, and the kids. Can you do that?"

Alex started pacing. He stopped. "Yes. I'll do it, but I want you to know I'm not happy about it. I don't agree with what you're doing. --But I'll respect your decision."

"Thank you, Alex."

The door to the study creaked open, a man from the Bomb Squad entered, a tall freckly man. The patch on his shirt said, *Quincy.* "Am I interrupting?"

"No. Come in," said David.

"I want to thank you for your cooperation. I know you've been through a lot this morning." He offered his hand to David, then Alex. "We're going to remove the bomb from the premises now, which means you need to leave." He handed his business card to David. "Give me a call if you see anything else suspicious."

David looked at the card. "Yeah. Will do." The man turned and left.

The card said: Sgt. James *Quincy,* Boston *Bomb* Squad, 2331 *Market* Ave., Boston MA. In the corner was a slogan. "Honor *is* Courage *in* Crisis." David's mind unscrambled the words, and a sentence formed. *Bomb is in Quincy Market.*

David's heart skipped a beat. "Here we go again," he said under his breath.

"David?"

"It doesn't get any clearer than that."

"What are you talking about?"

David looked at Alex. "I know where the bomb is."

"What?"

David spoke low. "It's in Quincy Market."

Alex's jaw dropped. "It just told you that? Point blank? Just like that?"

"It's on this card." He held it out.

Alex grabbed the card and examined it. "So what are you going to do?"

205

David scowled at him. "I don't *know* what I'm going to do! I wish you'd stop *asking!"*

"Are you going to tell the police?"

David stared blankly at his friend. *Should I?* The messages were coming to him, and him alone. Was he the only one who could get to the bomb? Would the mobilization of an entity as large as Homeland Security cause the terrorists to detonate the bomb early?

"I don't know, Alex. At this point I'm going to keep it to myself. The message was sent to *me,* so I have to assume that involving the authorities might force the terrorist's hand. Maybe the message was sent to me because I'm the only one who can slip in under the radar."

"Slip in *where,* into the middle of a terrorist encampment? Do you think the messages will protect you from men with guns?"

"I don't know."

"Think about it, David. You're working with *slivers* of information. You know where the bomb *is,* because the messages were nice enough to tell you, yet there are no instructions on what you're supposed to *do* with this information. You don't know whether to go, to stay, or even if you're supposed to tell anyone."

Alex was right. David felt like he was walking from streetlight to streetlight on a pitch dark night, with no idea of what might jump out at him from the shadows. He had one piece of information, but was left to guess the rest. What if he guessed wrong? What then? He looked at his friend. "Do you think I haven't thought of that? I am well aware of the pitfalls. But I'm going to follow this to the end."

"To the *end* all right. Your *end."*

David leveled his eyes at Alex. *Why is he so against me? Is it because HE's not the one getting all the action?*

Does it bother him that I'm the one in the spotlight for a change? "Are you going to help me or not?

Alex paused. "--Yes. *Whatever!* I'll take your family and leave you to your fool's errand." He scowled. "Man! I'll be glad when this is *over* so we can go back to liking each other again."

34

"Hi. You got Larry. I'm out *whoopin'* it up. Leave a message and I'll holler at ya later." *Beep.* Karen canceled the call and tried his cellphone.

"Hello?" said Larry in his thick Texas accent.

"Hi, Larry. It's Karen."

"Hey there, darlin'. You got banged up pretty good last night. How ya feelin'?"

"I'm okay. I just wanted to touch base."

"Sure thing. I got somethin' I want to show you."

"Are you standing in an empty room?" she said. "There's a horrible echo."

"Nope. I'm in a room full o' people."

She pulled the phone away and turned slowly in her chair.

Larry stood behind her with a broad grin, the phone still to his ear.

"You're pretty pleased with yourself aren't you?"

"Pleased as punch."

"What'd you want to show me?"

"This." He flipped his phone closed and slapped a crumpled napkin with pen etchings on her desk. The napkin was frayed where the pen had dug the name Ali Al-Kabim into it."

"Who's this?"

"That, darlin', is a name I may or may *not* have got off one of the cellphones put into evidence from the raid on the farm last night. Of course, that would be illegal, therefore

one can only figure I must have got it from another acceptable and reliable source."

She covered the napkin with her hand and looked at him. *"Larry!"* she whispered.

Larry's brows rose. "You want to find Brad or don't ya? This man might know where he is."

She closed her mouth. "Isn't this the guy who did an interview with Brad a few weeks ago to generate publicity for his pawn shop?"

"Yup. Same guy."

She looked around then leaned in toward him. "Why do you think he knows where Brad is?"

"While we was at the pawn shop I noticed some pictures on his desk and I asked him about them. One was his wife, the other his brother. Here's the real interestin' part. His brother was picked up last night in the farm raid, and that there name wasn't taken from his brother's cellphone."

"Okay, so someone *else* from the farm had him on their cellphone. Your point?"

"It wasn't his pawn shop listing, it was his name. It's a personal connection. Which means he has at least two points of contact with the terrorists. Are you catchin' my meanin'?"

"So-- we should question him?"

"Couldn't hurt."

She rubbed her hands across her desk. "Well-- I don't have anything better at the moment, we might as well."

"Great. Let's mosey on down to the carport and see if we can't rustle up a ve-hicle."

35

David said goodbye to Sharon and the kids and headed off to Quincy Market. His heart was heavy, not simply for the task ahead, but for how he was forced to leave things with Sharon. She wanted to understand why he had determined it was his responsibility to stop the bomb, but how could she? She had not experienced the things he had, and she did not share his driving passion to answer the question of God's existence. To David, it was more than stopping a bomb or saving a city. He was in communication with something greater than himself, possibly the God of everything, and he had to see where it led. She could not understand this, and he could not make her understand.

The city seemed dark and foreboding as he made his way through the busy streets. News of the terrorist activity had not disrupted business as usual, but apprehension was in the air. His skin tingled and his stomach roiled as he approached Market Square. It was the weekend, Quincy Market was always crowded on the weekend. The open-air market was filled with happy shoppers, blissfully unaware of the danger in their midst. He parked in a nearby garage then followed the flow of pedestrians to the main thoroughfare where people crossed to and fro from store to store, carrying shopping bags of all shapes and sizes.

There was a message here. There had to be, somewhere hidden in the endless array of advertisements, lying dormant, until each piece assumed its position in choreographed splendor upon the stage. David had never stopped to notice, but almost everyone had something to say. They put it on their shirts, their pants, their hats, even their skin. It was on bumpers, windows, backpacks, notebooks, shopping bags. Everywhere. The world was covered with words. Somewhere among the signs, posters, marquees, and window displays was a message just for him, a message leading to the bomb.

But would he find it set to explode-- or would it be another harmless bluff?

His eyes scanned the crowd.

A woman bent down to speak with her daughter. The bag on her arm said Record Town but the words did not speak to him. To her right was a man in a t-shirt. The shirt said Dare To Speak but there was no sense of confirmation. He turned and looked at a man pushing an empty wheelchair. Allstar was written in bright white letters across the seat back. He broke the word in half, All and star. Neither had any meaning. *Am I doing something wrong?*

He began walking, half in a trance, scanning and deciphering, gathering word after useless word, generating one garbled sentence after another. Nothing. *Why send me here only to abandon me? There are words everywhere! Why don't you speak?* He remembered the message from the study and pulled up his sleeve. Maybe now it would make sense. *I am that still small voice. Fear not the distant horn sounds signal run left bullet stairs she waits.* He cocked his ear. Nope. No small voice. No horn sounds. Still nonsense.

He turned and headed down a covered walkway toward the entrance of a restaurant. The colors of the menu lining the side of the brick wall were warm and welcoming. His eyes began their search: Tenderloin, to, poached, with, topped, creamy, delectable, perfection... Lobster Tail. Baked Salmon Roulade. Beef Tenderloin with Stuffed Mushrooms and Shallot Dressing served on a Tomato Garnish. *Mmm. That sounds really good.* His stomach rumbled.

He turned to the desert menu. Strawberry Cream Torte, cream cheese and fresh strawberries on a baked... Something stung him on the neck. His hand shot up, trapping the object. It felt like a bee sting, but it didn't feel like a bee, the object was hard and bristly. He kept the pressure on it and slowly pinched, hoping to trap whatever it was safely between his fingers. The covered walkway began to tilt. His vision blurred as he pulled the stinger from his neck. His eyes closed slowly-- *so slowly*. He forced them open and tried to focus on the object in his hand. It was a feathered blow dart. He stared at it, unable to comprehend what had happened. His brain slowed, his body began to go numb. *Who...* He put his hand on the wall to stable himself and turned toward the street.

Through melting vision he saw the wavering figure of the man he'd seen a short while ago with the empty wheelchair. Firm hands gripped him from behind and sat him down into the chair. He turned lethargically and looked up at the owner of the hands. *My Arab neighbor! Hamid!* David's eyelids slid down like a warm blanket as his brain sank helplessly into placid darkness.

The pawn shop rested in the heart of a neighborhood heavily populated by Muslims. Arabic words were everywhere, on windows, posters, neon signs. A woman in a berka strolled with two children up the cobblestone sidewalk, two men with full black beards and white linen robes stood talking next to a mailbox with an Arabic sign posted on its face.

Larry pulled the news car up to the front of the pawn shop and peered out the window. "Looks like it's open."

"What's our angle with this guy?" Karen looked up and down the street. "Do you think he'll talk in exchange for more publicity?"

"At this point, I doubt it. His brother was just thrown in jail. He's likely orneryer than a bobcat full o' cactus quills."

"Please tell me you have a plan."

"You're the reporter."

She furrowed her brows. "Okay. We'll do a human interest piece. Ask him how the current terrorist threat is effecting the Muslim community here. Maybe he'll open up and share more."

"Sounds good to me, darlin'."

"Fine. You go first and break the ice." With her one usable hand, Karen adjusted her wavy black hair, smoothed her suit jacket, and stepped out of the car. It felt like every eye on the street was on her. She was used to being the center of attention, but not *this* kind of attention. The memory of last night hung over her like a suffocating shadow, she couldn't shake the feeling that she was still a possible target.

Larry grabbed the camera case from the back seat and headed up the small cement stairs. Karen followed uncharacteristically close behind. The door jingled as they entered. The shop owner, a young Arab man in a white dress shirt, recognized Larry immediately. He waved him in. "Come. Come. I welcome you."

"We ain't interuptin' are we?"

"No. No. Not a- tall." He walked down the length of a glassed in counter filled with jewelry and watches and other assorted trinkets, to the end where he opened a small swinging divider. "'Tis good to see you, Mr. Larry Turner." The man offered his hand, and Larry took it.

"How's business?" said Larry.

"Business is very good. I thank you that you did not make me look like a rat. I was worried people would stop coming."

"Naw. That's not how Brad works. If he says he's gonna do somethin', he does it. And we was just lookin' for a confirmation from someone in the Muslim community, that Americans can sleep easy at night because there *are* Muslims who love this country and are watchin' out for us."

Karen shot him a glance. Was *that* what they'd interviewed him about? She hadn't bothered to ask. Of course, it made perfect sense. Why would they interview an Arab business owner about terrorist money laundering? He would only ostracize himself from the community he was seeking to win business from.

"Brad is a good man. I saw on the television about him. Very sad. I hope he is not harmed."

"Well, he's kinda why we're here." Larry moved aside. "Here's Karen Watson. She's doing a piece about the impact this terrorist activity is having on Muslims in Boston. Could she have a word with you."

"Yes. Yes, of course."

Karen held her hand out to him and he took it. "It's good to meet you, Ali."

He released her hand, stepped back and held a finger up. "Wait one moment. I will call Jamil down to run the shop, and we will talk out back." He made a call on his cellphone, and soon a young teenager came to take his place. He guided Larry and Karen into the back room where piles of boxes sat among old appliances, musical instruments, and assorted electronics. Ali stopped in the middle of the room and turned to face them. His countenance had turned serious, the single dangling lightbulb cast a foreboding shadow across his dark skin. "I am fearing for my life to talk to you," he said in a whisper.

"I promise we won't ask anything that would endanger you," said Karen.

"You do not understand. I know these people who have took your Brad."

Karen could barely keep her composure. "Wh- Who? Who took Brad?"

"I must ask you a most important question."

She stood silent, her eyes studying his face.

"Do you look for a story, or do you look for answers?"

She glanced at Larry, then back at Ali. "What do you mean?"

"If I tell you what I know, *you* cannot do the report. They have seen you. They know I have met with you." He looked at them with growing intensity. "But I tell you for fear of what is coming."

"You want me, to give the story, to someone else?"

"It cannot be you. You must promise."

215

"You have my word."

"And you, Mr. Turner?"

"Yeah. Mum's the word."

He gave the Texan a confused look. "Your mother, is-- the *word?*"

"That means I swear." He held his hand up in scout's honor.

Karen shook her head.

Ali's expression was void of humor. Whatever he knew brought him great anxiety. "Follow me." He led them out the back door and up a rickety staircase to the door of the upstairs apartment. A crooked broken number 2 hung from a single nail. "I am living here with my brother and his son Jamil." The door creaked as he pushed into a cluttered room which looked more like a storage closet than a living room. Light filtered in through multicolored curtains bathing the room in swaths of primary colors.

"Come." Ali gestured. "My brother's bedroom is this way."

Karen touched his arm. "Wait a second. Who lives here?"

"Me, my brother, and his son, the boy downstairs."

"The same brother who was picked up by the FBI last night?"

"Yes."

She looked at Larry. "We can't be here, the feds will be all over this place."

"No. It is safe. My brother is living in another apartment as well. No one knows he lives here with his son. They think he lives there and that his son has gone away with his mother."

Karen and Larry looked at each other. Larry shrugged.

"I am telling you. It is safe."

Hesitantly, Karen followed the men through the living room, down a hallway, and into a bedroom. Faint light penetrated the drawn curtains, revealing a small cluttered room filled with electronics. A computer sat on a desk in the corner. Ali switched on a lamp. He turned to face his guests. "One year ago, my brother began to act strangely, spending much time in here, his room, and not talking to me very much. When I heard of the other apartment, I asked him, but he said he could not tell me; he wanted me to stay out of it. I was safer not to know." Ali got down on all fours and slid an old suitcase out from under the bed. "I was worried for him, so I searched his room." He slid the zippers and flipped the top. Inside was an odd collection of items.

Larry crouched down. "Four galvanized pipes, some end caps, BBs, batteries, and two bottles of somethin' liquid." He looked up at Ali. "I could probably put a guess to what *this* is."

"When I found this, there was also a cellphone that was taken apart, a laptop computer, and many papers on how to make a bomb."

"Yep, a bomb alright. A small one, but still deadly."

Karen took a step back. "Did you confront him?"

"No. I was afraid. Not of my brother, but his friends. They are zealots."

"Well, at least he never used it."

Ali stood up and sat on the bed. His eyes appeared sunken in the shadows of the room. "I watched him. If he tried to use the bomb, I would have tried to stop him. But something else happened, something much larger than this, around the same time he got the apartment. He would go for a long time, then come home with expensive things, like a new digital camera, a new computer. I asked him where he got them, but he said don't ask. He could not lie to me, his brother, and I would be in danger. So I stayed quiet and watched."

Ali went over to the dresser, crouched and pulled out the bottom drawer. It was empty. He reached in and up to the bottom of the drawer above it and ripped off a piece of velcro. A container dropped down. "If he knew I found this, he would be very angry with me." He lifted the flimsy blue plastic container and placed it on the footlocker at the end of the bed. He popped it open and looked up at Karen and Larry. "These he has been collecting. I knew he was into something deadly, but this is far worse than I thought. I did not think he could do such things." His eyes turned down. "My brother is not evil. Before you look in this box, I want you to know, he is a good man, but he is frustrated with the evil of this world. He believes he can help bring the age of peace, by doing the will of Allah. Evil men are warping his mind."

Karen gave him a gentle look, then reached for the container. "May we?"

"Yes. But please, I beg you, do not use this to incriminate my family. Use it to tell the police of this terrible danger."

She placed it on the locker and slowly began removing items. Larry stepped closer. Ali got up and stood in the doorway.

Based on the numerous pictures and printed biographies, it was clear Ali's brother was in charge of gathering information and researching potential recruits. The photos had numbers in black ink corresponding to numbers on the printouts. Numerous web page resources outlined the construction of various types of bombs, including a dirty bomb. Finally, Karen pulled out two eight gig thumb drives. She could only imagine what was on them.

She turned to Ali. "Do you have access to that computer?" She pointed.

"No. It is password protected."

She rolled the tiny black thumb drives gently in her hand. If only she had brought her laptop. "Do you know what's on these?" She displayed the drives in her palm.

"One is nothing. The other has more research from the Internet."

She set them down on the foot locker, picked up the photos, and began laying them out. Her hand stopped.

"What is it?" Larry leaned in.

She slid a photo out from the rest and lifted it up. There were two men in the picture.

Larry's jaw dropped. "Is that David Chance?"

"It certainly looks like him." She flipped the photo over to reference the number on the back. There was no biography with a matching number. She flipped it back over. "Do you recognize this other guy?"

"Nope."

Karen held the photo toward Ali. "Do you know who these men are?"

He stepped closer. "Yes. That is the professor."

She looked at the photo again. "Which one?"

"The man on the left."

"What about this one?" She pointed to David.

"Him, I do not know."

"Who is this professor?" She studied the picture closely. "How does he fit into what's going on?"

"He is the one making the bomb." He pointed. "The information is on one of the flash drives."

David Chance knows the bomb maker? She pulled her phone from her purse and took a snapshot of the picture. "I'm going to email this to Nerd to see if he can find anything on this professor." She looked at Larry, he raised his eyebrows.

She scanned through the rest of the materials, but there was nothing referring to Afif, or the money laundering. It was all focused on creating a bomb and recruiting people who could make it happen. There were no clues to Brad's location, and she was about to pack the materials back into the box when she noticed some numbers on the corner of a printout. 42.360262 / -71.054839 "What do you make of this?" she said, showing Larry the page.

"No idea."

She held it out toward Ali. "Do you recognize these numbers?"

Ali came over and looked. "I am sorry. I do not."

She took a snapshot of the numbers and the top of the page, and emailed them to Nerd. Carefully she started putting the items back the way she had found them. "You should bring this to the police."

"I cannot, it would put my family in great danger. Use what you can, and have the story told, but please, it cannot be linked back to me. My brother is paying for what he has done, but my family and his son are innocent. Please. I am trusting you."

"Where am I going to tell everyone I got this information *from?*"

"Can you not say it is anonymous?"

"Not in something like this. It would be withholding evidence to an official investigation, that's a *serious* charge."

"We could film it," said Larry.

She shot him a look. "What?"

"I could put it all on tape, and we could say it was dropped off anonymously."

She gave him a startled look. "*That* is a brilliant idea.

But what if they track it back to us?"

"Back to me," he corrected.

"You're willing to take the heat?"

"To protect Ali and his family. Yes I am, darlin'."

"Would that be acceptable to you, Ali?"

Ali gave a reluctant nod.

"Fine. We'll shoot it all, but we have to make it quick, we only have a little over an hour and a half before the deadline." She started taking the items back out of the container.

"Deadline?" asked Ali.

"If we don't find Brad by 11:00 a.m..." Karen bit her lip, "they say they're going to kill him."

Ali looked alarmed. *"Why?"*

"Because the FBI will not allow the second terrorist tape to be aired." She continued laying out the items.

A light of understanding came into his eyes. "Yes. I saw this on the news. The man said he would kill him if the tapes were not run. Why would the FBI do this?"

"They're worried about causing a panic. I don't have time to explain it, but if you have any idea where Brad is being held, I would be very grateful."

He ran his fingers through his hair and stared at the wall. "All I know is what is in this room, and the name of the businessman my brother is working with. He goes to our Mosque. His name is Afif Al-Qadir."

"That's all you know?"

"Yes. I am sorry. But I do not think my brother had anything to do with hostages. All he has is information on how to make bombs. I think that was his only job."

She stepped back so Larry could start filming. "Thank you, Ali." She offered her hand. "I know the personal risk you're taking to give this information to us. We'll keep your

221

identity silent."

"I wish I could do more."

"The day is young." She gave a weak smile. "You may get your chance."

37

David's heavy eyelids opened to slits as a pair of brown loafers passed within inches of his face. The fake leather squeaked as the wearer crouched above him. Pain stabbed into David's shoulder and cheek bone where the majority of his weight was resting. His hands were twisted behind him, his legs pressed tightly together. He wanted to move to relieve the pain, but his captors didn't know he was awake-- and he wanted to keep it that way.

"Are you hungry?" said an Arab voice.

A shock wave ran through David's body. Was he wrong? Did they know?

"Yes," said a dry scratchy voice.

The man in the loafers was talking to someone else. "I know it is late, but I get you some breakfast or something."

"Thank you." This time, when the man answered, David recognized the voice. Brad! A wave of fear produced a shiver in his chest, he fought desperately to remain still.

The loafers squeaked again as the man stood and walked to the door. "I get you a juice too. You like juice, yes?"

"--Yes." His speech was slow and slurred.

The door closed, and David waited as the footsteps grew fainter and fainter.

"Brad." David spoke in a terrified whisper.

"You're awake." He sounded a little more alive.

"Do you know where we are?" David continued to whisper.

Brad whispered back. "It won't help to whisper. There's a camera by the door. They can see and hear everything."

David's breaths were short and labored as he shifted his head to see the camera. A little red light blinked above the lens, indicating it was on, or recording, or both.

David rolled onto his belly then back up onto his shoulder. He straightened out his legs and with several rocks managed to get himself up into a sitting position. He scooted back against the wall. The drugs were still working, the walls wavered and swayed. He squeezed his eyes shut, trying to take control of his equilibrium.

"What did *you* do to get thrown in here?"

David responded with his eyes still closed. "Tried to stop the bomb."

Brad let out a weak laugh. "Oh you're dead for sure."

David snapped his eyes open and glared at him.

"Kidding. Sheesh. Take it easy."

"How can you *joke* about this? We're being held hostage by *terrorists!* You've seen the videos. They behead people in orange jumpsuits!"

"Maybe it's the jumpsuits." Brad looked down at his clothes and smiled. "Maybe they hate orange jumpsuits. Maybe if we take 'em off they'll let us go!" He started giggling uncontrollably.

It was the drugs. It had to be. David had never known Brad to act like this. He was usually very reserved and dignified. "I wish they'd give me what they gave you. I could use a good laugh." --He had never been more frightened in his entire life.

Brad composed himself. "Sorry, Dave. I'm not myself."

"What *did* they give us? You have any idea?"

"Whatever it is, it has more than one effect."

"Have you learned anything about where we are or how we can escape?"

"If I had would I still be here?"

David leaned his head back against the wall. "Good point."

The door to the room opened and Hamid stepped in. "I see you are awake, Mr. Chance. Good. It is time to eat."

David squinted at him. *You!*

He took out a switchblade and removed the tape bindings from their ankles. Behind him, another man entered the room carrying a small submachine gun, or an Uzi, David had no idea. But he knew the man, he was one of the Arabs from the U-Haul truck. Was the bomb at the hostage house? "Please do not try anything. I assure you, my brother will not hesitate to kill you." Hamid stood and stepped back. Brad rose out of his chair. David shifted to his knees and stood. The room took a twist. "Please follow me." Hamid led them out of the room and down a short hallway to a living room, which was empty save for a card table, two wooden chairs, and a small television set. They were directed to sit. The man with the gun took a position behind them.

Hamid taped their ankles to the legs of the chairs and cut their bindings. David rubbed his sticky, wrinkled wrists. A third man, whom David recognized as the other man from the truck, came in and placed a plate of eggs and toast in front of each of them. "I will let you watch your TV station while you eat. Perhaps you will be fortunate to see your news break in for a special report-- or, you will be very disappointed when the clock strikes eleven, and it has not."

The old clock above the television said 10:22.

David looked confused. "What happens at eleven?"

"If your news does not play our tape--" his voice held

no emotion, "Mr. Knight will be executed."

Brad did not react, he picked up his fork and began eating with groggy automation. *They must have given him an extra dose.* He looked utterly numb.

Hamid switched on the TV and left the room. An infomercial for a new and exciting fat burning regimen came to life on the screen. David slid his plate away. The thought of eating made his stomach roll. *Will they do it? Will they follow through with their threat?* They had killed John in cold blood and shot at Karen. Clearly these were dangerous men, despite the unarmed bomb and the warnings they had given to him. *Should I ask their intentions toward me and my family? Why play games? Why not just kill me? What good am I to them? Should I ask? Should I speak up?* The man with the gun shifted his feet. David realized his hands were shaking. He also realized, in all his chasing after the messages, there was no apparent tie between the terrorists and the impending Presidential assassination. --The entire crisis centered around the bombing of Boston.

It didn't matter.

Even if he had the courage to ask, they wouldn't tell him; they had no reason to. David thought back to the times he had seen Hamid sitting on his steps, right down the street, right under his nose, plotting and planning unimaginable violence. David had been oblivious-- perhaps purposefully so.

The second hand ticked and started another round. Another minute gone. He looked at the TV. Still talking about fat burning. *God. If you're up there. Now would be a good time to speak.* He recalled a message from the library in Stan and Claire's house. His mind whispered-- *Fear not.*

Karen followed behind Larry as he pushed his way through the newsroom. She was surprised to see so many people still working.

"Look out," Larry shouted, "big scoop comin' through." He swung the news director's door open.

Jim looked up with a phone between his shoulder and ear. "I'll call you back," he said, and set the phone in its cradle. "Please tell me you've got something."

"This was left on the wiper of the news car, so I put it in my camera and took a look at it. It's video of terrorist recruitment records, *lots* of them, and bomb schematics."

"You better not be messing with me."

"See for yourself."

Jim picked up the tape and examined it. "Cheap tape stock but a broadcast format." He pushed it into the tape deck next to his computer and turned on the monitor. The screen flickered and came to life. A biography slowly scrolled up the screen. Jim leaned in and squinted. "Well I'll be a..." He forwarded the tape and watched as footage of photos and biographies and schematics streaked past. "Incredible. This was on your car?"

"Yep."

Jim punched the stop button and stared out the window. Karen knew exactly what he was thinking, she had known him for many years. He had in his possession what every news agency in the country wanted, and what he knew the authorities would demand to acquire. He was, no doubt, working through all the angles, wondering how he could exploit the opportunity sitting in his lap. At last he spoke. "We need to bring the FBI in on this. If we weren't so crunched for time, I'd say copy it and follow up on the leads, but this is sensitive material. Take this up to them immediately, but have Nerd stay with the tape; it's station property, I want it back when the Feds are done with it."

"Will do," said Larry.

Jim took the tape out and handed it to Larry. "Is there anything on there about Brad?"

Karen looked at the clock on the wall. Only thirty five minutes left. She fought to keep her composure. "No. Has the FBI done anything?"

"If by 'done anything' you mean sit on their hands, then yes, they have."

"I can't believe they know where he is, and they're not *doing* anything! Can't we find out what they know?"

"I wish we could."

"I might be able to help," said Nerd, who was standing just outside the door.

Karen's eyes fell on him, and she froze. She had sent him the picture of David and the numbers from one of the documents. He could link her to the contents on the tape. Did he realize? Would he give them away? She moved to prevent him from coming into the room.

"I found these," he said, holding up some papers over Karen's shoulder.

"Karen! Let him *in.*" Jim gestured for her to move aside.

Her skin tingled with terror, her hand shot out and snatched the papers. "Thanks, Nerd. Good work. I'll take a look at these and get back to you."

Nerd gave her a startled look. "Um, o-*kay.*"

Jim's eye narrowed. "Nerd, come *in* here and close that door."

Karen tried desperately to conceal her panic.

The door clicked shut.

Jim looked from Larry to Karen. "What do you two have going on?"

Karen glared at Nerd, then looked at Jim. "Nerd looked up some numbers for us."

"Numbers?"

"GPS numbers," said Nerd.

Jim held his hand out to Karen for the papers. "So why are you trying to hide them from me?"

"I'm not hiding anything." She was cornered. What was she going to tell him? If he looked at the pictures she sent to Nerd, he would make the connection between them and the tape, he would know it was they who recorded the footage. Her mind raced to find an excuse. "I..."

"What Karen's tryin' to say is, we played the tape in the truck and she took a coupla pictures with her cellphone."

Karen stood with her mouth open, then suddenly smiled. "I emailed them to Nerd."

"I thought you said you found it on the wiper of the news *car."* He looked at Larry.

"Car-- truck. I meant truck."

"What are you two up to?"

Karen furrowed her brow. "Alright! You want the truth? I think you're working a little too closely with the FBI. That's what I think. And I don't want them to know I took these numbers and that I'm following up on them so I can find Brad. Unlike you, *I* don't *care* what the FBI thinks, I'm going to find him!"

Jim took in a deep breath. "I'm just covering my butt, Karen. There are legal issues involved."

"I don't *care* about legal issues! Brad's life is in danger, I'm not going to leave it up to *them* to decide if he lives or dies!"

Jim held his hands up in defense. "All you had to do was ask me to keep quiet. There's no need to keep things from me, Karen."

She sat down and put her head in her hands. "I just need to find him, Jim. I don't care about the cost."

"I want to find him too, Karen. --Nerd, what did you uncover?"

Nerd shot Karen a hesitant glance. She looked up and nodded for him to continue. "The numbers are for something called a Geo Cache. It's a game people play using hand held GPS devices. They bury a box, or a can, or something and post its location on the Internet so others can find it. The numbers Karen gave me are a GPS location. When I referenced it on the Internet I came across a password protected website. It took me a little bit to break in, but it was worth it. The site was basically a shout out to all the terrorists working on something called *The Divine Gift.* The GPS location is their Geo Cache. Based on what I read, there is a high likelihood it contains information as a back up plan. Like alternate sites for..."

"A hostage house?" Karen looked hopeful.

"Precisely."

"How far away is it?" Karen was on her feet.

"'Bout fifteen minutes."

"We have a GPS in the news car."

Jim studied her standing there with one arm in a sling. "Karen, what are you going to do if this thing does contain information about a hostage house? Storm the house yourself?"

"I don't know. I'll cross that bridge when I get to it."

She headed for the door.

"Look," said Jim, "If you do find something at the site, call me. I'll send our security team over. We have some ex-navy seals and a couple of Marines who work for us. Maybe we can make something happen."

She twisted around. "What about the FBI?"

"You're right, Karen. Brad is one of ours, and we can't let him down. No matter what the cost."

Her heart lifted. "Thank you, Jim. I won't forget this."

Karen compared the numbers on the GPS to the numbers on the picture in her cellphone. She was close. The location was just off the right side of the road, somewhere in the woods. The tires buzzed as the car passed over the rumble strip. Wherever it was, she was going to have to drive to it; she didn't have the luxury of a hand held device.

The car bounced over a root between two trees and Karen struggled to keep the wheel straight with her one good hand. It vibrated and threatened to pull itself out of her grasp. A large rock scraped along the bottom of the car and spit out the back. She twisted the wheel again and zeroed in on the number, it looked like a few more yards straight ahead-- but a stand of pines prevented her from going any further.

She pushed the door open and climbed out. The trip had taken fourteen minutes. That meant she had twenty-six more before time ran out. She ran straight ahead scanning the brush and rocks. Whatever it was, it was probably buried. Her heel caught a root and she stumbled and landed hard on her arm. Pain rippled through every nerve ending, her teeth ground together in response. With urgency, she dug her polished fingernails into the soil and scrambled to her knees. Pain stabbed up through her shoulder and into her neck-- but she would *not* give in to it. She wiped the tears from her eyes and scanned the brush in front of her. At the base of a stump, not six feet away, was a moss covered opening between the roots.

She clawed toward it, ripping big holes in her nylons and scraping her knees. But all that mattered was getting to that box. The branches scraped her face and dug into her sides, but she pressed forward. With a swipe, the moss clump dropped away. Wedged inside the opening was a metal box! She pulled it free and opened the lid. This was *it,* what Nerd said would be here! There were maps with alternate routes, material resource sites, bank numbers, alternate bomb sites-- and an alternate hostage house. She wiped tears of relief with her arm. She had the location, now she could have someone go to the site and mount a rescue, that is, if the terrorists were operating from the alternate site. She had to believe they were. She pulled her phone from her pocket, flipped it open, and called the station. The screen read, *"Call failed. No signal".*

You've GOT to be kidding me! She shoved the phone back into her pocket, slammed the box shut, picked it up with her good arm, and struggled to her feet. Awkwardly she hurried back to the car, stumbling over rocks and roots as she went. At the car she tossed the box onto the driver's seat, then dug her phone back out. Still no bars! Anywhere! A thousand cell towers in Boston and she couldn't get a signal! She held the phone out at arms length and walked toward the road. One bar appeared. Quickly she dialed the news director.

"Hello. Jim Coldfield." The signal was very weak.

"Can you hear me?"

"Barely."

"I found the box. It was just what Nerd said!"

"That's wonderful!"

She hurried back to the car and rifled through the papers in the box, fearing she would lose the connection any second. "Take this address down!"

"Okay!" His voice crackled

She read the address several times to make sure he got it. If there was anyone who could put together a team to get Brad out, Jim was the one.

Oh, God, please let there be enough time! She moved the box to the passenger seat, climbed into the car and punched the address in on her navigator. According to the readout, she was forty-five minutes from the location. There was no way she could get there in time. But a team from the television station could. It was less than fifteen minutes. If Jim hurried, they would make it, just in time.

She leaned back against the seat. It was in Jim's hands now; she had to trust that he would take care of it. She took in a deep breath, then started the car. If she hurried, maybe she could get there in time to see Brad being brought out.

40

The second hand made its way around with no regard for the violence it would bring. Steady, and with purpose, the hand rounded the three, then the six... Five more passes and Brad would be dead-- and the clock would continue on, oblivious to what it had done.

David had taken every opportunity to grope for words in the room and on the TV screen, but no message had come. Maybe Alex was right, maybe he shouldn't trust the messages. They had lured him into the worst possible horror, and now when he needed them the most, there was nothing but silence. *Why? Why did I trust you! You ALWAYS let me down! You say you want faith! But you make it impossible to trust you! Why have you left me? Didn't I do everything you asked?*

The anguish tasted bitter in his mouth. He'd always wanted to know God; it was the deepest longing of his heart. Yet here he was, being let down-- again! He *wanted* to have the unshakable faith of Frank Johnston, but even with God speaking directly to him, he felt more distant than ever. What was the *deal* with God? *Why* all the parables? *Why* all the mysteries? Why hide up in the clouds and leave humanity on this *miserable* rock to figure everything out for themselves? It was a cruel and terrible *joke!*

David stopped himself. Had he *lost his mind?* Again, he was assuming there *was* a God, when all the evidence pointed to the opposite conclusion. There was no *master* plan. There was no *perfect* will of God. It was just him,

David, following some weird extrasensory perception into a highly lethal and volatile situation. And now, because of his *stupid* wishful thinking, he was trapped in the worst of all possible nightmares.

Hamid entered with a roll of duct tape and crossed the room to Brad. The reporter offered no resistance as his arms were wrenched behind him and bound together. His eyes were empty, vacant and lifeless-- as though he were already dead.

David looked at Hamid's jet black hair. He was so close, even the pores in his skin were visible. This was it. This was David's only opportunity to save Brad, and possibly himself. His hands were still free. He had to do something before the Arab tied them. *The clock is ticking! I could grab him!* But what about the man with the gun?

His eyes fell on the fork sitting on the card table. *Can I use that?* His mind sped. What could he *possibly* do with a *fork* that would cause the other man to drop his gun? He began to tremble as he worked through the scenarios. Hamid was almost finished with Brad. *I need to act NOW, or the window will pass.* He brought a shaking hand up onto the table, and began inching it toward the fork.

"We interrupt this program to bring you a special report," said the television. The newsroom of Channel Seven appeared on the screen, then a close up of a nervous Cindy Coulter. "This morning a second tape from the terrorists arrived here at the offices of Channel Seven News. It contains a message the terrorists wish us to air, and if we do not, they say they will kill our field reporter, Brad Knight." Her voice cracked, she paused. "The general manager has asked me to make this appeal to the terrorists. Please know that we are battling with the authorities to air your tape, but we cannot do it by your deadline."

David's chest constricted. *What! Why* would the authorities do this?

Hamid began to pace, his dark features tight and fierce.

"We beg you, please wait while we plead our case to Homeland Security. It is our intention to air your tape. Please give us one more hour. And, Brad, if you're watching this, we are so sorry. We are doing everything..."

"Turn it off!" Hamid screamed. The man with the loafers reached up and pushed the button. "They play *games!* How *stupid* do they think we are? They are tracking our location! They think they can find us and stop us. *But they are WRONG!*" He slammed his fist down on the card table, the dishes bounced. *"Get the camera!"* The man with the loafers ran down the hall. *"They want a show of wills? We will give them a show of wills! Allah* is our strength. We will *not* be moved from our goals!" He grabbed a red and white speckled cowl and began wrapping it on his head.

David felt the barrel of a gun press against his neck. The man behind him spoke slow and clear. "Put- the fork-*down.*"

David's hand opened and the fork fell to the table. Hamid turned and looked at him. A cynical smirk formed on his face. "Were you going to take on all three of us with a *fork?*"

He had considered it. It wasn't a good plan, but it was all he had. He held his chin up in defiance as the Arab probed him slowly. What dark intentions lay behind those evil eyes, David could only imagine. The thought produced an uncontrollable rattling of fear in his chest.

"Set the camera here," said Hamid, his eyes still on David.

The man with the loafers, who was much younger than Hamid, could not hide his nervousness. With trembling hands he set up the tripod and plugged it in. He wiped the sweat from his brow.

"Bind him!" Hamid pointed at David. David's arms were gripped from behind, twisted around his back, and bound together. Immediately his shoulders began to ache. The man with the gun joined the man behind the camera. Hamid said something in Arabic and flicked his fingers at the younger man, who responded by hitting the record button.

"You consider us weak." Hamid looked deep into the eye of the camera. "You think we will not do what we say?" David fought back the emotion. Each horrible word from the terrorist sent waves of hopelessness rippling through his body. "For your *arrogance,* the reporter, *will die.* His blood is on *your* hands. *You* have brought this on yourselves. You will see, we do what we say." He walked to the camera and switched it off. "Put the camera in the room with the plastic."

The young Arab picked up the camera and tripod and carried it to a door off the living room. When he opened the door, David could see in. It was a dining room. Thick blankets were hung over the windows but yellow light from a chandelier lit up a large table. It was covered in heavy opaque plastic. Hamid ripped off a piece of tape and covered Brad's mouth, then David's. David's breath came fast through his nose. The man with the gun came around and grabbed the front legs of Brad's chair, Hamid grabbed the back. Together they hefted him up and carried him through the dining room door and out of sight.

Hamid spoke in Arabic again and the man returned to the living room. The young Arab stepped onto the threshold between the two rooms, his countenance revealed his uneasiness. "I- I thought, we weren't going to kill anyone," he said in a low voice.

Hamid came to the doorway, his lip curled as he spoke. David did not know the language, but he could guess what was going on. Hamid was *furious* that the young man had revealed that piece of information. That one sentence opened up volumes to David. Hamid put his finger in the other man's face and shouted one last rebuke before stepping back into the dining room and closing the door. The young man walked back toward the hallway, his face wracked with emotion.

David pleaded with his eyes, but the man looked away. *Come on! Look at me! You can stop this! It doesn't have to be this way!* David struggled against his restraints, his fury fanned by something primal. He wished desperately to save his friend, but now an overwhelming and uncontrollable urge to flee drove him to a state of savagery. He could not face what was coming, and his body reacted with anger. Anger at the terrorists, anger at God, anger at his own helplessness. It infused him entirely.

Through the door, through the shrieking in his head, through the tape on Brad's mouth, David heard a muffled scream of terror and the chopping of a dagger. The sound burrowed deep into David's mind like a worm, firmly planting itself. It was a sound that cannot be removed, the kind that returns in nightmares. And in waking waves of unrequited dread.

The young Arab was taking it even worse than David. Crouching in the corner with his hands pressed against his ears, he wept like a child as he rocked back and forth, with mumbled Arabic falling from his lips.

Gradually it became quiet, and the door to the dining room opened. *I won't look! I don't want to know!* But he had to know. He lifted his head and braced itself for the

239

possibility of the horror he would see. Hamid stood in the doorway, the bloody knife gripped in his hand. Behind the table, in the thick opaque plastic, lay the body of Brad Knight, neatly wrapped for disposal.

The man with the gun looked into the room and spoke in a low voice. What he said made Hamid reach out and grip the man's shoulder. From their body language, it was clear, neither one had wanted this to happen.

Hamid pointed at David. "Take him back to the room."

The man cut the tape from David's ankles. "Go," he said, waving the gun toward the hallway. David, trembling violently, stood mechanically and walked down the hall and into the room. The door slammed and locked, he pressed his ear against it. The men were talking in the living room, but the voices were muffled and they were speaking in Arabic. He pushed away from the door and began pacing. There was no escaping. The door was locked and there were no windows. And, like the living room, it had been stripped of all its furnishings. Footsteps approached. David considered hiding to the side of the door and leaping on the owner of the footsteps, but quickly assessed the idea as partially futile, and fully insane.

"Step away from the door, Mr. Chance." It was Hamid. The knob rotated, the door opened a slit, then further as Hamid saw that David was backed against the far wall. "Sit down."

David complied.

He shut the door and came over and crouched before him. It was not close enough for David to make any kind of usable attack, so he sat and waited.

Hamid's face became intense. "I must be brief," he whispered. "Listen closely. I am working undercover. Your friend is not dead. You are going to feel the urge to escape.

Do not. I could have drugged you, but I may need you as a distraction. Kalid, the man with the gun, has been sent on an errand. When he comes back, he may attempt to check the body. If you hear me raise my voice loud, cause as much commotion as you can. This is almost over. When my people find the bomb, they will storm the house. I need you to *stay calm.*"

David tried to wrap his mind around the words. An undercover agent? --*Is he just messing with me?* He stared at the man crouching before him. Was he really acting? Why would he *lie?* David was at his mercy. If it was an attempt to calm him down, drugs would have done a more effective job. Could it be true?

Hamid ripped the tape from David's mouth, David bore the pain silently.

"I am working closely with Agent Cooper. You met him did you not?"

David nodded slowly.

"I need you to cooperate. Are you with me?"

Again David nodded.

"Good. Stay calm, my friend. This is almost over." He turned and exited.

David leaned back against the wall in astonishment. Hamid, an undercover agent? He never would have guessed in a million years! But he was still in danger-- and according to Hamid, things were about to boil.

He wiggled and squirmed until his bound hands slid under him and out around his legs. Slowly he rose to his feet and looked around at the empty room.

--The words were never there when he needed them most.

41

The address from the papers in the terrorist's box led Karen to a secluded Westwood neighborhood, right up to a reinforced steel barricade on a dead end street. On the right, a dirt driveway trailed off through a thick grove of pines to a yellow townhouse with black shutters. An enormous oak tree, stately and proud, stood guard on the front lawn. From a massive branch, a heavy twisted rope dangled. At its end, a tire swing swayed slightly in the breeze.

According to the Navigator, she had arrived at her destination. She parked the car and looked around. There was no activity on the street, nothing going on around the house. Karen looked at her watch. *Why is everything so quiet?* They should have stormed the residence by now, it was past the deadline. *Maybe I missed it, maybe they've come and gone.* But still, wouldn't there be people around?

Karen grabbed her phone and put a call in to Jim Coldfield.

"Jim here."

"Jim this is Karen."

"I was just about to call you."

Sarcasm dripped off her lips. "Were you now..."

"Don't go near the house. The Feds heard us talking about sending a group of security, and Agent Cooper paid me a visit. "Karen, you *can't* go near that house."

"*Why?* What did they say?"

"I'm not at liberty to tell you."

She sat with her mouth hanging open. "--Then maybe

I'll just go in and get him my*self.*"

"Karen. No. Where are you now?"

She looked in her rear view mirror. "--Let's just say, I'm close."

"Well, turn around."

"Give me one good reason."

"Karen, *listen.* Agent Cooper told me in strictest confidence that they have a *mole* in the house. Forcing him to reveal himself will *jeopardize the recovery of the bomb.* He would have told us before, but they were trying to protect the undercover agent, *and Brad,* by keeping a tight lid on it. He just left my office. Calling you was my next priority."

"A mole? And you believe him?"

"Why wouldn't I?"

Her mind reeled. "Now that we know where the house *is,* we're just going to *sit* on it and *wait?* "

"Karen, Homeland Security is on top of things. Let them *handle it!* "

"I just think its..."

"Let them handle it, Karen!"

"Fine!" She pressed hard on the cancel button and threw the phone on the passenger's seat. She knew Jim had a keen sense about things like this. He had years of experience dealing with crises, and the nose of a seasoned reporter. In all her years working at the station, she had never seen him make a mistake. He was right. She knew it-- but that didn't mean she had to like it. *So now what?* She looked down at her torn nylons, then back out the window at the house. Her eyes narrowed. There was something eerily familiar about this place-- but she couldn't quite put her finger on it. The yellow house with its black shutters-- the tire swing in the yard-- the dirt driveway off a dead end street. She looked over at the mailbox with the number eighty-five marked in

rusted lettering. Her eyes opened wide.

The scene from the book? It can't be! Her mind leaped about in confusion. *How?* She remembered her conversation with David. He admitted to putting the note on her desk. He *must* have known the story was connected to the hostage house! But he acted like he didn't. Why would he put the book on her desk and *pretend* not to know what it was? *And the photo?* David was standing next to the man Ali claimed was the bomb maker. *But he's such a nice guy! This doesn't make ANY sense at all! David Chance-- a terrorist?* She gripped the steering wheel and pressed her head against it. None of this made *any* sense!

Suddenly she looked up, a strange sensation washed over her. --David said to do what the book said. He was very adamant about this. She tried to remember what she had read; it was-- something about childhood sweethearts who were grown up. Apparently she still loved him, but for some reason she wasn't allowed to see him. *So--* she would beep the horn to let him know she was there. She looked out at the house, and placed her hand firmly on the center of the steering wheel. Once. Twice. Three times she pressed firmly on the horn, then let her hand slide off and rest in her lap. She looked down at the horn symbol on the hard black plastic of the steering wheel, her heart skipped a beat. *WHAT did I just DO?!*

33421

Three short beeps. They were faint, but he was sure he had heard them. And the message from the study flashed in his mind. *Fear not, the distant horn sounds.* It wasn't *fear not the distant horn,* but *fear not,* and, *the distant horn sounds.* The horn wasn't some scary sound in the distance. It was a *signal!* David got to his feet. What next? He brought his bound wrists to his face and pulled his sleeve back with his teeth. *RUN!*

He tried the door; it was unlocked! Did Hamid leave it unlocked on purpose? It didn't matter. He opened the door-- and froze. But Hamid said stay! *Should I trust him? What if Brad really isn't dead? What if I need to be here to distract the gunman?* His heart raced. *God help me!* As quickly as he thought the words, he *knew.* The message *was* TRUE; he *knew* it in the very depths of his being. Even if Hamid was for real, David needed to obey the messages *first.* He burst out the door and ran down the hallway. *Left!* He took a left at the empty living room and ran through a door to a large open hallway with a set of stairs running down. *Stairs! No wait!* He looked at his arm. *Bullet!* There, at the top of the stairs, was an open duffle bag. Lying on top of a pile of gear was a box of bullets. He reached his taped hands in, fumbled out one of the bullets, and shoved it in his pocket.

Where were the terrorists? He looked back and saw shadows moving in the kitchen. There was no way he could check on Brad without getting caught. It didn't matter; the messages were leading him out. He took the stairs three at a time and came to a door at the bottom. He opened it, ran across the porch, and leaped over the railing. His feet dug into a flower bed, his hands touched down in the soft dirt. In the distance a Channel Seven News car was turning around on the street. *Are they leaving?* He broke into a sprint, keeping his eyes on the car as he dodged back and forth through a grove of pine trees. Was it the news car that sounded the horn?

He sprinted harder toward the road. Thoughts of what the terrorists might do if they caught him flooded his mind. His feet pounded the grass, his upper body struggled against the wobble caused by his bound wrists. He wanted to call out, but he knew better. The car began to roll away, David waved his bound arms frantically. *I'm HERE! LOOK!*

The brake lights flashed and the vehicle slowed. David skidded to a stop at the driver's side door, Karen's face came into view. She looked as startled to see him as he was to see her. He bolted around to the passenger side and fumbled with the handle. The window slid down a crack. "Are you one of them?"

"Am I-- What! Open the door!"

"Are you working with the terrorists?

"No! Do I look like I'm working with the terrorists?" He held up his bound hands. "Open the door!"

She probed him with her eyes.

"Karen, *please!"*

She unlocked the door and pushed the dirty box onto the floor. He jumped in, and the door slammed by itself as the car accelerated.

"What is going *on!* Why are you bound?"

"They grabbed me when I went to stop the bomb." He breathed heavily.

"Stop the...? What are you...?" She snapped him a look.

"You *are* connected to the terrorists!"

"Connec...? No! I was following a lead and they grabbed me!"

"But you tried to stop the bomb? You know where it is?"

"Well. Y- yes, but, no. Not exactly."

"Then why..." She shot him a glare, then squinted. "Was Brad in there?"

"Uh, yeah."

"Is he okay?"

"Ye-- um, I don't know. Yes, I think so."

"You *think* so?"

"I *thought* he was dead." The words poured out. "It was done behind closed doors. I could only *hear* what was going on but then the man who I *thought* killed him came and told me he was an undercover agent, and that Brad wasn't really dead!"

Karen's mouth hung open.

"Supposedly it was all an act, but I don't know *what* to believe."

Karen thought for a moment. "Wh-- why would he *pretend* to kill Brad?"

"To buy time so they could find the bomb. That's what he said."

She squinted at him. "Wouldn't he *know* where the bomb is?"

"Apparently not."

"You said *you* know where it is, why didn't *you* tell him?"

"I *just* found out he's an undercover agent! And, *HELLO!* I was in shock!"

She gripped the steering wheel harder. "I'm sorry. I'm just trying to piece this thing together." She looked at him again. "It's been a *LONG* coupla days."

As she spoke, he noticed for the first time what a wreck she was. Her hair was tangled, her suit coat and skirt were smeared with dirt, her nylons torn to shreds. "What happened to *you?"*

"It's a long story."

He looked at the dirty box next to his feet. "Does this have anything to do with it?" He reached his bound hands down and picked it up.

"Yes. It has everything to do with it. That box is how I found you. It has information about alternate hostage sites."

David fumbled through the contents. "Why is it covered with dirt"

"It was buried."

"Buried?"

"Yeah, we ah, found some information about the terrorists and Nerd figured out how to find this box. It's some kind of GPS cache."

He looked at her. "And *you* found it?"

"Yeah! *I* found it! I wasn't going to wait around for the *Feds,* who were doing *nothing* to find Brad!"

David continued to paw through the contents.

"Basically it's all Plan B stuff," Karen offered. "Alternate locations, targets, routes. That sort of thing."

"And alternate bomb sites?" David stared at one of the pages. "This stuff is creepy."

"I figured since Homeland Security had raided Ace Wrecking and the farmhouse, that the terrorists would have Brad at an alternate site. And I was right, but now Jim says..."

"Wait a minute." David looked closely at the sheet. "There's nothing in here about Quincy Market."

Karen looked at him. *"What?"*

"That's where the bomb..."

The car slowed. "Where the bomb is? Are you sure?"

"Ah-- no?" He really didn't know. "--Maybe they moved it by now."

She put her blinker on and shifted to the right lane. "Maybe they didn't."

"What are you doing?"

"According to the Feds, Brad is safe because they have a mole in the house. You confirmed that. So we should go to the bomb sight."

"I don't *want* to go to the bomb site."

"Why not? You were just there."

"Well maybe it's not *there* anymore. Listen. Let the Bomb Squad deal with it! I've had all I can handle of bombs and terrorists." *And messages from God.*

She gave him an examining stare.

He scowled back at her. *"What?"*

"I'm trying to figure out what your role is in all of this. Clearly you have inside knowledge, you're connected somehow, yet they *kidnapped* you. --Did you have a falling out?"

"What? No! I told you I'm *not* connected to them!"

"How do you know so much about the bomb and the location of the hostage house?"

"I never said I knew where the hostage house was."

"But the book you left on my desk. Page forty-nine? It *exactly* described the hostage house. Did *you* write that book?"

"No." He looked away and stared out the window.

"Do you *know* the person who wrote it?"

"No. --I, ah, don't even know what the book is."

She looked at him in astonishment. "Then *how* on *earth* did you know I was supposed to go to the house on page forty-nine?!"

He continued to stare out the window. *Oh, man. Here it comes.* "You wouldn't believe me if I told you."

"*Try* me!"

He sat silent.

"How do you know the bomb maker?"

He looked at her. *"--What?"*

"*How* do you *know* the bomb maker?"

"I- *don't!"*

David, I *saw* a picture of you next to the bomb maker."

David's mouth hung open. *"What? What picture?"*

"Just answer the question, David."

David's mind raced. Was it true? *Did* he know the bomb maker? That would explain how his family had been tracked so easily, and why there was a bomb in Claire's backyard.

"Why is there a picture of you standing next to the bomb maker?"

"I don't *know.* I have no idea what you're talking about."

"Don't play dumb, David. How did you *know* where the bomb was if you didn't find out from the one who made it?"

"I can't tell you."

"David. It's going to come out. Last time I checked, the FBI doesn't take *I can't tell you* as an answer."

"They won't know I'm involved if you don't tell them."

"They have the picture!"

David gripped his head in his hands. "Listen, Karen. You have to believe me. I am *not* a part of this terrorist thing. I'm *trying* to *stop* it. That's why they keep targeting me."

She examined him again.

"Please, Karen. Ask Nerd. He'll tell you. I'm going through some really strange stuff. And because of it, I'm stumbling onto things. I have no idea who the bomb maker is. I *just* wanted to *stop this bomb* and end this *nightmare!"*

She pursed her lips. "--Okay. I'll except that, *for now,* but I'm not done questioning you."

"Thank you."

"All I care about is getting the FBI to this *bomb,* so they'll release Brad. Hand me my phone, it's under your butt."

"What are you going to tell them?"

"That I have a credible source who claims the bomb is in Quincy Market."

"But I don't know *where* in Quincy Market, and if Homeland Security swarms the place, they're likely to set it off early."

"Then we need to find out *exactly* where it is."

David didn't bother to argue. He'd seen that look before, there was no reasoning with Karen Watson once she made up her mind. He was going to have to follow the messages further. But he was *not* happy about it.

Not happy at all.

A comedy troupe interacted with a small crowd in front of a white pillared building. Above them the golden letters of "Quincy Market" gleamed in the afternoon sun. David, still trying to rub the stickiness from the duct tape off his wrists, passed through and down the colonnade with Karen in tow. She had removed her torn nylons and tried to clean up a bit, but was still a mess. She called out to him over the noise of the crowd. "What are you looking for?"

"I'll know when I see it." He felt bad for being short with her, but whatever had fueled his faith in the messages was now fully depleted, and he felt utterly vulnerable. Sure they had rescued him from the hostage house, but they had allowed him to be *captured* in the first place! What else would they allow to happen to him? Was a little protection too much to ask for, while he ran his butt off trying to save innocent people from being blown to bits? David bounced his eyes back and forth, from signs to banners to clothing, and a message formed. *Moved to second site. Go alone.* --What? *WHY! Why me? Aren't there more qualified people, or more FAITHFUL people to lay this burden on?* David crouched down and put his head in his hands.

"David?"

He shook with desperation. "This is *never* going to end."

She put a hand on his shoulder. "I know you've been through a lot, but we have to keep going. Look around. These people need you."

"I didn't *ask* to be anyone's savior. I'm just an *intern.*"

"Listen, I don't know what you're going through, but you need to pull it together. If you can stop this thing, David, stop it!"

He smeared the wetness across his cheeks with his palms and looked up at her. "The bomb's not here."

"What? H- How do you know?" The phone chimed in her jacket pocket. "You've got to be kidding me!" She pulled it out. "It's Jim. I have to take this. Maybe he can help us." She flipped the phone open and turned her back to him.

David remained crouched. Her voice was distant in the swirling fog the drugs had left in his head. --The message said go alone. If he was going to go at all (which was unlikely) *this* was the time to get away from Karen. He studied her, waiting for the right moment. She twisted further away and began speaking in a low voice.

He stood silently and slipped into the crowd.

By the time Karen noticed he was gone, David had already melted into the sea of moving bodies. In the distance, he heard her shout his name above the noise of the crowd, but he didn't look back. He left the colonnade out through South Market to the parking garage, where he had left his car earlier. It was still there, in the same shadowy corner, untouched. David pulled his keys out of his pocket.

He got in and put the key in the ignition, but he couldn't bring himself to start the car. He was free to pursue the messages to the second bomb site, but doubts ate at him like a cancer. Doubts about himself, doubts about the messages. He felt like a rat in a maze. *WHY is God putting me through this? --Was* it God? Would a loving God do such a thing? *I'm going to live the rest of my life permanently scarred from this whole stupid mess! Is that your so-called perfect plan?* David saw his phone sitting in the passenger seat. He took in a deep breath and exhaled. There was only one person he knew who might be able to give him some peace of mind. He snatched the phone and dialed.

The gurgling ring on the other end seemed to go on forever.

"Hello?"

"Frank?"

"David! I didn't expect to hear from you again."

"I didn't expect to call again. Hey look. I have another God question. You in the mood to field it?"

"I'll do my best."

"Why does God let bad stuff happen to good people, even people who are *trying* to do what he wants them to do?"

"You're assuming there are good people."

David thought about that for a second. "Why do I even call you?" he stated flatly.

"Do you want my answer?"

David held his tongue.

"You're caught up in relativism. You think because you're not as *bad* as the next guy, that makes you *good*. If a thief stood before a judge and said, I know I took all that money from the bank, but I'm not as *bad* as that other guy who kills people and likes it, do you think the judge is going to say, 'You know, you're right. You're a pretty good guy. I'll let you go.'? Of course not!"

"Frank. You're comparing thieves and murderers. I'm talking about *regular* people who try to do what's right."

"That's right, we *try* to do what's right. Most people in the world *try* to do what's right, but no one can measure up to the perfect law of God. No one is *perfectly* good. When we compare ourselves to God, we are nothing more than varying degrees of bad."

"Varying degrees of bad--"

"Right. Because we're born that way. God gives us free will to choose to obey or disobey him, and from the very first people he created, we've *all* chosen to disobey in one way or another. We're *all* sinners."

"What about Mother Theresa?"

"Sinner."

"Oh, come *on!* No one's good?"

"Nope. Not one. As soon as the first people sinned in the Garden of Eden, sin entered the world and was passed from generation to generation. But it's not *God's* fault. He created a perfect paradise. But like I said, he gave people free will, and every one of us is messed up."

"Why not just make it impossible for us to sin? Then the world would be perfect."

Frank paused.

"Ah! I got ya on that one. You don't know do you."

"No. No. I'm just thinking of the best way to explain it. --You see, David, I believe God created us because he wanted fellowship with us. He loves us and he wants us to love him too. If he didn't give us the free will to *choose* to love him or not love him, then it wouldn't be *real* love. It would be forced, like a programmed doll that says, 'I- love- you,- Mama.' It wouldn't *mean* anything."

David took a moment to digest this new information. "--Okay. That makes sense."

"So yes, bad things *do* happen to people in this world, but it's not *God's* fault. Bad things happen because of our own bad choices, *or* as the result of someone else's."

"So even if *I'm* doing everything right, or at least *trying* to, bad things can still happen to me as the result of *other* people's bad choices?"

"Exactly. But also, sometimes God allows bad things to

happen to people who are following him because it's *good* for us, because we need to be purified."

"Huh?"

"Like smelting gold. The goldsmith brings the heat up, and the impurities rise to the surface. When he skims the junk off the top, he looks into the vat. The clearer he sees his own reflection, the purer the gold. That's what God does with us. He turns up the heat, allowing us to go through bad things, so we can be purified, so we can *grow.*"

An image formed in David's mind. "--Like the flower in the rain." His voice trailed off.

"What?"

"--Nothing, just something my daughter drew." He took a deep breath. "I just wish he'd choose someone *else* to *purify*. I'm going to be messed up for *life* when I'm done with this stupid mission!"

"How? Physically?"

"No. Trauma!"

Frank laughed.

"It's not funny, Frank!"

"I'm sorry. I have no idea what you're facing. All I know is, I'd take mental trauma over losing a limb or something."

"I don't want *either.*"

"David. You have no idea how special you are. Out of all the people in the world, God chose *you.*"

"Let him choose someone else."

"When God is done with you, you'll be a better man. He won't leave you with trauma, he's turning you into something new."

"What*ever!*" Even as the word left his mouth, something deep inside David was stirred. How had he been so blind? It was the one burning desire of his heart. He had tearfully prayed on bended knee for years, asking for God to make himself *real* and *tangible*. David knew his own cynicism would never allow him to believe in God, no matter what the evidence. He needed *more* in order to believe-- and God was giving it to him. God was speaking in a powerful and miraculous way, yet he was *still* resisting.

God was giving him more of an opportunity than he deserved, yet he was *complaining* about it! No matter how many times David had messed up, God *hadn't* given up on him. He was boiling out the bad, changing him into something new. Something better. Tears trickled down his cheeks. The weight of the stress, and the revelation of God's patience with his doubt and rebellion caused something deep inside him to break. The frustration melted away and was replaced with gratefulness and humility. "I'm *such* a *fool.*" David's voice shook. "God's been changing me-- and I've been *fighting* him the whole way!" David smeared the tears on his eyelids. "Thank you, Frank. I needed to hear that."

Frank sniffed. "Glad to help."

"Are you crying?"

"Nah. It's just allergies."

"Hey..."

Frank sniffed again, then chuckled. "Are you going to be okay?"

David thought a moment. "--Yes. Amazingly enough, I think I got what I was looking for." He wiped his eyes. "I'm *going* to finish this thing."

"Good. And maybe sometime you can actually tell me what's been going on."

"Yeah. I need to. When all this is over, I promise to tell you everything."

"I bet it'll be one heck of a story."

"It already is, Frank. --It *already* is."

44

Karen pushed through the crowd, but the top of David's bouncing head had disappeared. She cursed under her breath and brought the phone back up to her ear. "He took off!"

"Did he hear you talking about his brother-in-law?"

"I don't think so, I was speaking pretty low. He was probably just spooked by the phone call in general. You should have seen him earlier in the news car. He's a *mess.* Somehow he's wound up in this thing, *clearly* in over his head."

"Maybe his brother-in-law had second thoughts and gave him information to stop the bomb."

"There's more to it than that. He saw something that caused him to break down into tears. He said they moved the bomb."

"The bomb could be in something large and movable, maybe he was expecting to see it but it wasn't there."

"So the question is, where did they move it *to?* Somewhere else in Quincy Market, or to one of the alternate sites?"

"You need to get that box into the station so the Feds can go over it."

"Not till I've located this bomb."

"Karen. Leave that to the authorities."

"David doesn't think the FBI can get close to the bomb without the terrorists setting it off. They need to know *exactly* where it is so the terrorists don't have time to react."

"So you're going to hunt the bomb down, and call it in *yourself?*"

"That's the plan at the moment."

"Karen, come back to the station. You're talking crazy."

"Sorry, Jim. I have to at least try."

"Do you have any idea what you're doing?" Jim did *not* sound happy.

"Of course not, but that's never stopped me before."

There was a long pause. "Just be careful."

"I will. I'll call you in a bit."

She hung up and gave David's cellphone a try. It rang five times then dumped her to his voicemail. "David, this is Karen. Your brother-in-law has been linked to the making of the bomb. We need to talk. Call me when you get this."

Soft light filtered through the arched glass ceiling and reflected in the turquoise water of Alex's indoor pool. Sharon dipped her feet in the warm water and fixed her gaze on the waves playing around her ankles. Terrorist plots, the safety of her family, her husband, the death of her brother. It all swirled inside her like a tangle of cords. She'd hoped a little seclusion would bring relief from her worries and grief, but the solitude of the pool room was only making it worse. She pulled her feet from the water and stood. *I need something to occupy my mind.*

She found her children right where she had left them, in the living room, watching cartoons on the high definition screen. Their somber faces and slouched postures betrayed the fact that they were not finding any enjoyment.

"Would you like a cup of coffee, Sharon?" Alex stood in the archway to the kitchen.

She looked at him as through a fog. "That would be nice, thank you."

"How are you holding up?"

"I do better when I don't think about it."

"Gotcha." He turned. "One coffee coming right up." He disappeared behind the mahogany shelving that separated the living room from the kitchen.

Sharon walked over and sat next to her daughter on the couch. The girl's eyes looked sallow as she sat mindlessly absorbed in the activity of the characters on the screen. Sharon envied her. If only she could so easily block out all the horrible questions and dark feelings waiting just on the edge of her perception. From somewhere a muffled tune began to play. Sharon went to her purse and pulled out her phone. Maybe it was David. *"Hello?"*

"Sharon, it's Jerry. I'm at Claire's. They told me what happened. Are you guys okay?"

"Yes. We're with Alex."

"I'm sorry I left, but I was called over to the University..."

"I know. Claire told me you had some kind of breakthrough."

"Yes. But it was more than that. We needed to move the whole project out of Boston, just in case. I came over to pick you and the kids up to bring you with us."

"David figured we would be safe with Alex. We're going to head out of state soon."

"Well, I'm heading to a facility about fifty miles outside of Boston. It's a high security installation, they said I could bring you and the kids. If you come with me, you'll be safe for sure."

"What about Alex?"

"He could go help David. It wouldn't hurt to have a little muscle with him."

"You're sure this place will take us in?"

"They've already okayed it."

"Alright. I'll get the kids ready. We're at Alex's house."

"Tell him I'm on my way. I'll be there in about thirty minutes."

"Who's that?" Alex stood in the doorway with two cups of coffee.

"I'll tell him right now. Thanks, Jerry. See you soon." She closed the phone.

78946

The sign said, "Right *Turn* Only." David's eyes bounced to the Comfort *Inn* sign beyond it, and then to a billboard with the words, "They're *here.*"

Turn inn here.

It was the parking lot of a strip-mall. David drove through the rows of cars and parked next to a truck with a vanity plate reading VDOGUY. Directly in front of him were the large glass windows of a video store. He heaved a sigh and started staring at the movie posters. He felt like an idiot savant. Well-- like an idiot anyway. This was the place. He was sure of it. But there didn't appear to be any messages outside. *I guess I have to go in.*

An electronic ding sounded as he passed through the doors. An attractive young woman behind the counter said, "Welcome to *Jack's Video Barn.*"

David gave her a nod of acknowledgment.

The store was *huge,* with rows upon rows of movies. *Which row?* The choices were endless-- and they all looked the same. He stood for a moment, staring at the aisles. Nothing spoke to him. *Apparently I have to guess.* He picked a row and started walking. His eyes bounced from title to title until he reached the end. Nothing. He moved to the back and worked his way around the outer wall. Title after title crawled by as he scanned one after the next, slowly moving from the top to the bottom of every rack. Not *one word* spoke to him.

David gritted his teeth. *This is ridiculous! Am I not*

*standing in the EXACT spot I need to be in? Am I not
looking in the PRECISE direction I'm supposed to look? I
followed the messages. What more do you WANT from me?
Is this the right place or not?*

His eyes fell on a movie titled, *Trust Me.*

He stared at it. *--I'm trying to trust you, but you lead
me on these crazy word hunts and all I can think about is
that there's a BOMB about to explode and I'm running
around a movie store like a moron!*

His eyes grabbed another word from a movie.
Patience.

Okay. Maybe he *was* trying too hard. But was it his
fault? There was a *lot* at stake. *Relax, David. Be patient.
The message will come.* He looked out across the aisles of
the enormous room, and stood still. Watching. The message
was here, he just needed to let it come to him. His eyes
scanned the posters on the walls above the movie racks, one
by one, until two words stood out. *Pretty Woman.* Finally!
But what was that supposed to mean? He looked around.
Maybe I'm supposed to talk to the woman at the counter. He
went back up front.

"Hey, there," he said to the pretty woman.

Her demeanor was relaxed and friendly. "Hi."

He pursed his lips and stood expectantly.

"Can I help you?"

What was he supposed to say? All he knew was that he
was supposed to talk to her-- and he wasn't even sure about
that. "Well... I..."

"Are you having trouble finding something?"

"Yes," he blurted. "I am. Yes. That's what I'm doing.
Having trouble."

She smiled at his odd behavior. "What kind of movies
do you like?"

263

He thought about it. "Um. Action?"

She came around the counter and started walking down an aisle. "Action's in the back. Here, I'll show you."

He followed her down to the end until she stopped and pointed at a little yellow sign that said, "ACTION."

He shrugged sheepishly and grinned. "Yup. Says it right there. Ac-tion." He enunciated the word.

Her eyebrows rose and she returned his grin. "So-- You're all set?"

"All set." He parroted.

She walked away shaking her head.

Well, that went well. He tried to shake off how ridiculous he felt and looked down at the rack in front of him. The movies, *Remember* the Alamo, and *North* Dallas Forty, sat on the second shelf. Immediately the message jumped out at him.

Remember North.

What else? There had to be more. He scanned the rest of the movies on the shelf, another string of words came together. *Follow Security 6622 meters 0 out red yellow blue.*

Another series of instructions? Like the ones he used to get out of the hostage house? He repeated the words several times until he had them memorized. Follow a security guard maybe? Did he have to follow a security guard six hundred and twenty two meters? That was around four miles, maybe more. No, it was probably something else. Perhaps a security vehicle of some kind? Maybe he was going to follow a security guard somewhere on the road? The rest of the message was gibberish. Could mean anything. He scanned the rack behind him and came up empty. That was it. He had his marching orders. Now the hard part; following them.

He walked to the front of the store. The pretty cashier smiled at him. "Didn't find anything?"

"Nope. Nothing." He smiled. "Guess it's just not a movie kind of day." The door dinged as he walked out. *Could I possibly look ANY stupider?*

He continued scanning for words as he walked back to his car. Nothing more jumped out at him. Well, he had his two cryptic lines. Apparently that was all he needed. He opened his car door, plopped down in the seat, and leaned his forehead on the steering wheel.

Why do I continue to doubt? I've seen over and over how the messages come when I need them. They knew Karen would see the note and follow up. They knew when the terrorists would be in the kitchen so I could escape. They even knew where the winning lottery ticket was. So why do I continue to doubt? If two cryptic messages were all God felt he needed, then they were all he needed. Plain and simple.

Bleep.

David lifted his head. Was that his phone? He reached over and picked it up. There was a new voicemail message. He brought it up.

"David, this is Karen. Your brother-in-law has been linked to the making of the bomb. We need to talk. Call me when you get this." His arm went slack, his hand landed in his lap. *Jerry*, involved with the bomb? *Why...* Before the question could fully form, he knew the answer. Jerry *hated* the government. He *hated* the war. --But *still*. A *bomb?* Was it possible?

Jerry?

David thought about everything that had happened. The cat and mouse game with his family, what the young terrorist had revealed at the hostage house-- that no one was supposed to get hurt. Was it all a harmless scare tactic? They shot John in cold blood and wounded Karen. Maybe Jerry didn't realize how dangerous these men were. Maybe he went into it thinking it was only going to be a bomb scare but ended up in the middle of something far worse. Maybe he was purposely kept in the dark, like the young terrorist at the hostage house. Maybe... *I left my family with him!* Thank *God* they were with Alex now. He shuddered. The whole thing made his mind twist.

He went back over every detail, every event, every message. It all made sense now in light of Jerry's involvement, everything that is, except for one point: How did the *President* fit into it? The assassination was only mentioned once. All of the other messages pertained to the terrorist plot. There had to be a connection. But what? The hostage play made sense. It was clearly the leverage the terrorists needed to make the television station air the story that would have caused the city of Boston to evacuate. And with stolen nuclear material, the authorities would have bought into it, if it hadn't been for the mole. He kept feeding the Feds the leads, and they kept making the busts, and when it came time to have the television station air the message, Homeland Security didn't comply.

Were they backed into a corner now? Would they set the bomb off as a last resort? Maybe, but that still wouldn't bring the President anywhere near this place. When the terrorists attacked the trade center towers in New York, it was with non-nuclear material, and the President didn't go to *that* site until many days later. There was no way a dirty bomb threat, real or otherwise, would lure the President here. So how did this have *anything* to do with him?

Maybe it didn't.

Maybe the two events were unrelated.

When he asked about the assassin, the message said he was near, and the other message said, *two days.* That's all he knew. It didn't matter. Whatever reason the terrorists had for creating the bomb threat was irrelevant. The bomb was sitting, ready to go off. And David was supposed to stop it.

85471

Sharon watched Alex prepare sandwiches for the kids on the hardwood cutting table, next to his chrome plated oven, in the ambience of inset cabinet lighting. He had done well for himself over the years and had acquired many luxuries. But at what cost? Would he ever settle down, as he had been claiming for the past fifteen years, or would he miss having a family altogether, choosing instead to keep chasing the ever elusive carrot?

Alex wiped his hands on his apron and pulled two plastic cups from the cabinet. One was Barbie, the other, Transformers. He was always getting things for Emily and Ben. The Teletubbies sippy cup he'd bought for Emily when she was two was still sitting in the cabinet. Sharon's heart warmed. *He would make a great father.* "Are you going to let me give them soda?" he said over his shoulder as he opened the brushed metal refrigerator.

"After the day they've had, let 'em have anything they want."

"And you're sure you don't want anything?"

"I'm sure."

He put the lunches on a tray and picked it up. A yellow light began flashing on the security panel by the door.

"Wow. Is that Jerry already? That was fast." He looked down at the tray. "You want me to pack these up instead?"

She sighed. "Could you? Would that be a lot of trouble?"

"No trouble at all. I'll pack. You get the intercom."

268

"Okay." She went over and pressed the button on the glass panel. "Who is it?"

"It's me."

"Hi, Jer." She pushed the lock button. "Here you go." The buzz from the gate filtered in through the intercom. She let her hand drop and placed her weary head gently against the wall. *Please let this be the last move.* She straightened and took a deep breath. *The kids.* She dreaded the thought of pulling them from their source of artificial comfort. But, it had to be done. They would all be safer at the high security installation. And David would be safer with Alex at his side.

She walked into the living room and sat next to her daughter. "Em, we're leaving in a few minutes. The TV will have to go off." Emily needed a little warning time to help her shift gears. Ben, on the other hand, was much more resilient. He didn't need warning for anything.

Emily turned her pretty blue eyes toward her mother. "Do we have to?"

Sharon rubbed her back gently. "Yes. I'm afraid so."

Emily frowned.

Alex came and stood in the doorway. "Hey. I have an idea. You want to take my portable DVD player?"

Both kids looked up and nodded stoically, then returned their somber attention to the television.

He looked at Sharon and shrugged.

"Thanks, Alex. That will help."

Sharon stared blankly at the TV until a knock sounded on the door. "Alex, can you get the security alarm?"

"Sure thing," Alex called from the kitchen.

She walked to the front door and put her hand on the knob. "Kids, Uncle Jerry is..." The door smashed her in the face and she was on the floor. A black shrouded figure loomed over her with a pistol.

269

"Don't forget the..." Alex came to an abrupt stop in the doorway. Two lunch bags dangled from his grip.

"Stop!" The man pointed the gun at Alex. His accent was unmistakably Middle Eastern, his dark eyes pierced like daggers. "Do not move or you will *die!"*

Emily screeched and Sharon started to scoot toward the living room.

The man spun around. *"Stop!"*

Desperate hands shot up in front of her face. "I'm sorry! Please! We're not a threat..."

He pushed the gun at her. *"Shut up!"*

Alex shifted his weight

"What are you doing!" the man screamed.

"Just stay calm." Alex's voice was cool and level.

"You think I'm *stupid?"*

Alex dropped the lunch bags on a nearby shelf and raised his hands. "No one needs to get..."

Two shots exploded and Alex collapsed into the kitchen.

Sharon screamed. Where was Jerry?! She tried to see out the doorway. *Did they kill him too?!* She scooted backwards into the living room and crawled to the kids.

The smoking pistol swung toward the three cowering on the couch. The kids' faces were streaming with tears. He walked slowly towards them. "Your *life,* is in the *hands* of your *husband.* If he is *wise,"* he enunciated the words, "you will live. If he is *not,* you will die."

Sharon's body quaked.

The man crouched before her, so close she could smell the burning powder from the gun barrel. Above the shroud, his piercing stare forced her back against the children. "Your husband has been *most* difficult. He *thinks* he is saving the city from a bomb, but he only puts the city in *danger. You* must explain this to him. Tell him we do not wish to detonate the bomb, we want the city *evacuated.* If he will simply *walk away,* his family, and *he*, will be safe."

Sharon stared wide eyed, unable to move.

"I assure you, I am more than capable of releasing the full power of that bomb. Do you understand?"

She could barely breathe, but managed a small nod.

"Good." His eyes became narrow. "Call him." He gestured to the wireless phone on the end table.

The keypad was unreadable through her tears. She dug the back of her hand into the sockets to clear her vision and began typing in David's number.

"Put it on speaker," he said evenly.

She lifted a shaking finger and pressed the button. Ringing filled the room, steady and even. Behind her, the children cried quietly. With each ring her dread increased. *Why doesn't he answer!* A recorded voice came on. She looked at the shrouded man with wide tear soaked eyes. "Do you, w- want me to leave a message?" Her voice wavered.

"NO! I want you to speak with your husband!"

She recoiled with a shudder, her eyes knitted shut in anticipation of violence.

"Call him AGAIN!" he shouted over the sound of David's voicemail greeting.

She stabbed the phone button, and hit redial.

The terrorist stood and paced.

Again David's voicemail picked up. Sharon looked at the shrouded figure, her shoulders hunched and cowering. He stopped pacing and slowly turned towards David's recorded voice. A raging scream exploded from behind his veil.

The children echoed his scream.

"WHAT NOW?" He began looking around wildly, he

suddenly stopped and brought his hand to his mouth. The pistol dangled in his grasp, his eyes were locked onto the floor. His breath came hard and fast through his nose.

Fear gripped Sharon's belly as a haunting thought entered her mind. He was going to kill them; there was desperation in his eyes. She was supposed to convince David to stop-- but she couldn't reach him. She dropped the phone and wrapped desperate arms around her children. She squeezed her eyes shut. *Oh, God, no. Please, God. Please don't let this happen.*

Not now, God.

Not now.

Not ever.

PLEASE!...

Silence.

Slowly Sharon opened her eyes-- to a gun pointing in her face.

"Call *again.*"

The phone went off in the passenger seat of David's Plymouth Neon-- but he didn't hear it. He was standing on the moist brown mulch of the parking lot island in front of his car, staring at the distant sign for JC Penny. The parking lot of the double decker mall was full to the brim with holiday shoppers taking advantage of pre-Christmas sales.

The newest message had said *double mall.* So here he was.

The smell of damp tar filled David's nostrils. He closed his eyes and tilted his head back. A light drizzle speckled his face, he drew in a deep breath and let the cold gentle taps absorb into his skin. For a brief moment a sense of peace washed over him, but it retreated as quickly as it had come. His eyes snapped open, he looked around. People were *everywhere.* On the sidewalks, in the parking lot, passing in and out of the mall's entrance, blissfully unaware that this could be their last shopping trip-- their last *anything.* A massive explosion flashed violently in David's mind, so vivid it made him flinch. He stepped off the island and headed toward JC Penny with a new resolution forming in his chest.

Through the vestibule, down the sand colored walkway, and into the men's section he strode. Around holiday shoppers, between the clothes racks, then back out onto the tiled walkway. The people crawled along with their swinging bags and wide searching eyes. *Tis the season for guilt driven sensory overload,* David thought. The bargain shoppers were out in force.

He emerged from JC Penny into the long center corridor of the mall and moved briskly to the railing overlooking the floor below. *What next?* Was there another message? He surveyed the words around him with familiar automation. A sign in the window of an empty glass case read, "Advertise *Here Now.*" A credit card ad read, "*Gotta* have it." A poster for running shoes said, "*Run hard,* Soft ride." And finally, in large golden letters, part of the word, *Dire*ctory added itself to the message in his mind. *Here now. Gotta run hard. Dire!* His head snapped left and right. *Run WHERE?* There were no more words. He looked at the escalators to either side of him and picked one.

Three steps at a time he squeezed past startled and angry people-- in that order. He jumped off at the bottom. He was at the far end of the mall, so logically there was only one way *to* run. *To the other end!* He took off in a sprint and ran as hard as he could. *Run hard! Dire!* He paid no attention to the man who cursed at him, he didn't stop to help the lady whose bag went sliding across the floor. He cut and weaved in desperation, working his way into the heart of the mall. In the center court, another corridor crossed over the main one. David stayed on the main. His lungs and legs began to burn, but he pushed on, dodging and cutting, accelerating and decelerating, pushing himself beyond his endurance.

Eyes scanning. Words in a blur. To see them he'd have to slow down, but he wasn't going to second guess. The message said *run!* When he needed another message, it would come. He was sure of it. Out of the corner of his eye he saw the uniform and came to a stop. The letters across the man's back spoke loud and clear. *SECURITY.*

Am I supposed to follow him? He panted over and

peered down the hall where the man had just entered. The man strolled to the end, David stayed at the corner, bathed in sweat, lungs on the verge of bursting. The guard stopped and shuffled his keys, slid a key in the lock, turned the knob, and entered. David smeared the sweat around on his face and headed down the hallway. As he approached the door, he heard a click. Had it taken that long to close? On the heavily rippled glass window was the word *Maintenance* and a sign reading, "Authorized Personnel Only." David tried the knob. *Of course it's locked, bonehead.*

Now what? He looked around. The men's room was across the hall, maybe he could wait in there until the guard came out then catch the door before it closed? He looked back up the hallway and shrugged to himself. *It's as good a plan as any.* He pushed the bathroom door open and stepped in. Two of the six stalls were occupied, but it was quiet. If it stayed quiet, he would hear the maintenance room door open. He pressed his hot sweaty head against the door jam and listened through the crack. Sweat trickled into his eyes. Doubts trickled into his mind.

Anything could go wrong. Someone could come out of the stall and talk to him. Kids could come in and be loud. Someone could flush... Maybe this was a bad idea. There were footsteps, distant at first, but getting closer. Shoes. Definitely not women's shoes. A man coming to the bathroom? David stepped back and pulled a paper towel from the dispenser. The door swung in and a tall teenager walked past him. David glanced out the door. The maintenance room door was slowly closing!

He lunged through the door and across the hall as quietly as possible so as not to draw the attention of the security guard, who was walking back up the hallway. David caught the door. The guard's keys jingled as he fastened them to his hip. David quietly slipped into the room. *That was close!*

He put his hands against the wall and slumped to catch his breath. The beating of his heart throbbed in his boiling head as he pushed off the wall and turned around. His breath caught in his throat.

In the dead center of what was half storage and half garage, was a U-Haul truck. It looked like the truck he had seen leaving Ace Wrecking. Was this the bomb? He gripped the yellow pipe railing and climbed down the cement stairs. A two foot gap separated the truck from a wall of cardboard boxes. He squeezed through to the back, grabbed the door handle, and pulled up. The truck was filled with white barrels connected by plastic hoses. On the floor, right in front of David's face, was the detonator box with two digital readouts, a rubber number pad, three colored buttons, and three thick colored wires in half hoops running from top to bottom. The buttons were red, yellow, and blue; the wires, green, yellow, and red.

One of the digital readouts counted down. 123, 122, 121… *If those are seconds, I have two minutes!* His mind raced. *Okay.* He swallowed hard and closed his eyes. *It's okay, David. Don't panic. Remember…* He closed his eyes and the words came back to him. *Follow Security 6622 meters.* He'd followed the security guard. That was done. But it wasn't 6,622 meters, so the 6622 had to be something else. The number code?

The numbers continued to decrease. 109, 108, 107, 106… He wiped his drenched forehead and began typing the numbers on the pad. 6- 6... They appeared in the smaller digital readout, one at a time. With each glowing red number his heart quickened. Could there be another application for the numbers? No. This had to be it. He had to trust his instinct. The message had been given to him specifically. It was designed to tell *him* what to do. Logically, it had to know what he would choose. There was no time to second guess. It had to be right.

His finger stabbed the enter button. And the countdown started moving faster! The readout with the 6622 also started counting down rapidly. *Did I do something wrong?* He frantically examined the device. *6622 meters 0 out red yellow blue.* The colors matched the buttons. Was he supposed to push the buttons? He brought his finger up to the red button and started to push-- but his mind screamed, *NO! --meters 0 out!* His hand snapped back. The meters had to zero out! The seconds counter and the smaller readout hit zero at the same time. David squeezed his eyes shut.

No explosion—he opened one eye.

Bleep. Bleep. Bleep. The seconds counter reset to ten and began counting down again. David's heart skipped a beat. *The colors! What were the colors?* They echoed in his mind. *Red, yellow, blue.* He stabbed the three buttons in that order, the counter stopped on the number six, glowing eerily, red on black. David eyes stayed locked onto it. Was it over, would they start counting down again? He stared. The number six stared back. No more bleeps. No more numbers. Nothing.

He backed away from the truck and crouched down, his muscles felt like sandbags as sweat dripped from his forehead onto the cement floor. He was thankful for the effect the endorphins were producing; a numbing buzz enveloped him. For a moment.

The bomb had been deactivated, but he still had to call the authorities. He patted his pocket. His phone was in the car! It was probably better if he didn't use his own phone anyway. He was already in enough hot water with his connection to Jerry. How would he ever explain *this?* He started to put his head in his hands, but then stopped. *Karen! I'll let her tell them where it is. She wanted in on it anyway!* He stood on wobbly legs, slid the door of the truck down, and made his way back out to the main corridor. A single pay phone sat against the far wall.

Briskly, he made his way to the phone and grabbed the receiver, but as soon as he dug in his pocket for change, he realized he didn't have Karen's number. It was in his cellphone-- in his car. He slammed the phone back on the hook.

It was a long walk to the other end of the mall, and the endorphins were no longer pulling their share. His muscles cried out with every step as his walk degraded to a limp.

Ding. "Attention mall shoppers and employees. Due to an increased threat level, the mall is being evacuated. There is no cause for alarm. The threat is under control. Please walk to the nearest exit. I repeat, the threat is under control. There is no cause for alarm. Please walk to the nearest exit."

How did they know? Did they find the bomb in the truck? Did Karen figure it out by using the information in the box? It didn't matter. David followed the current of people exiting the mall, and returned to his car where his cellphone sat on the passenger seat. He picked it up and noticed a message had been left. He called it up and listened.

"David." It was Sharon, and she sounded *terrified.* "The terrorists have us." Her breath came quickly. "They shot Alex. He's... David. Alex is…" David heard a man's voice in the background conveying something unintelligible. "He's dead, David. And they're going to kill us too if you stop the bomb." The man continued to speak. "Please, David. Call me back. He says they won't detonate the bomb

278

if you leave it alone. They don't want to hurt anyone else, but they will if they..."

The man spoke into the phone. "Pray you receive this *before* you stop the bomb."

Authorities from every agency in the government descended upon the double decker mall. Positions were set up at all exits to direct the traffic fleeing the enormous parking lot. The surrounding roads were barricaded. Overhead, police choppers circled the perimeter warning stragglers to evacuate the area. News teams from every major network, as well as reporters from newspapers and national news agencies, were perched on a highway overlooking the mall. Two network helicopters flew a wide pattern around the perimeter.

One lone truck made its way across the dead parking lot, carrying the Boston Bomb Squad, two FBI agents, three SWAT officers, one Karen Watson, and a very happy Larry Turner. Due to the urgent nature of the threat, the robotic bomb unit had been shelved in favor of a team that could work quickly to locate and dismantle the bomb.

Working from information from the Geo Cache, and evidence that the bomb could still be in the U-Haul truck, the team headed toward the far side of the mall. A U-Haul had recently been sighted entering a storage garage in that area. The SWAT team filed out and set up a perimeter around the garage, and the Bomb Squad began testing the area for radiation. The bomb *was* in the U-haul as they had suspected, and radiation levels were low, so the all-clear was given. The Bomb Squad began their work.

Karen was busy asking questions. Larry was allowed to set up the portable satellite box near the Bomb Squad truck.

He fired it up, got the sat-lock, and plugged his camera into the side. "Ready when you are, hon."

Karen listened through her earpiece to the news director in master control. "Are you set up, Karen?"

"Yeah, Jim. Ready when you are."

"Cindy's getting set in the chair. Hold on a sec."

Karen adjusted the suit coat Larry had brought to her and checked her face one last time. She was not looking her best by *any* means, but it would have to do.

"Alright," said Jim, "look alive. We're going to camera one on Cindy in five, four, three, two."

Karen could hear Cindy talking through her earbud. She gave Larry a nod, he brought his camera up onto his shoulder.

"We now go live to Karen Watson at the bomb site."

"Thank you, Cindy. Behind me, as you can see, the Boston Bomb Squad is assessing the situation. We have been told that the bomb has been deactivated, but the threat is still high. These men need to determine if the bomb can be dismantled and whether or not it has been rigged to explode if tampered with. The nuclear material is another hazard; a specialist is on site working closely with the team to handle the added danger. It is a grueling job, a job these brave men handle with professionalism and dedication. Earlier this morning authorities uncovered, through an anonymous source, information linking a Harvard Chemist named Jerry Cook to the construction of the bomb. His full involvement is unknown, and his whereabouts are also unknown at this time. This afternoon, FBI stormed the hostage house containing Brad Knight, he is said to have been recovered uninjured. Police and Federal agents have linked the money to a man named Afif Al-Qadir. Qadir is currently at large and is considered armed and dangerous. If you have any information about this man, or about Jerry Cook, please contact the Boston PD. Things are still tense here, as you can imagine, but authorities are at work, and the outlook is hopeful. --Back to you, Cindy."

She heard Cindy take over, and Jim's voice came on her earbud. "Excellent job, Karen. Have Larry get some live footage of the Bomb Squad. We'll go back to it a few times over the next few minutes and wrap up with you at the end. Kay?"

Karen spoke into her mic. "Sure thing, Jim."

She relayed the information to Larry; he repositioned beside the truck.

A tall Arab man came up behind Karen. "Excuse me, miss."

She looked at him blankly.

"I have information about your Brad Knight."

Her face came alive. "Yes?"

"I was told to give Mr. Knight anything he wanted, and against my advice, he wanted to come here-- to see you."

She turned and saw him, standing by a black Humvee. A blanket was thrown over his shoulders, his hair and pants were covered in blood. He looked like he had been through hell and back, and yet his face-- his beautiful face-- was strong and confident. Her eyes filled with tears. *"Brad!"* She ran across the parking lot and wrapped her good arm around him. Her face pressed into his neck, he pulled her in tight. "I was so worried... I... I... " Her voice gave out and she began to weep quietly in his arms.

His fingers caressed her hair in gentle swirls. "It's over, Karen. It's over."

She continued to cry. *Was it over?* Had they stopped the terrorists completely? Was this the end of the story? The end of the threat? She rubbed her cheek on his chest.

"I had some time to think." His voice sounded dry.

She pulled away and looked up at him. The tears were still flowing. "--About what?"

"Us."

The world seemed to slow as her mind attempted to decipher the implication of the word.

"Karen, I know this is unexpected, and probably the worst time in the history of worst times, but I don't want to ever have to face something like this again and regret that I never asked you to marry me."

She stepped back. A look of shock crossed her features. *Did he just...* Her eyes grew wide, then questioning. "Did you just-- *ask* me..."

"Karen." He got down on one knee. "Will you marry me?"

She didn't see the blanket, or the blood, or the toll the drugs had taken on his features. His soul was speaking too her. His strong, gentle, compassionate, wonderful, loving soul.

Her heart filled with joy. *"Yes!* Yes. YES I'll marry you!" She pulled him up, wrapped her arm around his neck, and kissed him passionately.

Larry hollered across the parking lot. *"Hey!* You love birds *mind?* We got work to do!"

She glanced back at Larry, then up at Brad. "I'd like to thank you."

He gave her a confused look.

"For choosing Larry as your cameraman. I was wrong about him." She looked again at the big Texan tapping his watch with a meaty finger. "--But don't tell him I said so," she said, smiling.

"Whatever you say, little darlin'."

She punched him on the arm. "Honestly, I don't think

I would have made it through without him. I guess I just needed someone to be angry at."

"Well now you have me back, and you can be angry at me *every day.*" He pulled her in and kissed her.

"If y'all are gonna stand there kissin' all day I might's well get in front of the camera myself!"

Karen pulled away and bolted across the lot.

David pulled off to the side of the road, put the car in neutral, and started punching the steering wheel. *"HOW! COULD! YOU! LET! THIS! HAPPEN! TO! ME!"* He gripped the wheel with both hands and shook it violently. Rage burned *hot* in every cell of his body. *"WWHHYYY!"* He pressed his forehead against the steering wheel. His best friend was *dead.* And for all he knew his family was too. Hate boiled in his heart. Hate for God. Hate for Jerry. Hate for the evil he had caused. *And for WHAT, Jerry? For some IDIOTIC political belief? Was it worth it? Was it worth sacrificing the only family you had left on this earth?* David lifted his head as a realization washed over him.

His grip loosened.

It *wasn't* worth it. Jerry wouldn't have made that choice. David's eyes grew wide. It was another bluff; it had to be. But *why?* Why would Jerry want him to think his family was dead? Was it a vindictive stab, meant to hurt him for stopping the bomb? No. The voicemail was left *before* he stopped the bomb. It was another scare tactic. David clutched for his phone. *They're still alive. They have to be!* He hit recall on the number for the voicemail. The phone rang and rang, but no one answered. He waited. Still nothing. The phone just kept ringing. *What now?*

He pressed the off button and immediately the phone buzzed in his hand. He flipped it open. *Go to the Internet Cafe on Brown Street and open a Google chat with me. Jerry.* Jerry? He stared at the message, then slammed the car back in to gear. The tires screeched into a u-turn and he headed back toward the mall. Brown Street was only a few minutes away.

The car skidded to a stop on the grass next to the cafe. The evacuation from the mall had created a frenzy of activity in the little Internet cafe, there were no spaces left anywhere. He ran in and pushed through the crowd. All eyes were glued to a large television on the wall. David came to a stand still and looked up at the screen. *Brad!* Brad Knight was reporting live from the mall! Hamid had told the *truth!* The image sparked a seed of hope in David's soul. If *Brad* was okay, maybe his family was okay too!

He grabbed a computer pass and called up gmail on a computer near the front window. "I'm here," he typed.

The curser blinked, but there was no response.

"I'm here! Jerry, answer me!"

Nothing.

What is he doing? Why doesn't he answer?

David's phone went off in his pocket. He pulled it out and flipped it open. *"Hello!"*

"David. It's Alex."

--*Alex?* His brain tried to process what he was hearing. It *sounded* like Alex. *"Wh- who?"*

"David. It's me. Alex."

"But. --Alex? Sharon, said you were *dead.*"

"I'm not dead. I'm in a lot of pain, but I'm not dead."

David was speechless.

"I had my vest on. The bullets embedded in the center plate, I lost consciousness for awhile, but I'm okay."

"Oh, thank *God* Alex, I thought..." His throat constricted with emotion. "Wh- where's Sharon and the kids?"

"I don't know. When I woke up, they were gone. It all

happened so fast! We thought Jerry was at the door, but it was one of the terrorists. I'm so sorry."

"Jerry? He came to the house?"

"Yeah. To pick up Sharon and the kids and bring them someplace safe. Based on your tone, I'm thinking you know about him."

"Yeah. I found out from Karen."

"I just heard it on the radio. I had no idea. I thought the terrorist had followed him or something. If I'd known he was involved in all this I *never* would have let him through the gate."

"How could you *possibly* have known? Jerry's the *last* person *anyone* would expect to be involved in all this."

"I know. It's crazy!"

"So you have no idea where he took them?"

"Not at the moment. But I have friends who are plugged in to everything that happens in this city. We'll find them."

David looked down at the computer monitor. A message sat waiting in the chat box. It said, "Are you there?"

"Where are you? I'll come and we can figure out the next move," said Alex.

David pulled his eyes from the screen. "I'm-- at the Internet Café on Brown Street. You know the place?"

"Yeah. I'll be right there."

David closed the phone, set it on the table, and typed an answer.

"Yes. I'm here."

"I'm very angry with you."

"Who am I speaking with?" typed David.

"Who do you think?" The words sat silent on the cold screen.

"Jerry?"

"This didn't have to happen this way. I did everything I could to deter you. But you wouldn't stop."

"Jerry. Why are you doing this?"

"You have forced my hand. Now I have to do something drastic. Something horrible."

"Why?"

There was a long pause. Then another message popped up. "Because this country needs a wake up call. We can't continue to export war and violence all over the world, and expect to live in peace and prosperity. This country needs to know that it is fueling hatred in Muslim countries, and that that hatred will bring our extinction."

David poked in a response. "They would hate us no matter what. They hate us simply because we're not Muslim."

"We never intended to detonate the bomb, David. It was to show what could happen if we continue down this road. But you have ruined everything. Now I will have to do something horrible, so something more horrible can be avoided. I've seen what they're planning. It's nothing less than the total economic destruction of our country."

David's eyes flew over the words "How will any of this help your cause?" he typed back.

"Our government will have to make a statement to the world community, promising to bring all of our troops home. That is the only thing that will stop this."

"You're mad."

"If you use your messages to stop me, I swear to you, David, I will allow my sister and her children to starve to death in the hole I have put them in, their deaths will be on your head."

The chat terminated.

They're still alive! David's heart surged. *I KNEW it!* He rolled back and stared at the screen. Was it possible that Jerry was bluffing? It certainly didn't sound like it. Even if he was serious, was he *capable* of following through with his threats? He could believe that Jerry had something to do with the bomb plot, *IF* he stretched his imagination. *Really* stretched it. But to let his sister and her children *die* of starvation? There was no way. He simply wasn't capable of such a thing. *And* it didn't match up with the conversation on the screen either. In Jerry's mind, he was doing all this for the greater good of the country. A man sensitive enough to be driven by civic responsibility was not the kind of man who would allow harm to come to those closest to him. If he cared so much about people he didn't even *know*, then how much more would he care about his own family? Having Alex killed was understandable. He never liked Alex much anyway. But letting his own *family* die? It would never happen. He *had* to be bluffing. *Okay, Jerry. You want to play hard ball? Bring it on! Only this time, we're going to play by MY rules!*

David watched the hostage rescue play out on the large HDTV screen for about the hundredth time, but there was still no sign of Alex. It was dark now, the evacuees from the mall had cleared out. David sipped his orange soda.

A picture of the President appeared on the screen behind the newscaster. "We have news from the White House that the President has decided to continue on with his scheduled appearance at the airbase in Bangor, Maine, an event he had canceled earlier due to terrorist activity in the Boston area. The President says he hopes to quell fears of more bomb threats by demonstrating his trust in the outstanding work of Homeland Security. With the recent capture of key suspects, and the apprehension of two dirty bombs, the President says he feels confident to move forward with his appearance."

David's mouth hung open. If the President was going to be at the airbase, he would be open to attack. Would Jerry try to kill him? Was *that* the horrible thing he had hinted at?

David felt a tap on his shoulder and looked up. Alex hovered over him. *"Alex!"* He jumped up and wrapped his arms around him.

"It's good to see you too, man." Alex laughed.

"Did you see what I just saw?" David let go and gestured toward the television.

"What?"

"The newscast about the President?"

"The radio said something about him giving a speech

up in Maine, is that what you're talking about?"

David gripped Alex by the arm and pulled him down into the seat next to him. "I think Jerry is going to try to assassinate the President just like the message said. It's the only thing that makes sense."

"Where? At the *speech?* Are you crazy? That airport is going to be locked up tighter than Fort Knox. How would he do it?"

"I don't know, but it's going to happen. The messages said it would."

"Do you know when?"

"It said on the news last night that he was scheduled to appear at 11:00 a.m. tomorrow, but I can check on the Internet to make sure."

"Well, let's do it."

David raised his brows. "What? No riot act? No long oration about how I need to rescue my family?"

Alex gave him a dirty look. "Where's your family, David? Jerry has them. Right? And where is Jerry? We don't know, do we? But we *do* know where he'll be *tomorrow.* And to rescue Sharon and the kids, we have to stop Jerry. Plain and simple."

"Yes." He grabbed Alex's arm. "That's true."

"And you know what else? If you'd listened to me in the first place, Jerry wouldn't *have* your family, would he?"

David pressed his lips together. He was right. This was all his fault. If he hadn't gone chasing after the messages, he and his family would be far away from all this right now. But instead, the Feds were surely looking for him, and his family was being held hostage. He shook his head in disgust. "The thought of my family being with him for the whole night turns my stomach."

Alex put his hand on David's shoulder. "Look, I have

friends in the police department. I'll go do the rounds and see if I can turn up some information on where they think Jerry is. If nothing shakes loose, we'll head up to Maine."

David thought for a moment. "Okay. I'll go back to the motel and lay low. The last thing I want to do is run into Homeland Security. They're going to have questions for me-- questions I can't answer."

Alex nodded. "Good. I'll get back to you as soon as I can."

David reached up and rubbed his neck. He was completely and utterly *exhausted,* it would be good to let Alex take over for awhile. If anyone could dig up the location of Jerry and his family, it was Alex.

The hollow din of the celebration going on in the newsroom could be heard all the way down in Nerd's office. But he tried to block it out. He *was* excited about Brad's rescue, and the finding of the bomb, and the announcement about Karen and Brad's wedding plans. But the video clip flickering on his screen kept him from the festivities. It was paused on a close up of the detonator housing. Although the serial number had been scraped off, there were still identifying marks he was sure his hacker friend Canary could track down. *Canary is an odd bird--* Nerd snickered to himself at the pun. The name said much about the man behind the alias. It was an anagram for anarcy, a purposeful misspelling, to symbolize the man's hatred for society, and anything else to do with organized civilization. At least that's what he claimed. But as far as Nerd was concerned, it was just a lame attempt to play off the fact that he couldn't spell. Nerd dragged the image he had captured from the video to the email directed to Canary, and pressed send. It would probably turn up as a dead lead, but it was worth a try.

"Are you coming up?"

He swiveled in his chair. It was Karen.

"Oh. Hey there." He looked at the screen, then back at Karen. "I was just following up on something."

"You've had a busy day. Don't you think it's time to take a break? We're telling stories about John, some of the stuff he use to do. You should come up."

293

He sprang to his feet, trying to smooth the tangled mess of red hair on the top of his head. "You're wish is my command, Karen." He snorted. "Don't want to keep my fans waiting."

She smiled, and her eyes twinkled.

That Brad was a *lucky* guy. *Lucky for him he moved in when he did.* She was Nerd's kind of girl. The kind who paid any attention to him at all.

*"LEAVE HER **ALONE!**"* David sat up in bed, panting, covered in sweat. His alarm was going off, he reached over and hit the button. Silence filled the dark motel room.

But he could still hear her screaming.

A black shrouded figure had been dragging Emily by the hair into a gaping hole in the ground. David shuddered and tried to shake the image from his mind. He looked at the clock. It was 4:00 a.m. Where was Alex? He turned on the light and clutched his phone. No messages. He flipped it open and punched the number.

Alex answered with a scratchy, "Hello?"

"We're you *sleeping?"*

"Just for a couple of hours. I was up all night following leads."

"We have to get out of here."

"There's plenty of time. The President doesn't speak till eleven."

"But we should get there early. What if the car breaks down?"

"Then we'll get a cab. Don't worry. We'll get there." The sound of squeaky bedsprings came through the phone.

"Where *are* you?"

Alex groaned. "I'm at the police station. They've been following Jerry's trail from Harvard, we're waiting to see where it ends."

"How close are they?"

"They've been saying any minute for the last six

hours."

David ran his hands through his curly hair. "We have to *go*. We can't *wait* for them. How soon can you get here?"

"I don't know. Thirty minutes?"

"Get here, or I'm going without you."

"Okay. Don't snap at me. Wait, okay?"

David closed the phone.

Forty-five minutes passed, and David paced. Every passing minute meant one more opportunity for failure. This was *not* an appointment he could be late for. *That's it! I'm leaving.* He gathered his few things and headed down to the office to leave his key. As he jogged through the dimly lit parking lot, Alex pulled up beside him. "Come on, get in. I just filled the tank so we won't have to stop on the way." He hopped in, Alex pulled the car out onto the road. Alex drove, and David stared out the window. Neither one felt the need to speak. And the road passed under them.

For an eternity.

Nerd flicked the switch, and his office filled with the green tint of florescent lighting. He set his coffee mug down next to his mouse pad and tapped the spacebar; three flat screens came to life. In the lower corner of the center screen a number four blinked. He had four new messages. He clicked the icon, and his groggy eyes scanned down the page to the entry he'd been waiting for.

Subject: *You owe me big.*

It was from Canary. *Did he find something?* With a click, the email opened. The contents were exactly what he had requested. Canary had come through for him. In spades! "Hey, Nerd. This unit was sold to an American demalition company working in Egipt. Up til a few weeks ago it was being used for excavation work. Then was perchased by a company whos name came up defunct when I did a search for it. But that didn't stop me and my *superlative intillect!* I accessed CIA docs, (thanks to Homeland Security's new efforts to share info.) and uncovered the name of a suspected arms dealer..."

Nerd's mouth dropped open as his gangly fingers reached out and picked up his coffee mug. He drew it in and took a sip as his eyes peered through the steam at the name glowing on the monitor. Part of him was elated at uncovering what was sure to be big news. It was sure to impress Karen, and would virtually guarantee her taking him with her when she moved on to a larger market, maybe even to national. But a larger part of him wished he had never dug it up in the first place.

He picked up the phone and began dialing, but then placed it back in the cradle. He didn't want to hear the reaction. He didn't want to hear the agony as the inevitable questions came firing at him. He didn't want to be the one to have to swear it was true, even though he wished it wasn't. He ripped open the velcro pouch on his belt and pulled out his cellphone. News like this was best delivered with text. That way, if there was a response, he didn't have to hear the emotion, he didn't have to hear the pleading for answers. It would be a share of information. Nothing more. He thumbed down through his contacts to the one he was seeking, *David Chance.*

David watched the mile markers of the Maine Turnpike pass. His brain had finally shut down. It was no longer churning through all of the possible ways he would search for messages once they arrived at the airbase. It was no longer running through endless variations of the conversation he would have with Jerry.

He simply stared. Too tired to think. Too tired to focus.

And the landscape passed by.

Rock music played on the radio, a cold breeze circled around from the driver's window. Alex yawned again and stretched over the steering wheel, arching his back like a cat. David turned his head. "You want me to take over?" he mumbled. "I've had more sleep than you."

"Nah. I'm all set. I've got my tunes to keep me awake. How are you holding up?"

"Never better." It wasn't true, of course, but it wasn't a lie either. It was *denial,* a trait he had learned from Alex. Men *deny* pain. The stronger the man, the greater the denial. In David's mind, there was no greater proof of strength than to have a bone sticking out of your arm and to say *'What? That? Oh it's nothing.'* So to David, it wasn't really a lie. It was a demonstration of toughness. Alex had taught him many such lessons growing up on the streets of Boston. David's phone vibrated in his pocket; his body jerked.

Alex laughed. "You okay?"

"Phone," muttered David as he shoved his hand into his pocket. There was a text message. *"Thought you should know. The detonator was purchased by Alex Blackstone. Sorry. I know he's your friend. Nerd."*

The text burrowed through layers of drowsiness, and embedded itself into David's weary mind. *What?* He squeezed his eyes shut, then reopened. *Am I dreaming?* He looked over at Alex, then back at the message. *That's not possible.*

Alex?

He stared straight ahead at a spot on the windshield. *No. I don't bel... It's a mistake. It HAS to be.* David stuffed the phone back in his pocket.

"You okay?"

"Yeah."

"Text message?"

"Yeah. Just a co-worker. I'll deal with it later."

Alex knew David better than anyone, even better than Sharon. He knew all the tactics David used to avoid lying.

He was using one of them now.

"What did it say, David?"

"Nosey much?" said David, trying to muster as much nonchalance as he could.

Alex lifted a brow. "So we're keeping secrets now?"

David glanced at Alex with a casual expression, then listened in horror as the words slipped from his lips. "You tell me." The words *dripped* with suspicion.

Alex slammed on the brake and jerked the car into the breakdown lane.

David slapped his hand to the dashboard. *"What are you doing?"*

"You tell *me?"* Alex parroted the comment. The car slid to a stop. Alex turned a fierce expression toward David. "Are you *implying* that *I'm* keeping secrets?"

Was he? Maybe the name Nerd found was a different

Alex Blackstone. But why did he react so violently? David's mind raced. The terrorists spared him and his family. *Why?* Because *someone* among them *cared* what happened to them. He had thought it was Jerry, but that *still* didn't add up. He *just wasn't capable* of such things. But *Alex?* He was *more* than capable.

"Well?" Alex glared at him.

The magnitude of the betrayal seized David, and rational thought departed. He shoved his hand in his pocket, yanked the phone back out, and yelled at his friend. "I just got *this!"* He thrust it at Alex. "You want to talk about *secrets?"*

Alex looked at the message, then out his window.

The silence was deafening.

"Is this *you?* Has my *best friend* betrayed me?"

Alex turned. His eyes grew cold and his voice sent a chill down David's back. "You figured it out. How fortunate for you." His hand came up from between the seat and the door. He was holding his pistol.

David's hands flew up. "Are you kidding me!"

"Get out."

"What..."

"GET OUT OF THE CAR!"

David fumbled the door open and climbed out onto the grassy slope. Alex climbed out the other side.

David put his palms up. "Come on, man, this is *crazy!* Whatever you're caught up in, I'll understand. We can work through this."

"Shut up!" Alex looked up the highway at the sparse early morning traffic. "Head down to the tree line."

"What are you..."

"Now!"

David stumbled down the embankment to the tree line

and turned. Alex shoved him around and into the trees, forcing him forward deep into the pines. Until the traffic was barely audible. And still they continued on. Stumbling through the branches. Tripping over roots.

Finally David spoke. "So this is it? Years of friendship coming to an end when you put a bullet through my head in the mid..."

Alex shoved him to the ground.

"If I was going to put a *bullet* in your head, you'd be *dead* already! Man! *Take a hint!* I've been *trying* to keep you alive for the past two days!" He waved the gun through the air. "I *protected* you! They wanted to kill you and *I* protected you!" A look of hopelessness crossed his features. "You should have *backed off!* But you wouldn't *listen!* I thought if I pretended to be the Arabs, you'd lose your nerve. I thought if I put your family in danger, you'd give in. But NO! You had to keep on *sticking* your nose where it didn't belong! I threatened your *life,* and the life of your *son!* BUT YOU JUST KEPT COMING!" He began pacing wildly.

"You could have just- talked to me. We could have dealt with..."

"YOU WEREN'T SUPPOSED TO KNOW!" He rubbed his face with a heavy hand. "It was *my* burden to carry. *I* was going to make *one big score,* and we'd be *set* for *life!* I could finally have the family I've always wanted! And you wouldn't have to work at that *stupid* station editing tapes. You deserve better than that!"

"So this is about-- *money?"*

Alex glared at him. "It's about not letting life pass me by! I feel like I'm on a treadmill that never stops. In a few years I'll be forty, and my life hasn't even started yet! This was my chance to break free of the cycle. To have the family. To have the kids."

"By *killing* thousands of innocent people?"

He stood with his mouth open and his eyebrows raised. "No one was supposed to die, David. It was all political posturing, a planned event that would smear the President's *no terrorism on American soil* record. But you've *more* than sufficiently ruined *everything.* " He started pacing again. "They wanted an evacuation of Boston, and thanks to *you, I* gave them a successful Homeland Security sting operation. They wanted the authorities to look like they had been caught with their pants down, and *I* made them look like heroes! So NOW, because of YOU, *I* have to do something terrible!" He stopped. David could see tears in his eyes. "-- *Why,* David? Why did you have to keep coming?"

"Are-- you going to try to kill the President?"

He wiped his arm across his wet face, his wild eyes pierced David's heart. "I got the idea from *you* actually."

Me? The thought bent David's mind. "You'll never get close enough to him, not with all that's going on."

"The people I work for have it all set up." He chuckled. "They're more powerful than you can possibly imagine. These people get what they want. All I need to do is execute *my* part of the plan, and I get what I want. If I don't-- I'm dead."

"Alex..."

"This was supposed to be for all of us." He hung his head. "I could have lived with the guilt. It would have been my secret. But knowing that you know..." He looked up. "Knowing that you will always look at me like you're looking at me right now-- *that* I can't live with." He cocked the gun.

"Alex! Please! We'll work something out!"

Alex circled. "You know the weird thing? The thing I

can't for the life of me figure out?" He pressed the cold hard barrel into David's head. "Do you know, David?"

"Wh- What?"

"Why did your messages hide this from you?"

"Please. Don't do this." David's body shuddered.

"You should have *listened.* You should have stopped. I gave you *every* chance. And all you had to do was listen. All you had to do was stop!"

David squeezed his eyelids.

"And you know what else, David?" The words were cold and filled with bitterness.

"Wh- What, Alex?"

He pressed the barrel harder against his head. "*You--* killed our friendship."

He pulled the gun away.

There was a bright light.

And then darkness.

David's eyes fluttered open, then shut tight. The light was unbearable, the pain swelled in response. He rolled onto his back and gripped his head with both hands. There was a damp spot on his hair, pine needles clung to the wetness.

He let me live.

He rolled to his side and opened his eyes a slit.

He's risking his life to let me live. He's not a heartless monster. Maybe there's hope. With one hand on the ground, he pushed up to his knees. The pain was excruciating. He almost passed out again. *How long have I been out?* He looked at his watch. It was gone. Slowly he tried to rise up, but fell back again. *I HAVE to get up.* He crawled to a birch, pulled himself up, and held tightly to the trunk. He let go and teetered to the next tree. The world pulsated in rhythm to the pain in his head, but he ignored it, and stumbled forward like a drunk, shoving himself from one tree to the next.

After awhile, he stopped and listened. *I must be nearing the Interstate.* But all he could hear was the whispering wind, the chattering birds, and the pounding in his head. *Did he move me deeper into the woods? Why can't I hear the cars?* In every direction there was nothing but trees, no paths, nothing to indicate where he was. *Even if I started off in the right direction, I could go in circles-- or walk parallel to the highway for hours.*

He collapsed to his knees and held onto his head. His friend was making the biggest mistake of his life. The life of the President was hanging in the balance. There was too much at stake to rely on dumb luck. There had to be a way. Were there any messages he hadn't used? He clutched his head harder and slowly went back over the events of the last two days. Suddenly he looked up. *Remember north!* That one hadn't been used yet! *Okay, which way is north?* He looked up at the clouds. *Clouds? HOW am I supposed to know which way NORTH is?* He hung his head in defeat-- then looked up again, remembering something-- something Alex had taught him when they were kids. *Moss grows thicker on the north side of trees!* He struggled to his feet, examined the trees, then turned and stumbled back the way he had come.

It wasn't long before he heard the cars, and soon after emerged from the tree line. His brain rolled in his head as he struggled up the bank to the side of the Interstate. The sun was peeking out from about a nine o'clock position in the sky. David's heart sank. *Even if I can catch a ride, I'll never get there in time!* The message pushed its way back into his mind. *Remember north. YES. I did that. NOW what?*

Above the noise of the cars racing by and the pounding in his head, David heard a distinct and familiar sound. At first he thought it was his imagination, but as it grew louder there was no mistaking it. *A plane!* He looked at the tree line on the other side of the Interstate, and it appeared, not far above the tips of the trees. Apparently it had just taken off.

He waited for a break in the traffic, and sprinted northward, to the other side.

24357

The airport was small compared to what he was used to, but inside the terminal was spacious, and appeared even more so by the complete lack of activity. David rushed across the large hollow room to the ticket counter. A stout dark haired attendant sat with her head in her hands and her cheeks squished into her eyes.

"Excuse me, miss." He panted. "I need to-- get to Bangor immediately. I need-- whatever is taking off right now. Please-- it's a matter of life and death."

She sat up and eyed him, then wheeled her chair over to the computer terminal. "I'll see what I can find, but I don't think anything is leaving within the hour." Her fingers tapped the keys as her brows descended. She squinted at the screen. "I can put you on a flight at twelve-thirty."

David shook his head. "No. That's too late. Is there a charter flight? A sight seeing flight? *Anything?* "

"I don't handle those at this counter."

"Who does?"

"Various companies operating around the airport." She gestured here and there with her hand.

David gripped the counter. "I don't have *time* to..." He stopped himself. The last thing he needed was a run in with security. "Never mind. Thanks for trying."

She gave him a blank stare as he backed away.

Now what? According to the clock behind the desk, it was 9:45. Time was draining away, and with it, all hope of stopping Alex. He frantically looked left, then right. *Okay, stay CALM, David. You're missing something. Look for it. The answer is here. Somewhere.* He took a deep breath and let it out slowly. There were words all over the airport. In all the buzz of written instructions, there *had* to be another clue. That's how it worked. There was *always* another message, he just needed to *trust.* He began walking forward, letting his eyes bounce from sign to sign.

Then he stopped.

His eyes narrowed.

It couldn't be-- He stood transfixed on a man entering the glassed-in front doors of the airport. He was wearing dark blue pants, a crisp short sleeved white shirt with tie, and on his pocket, the silver wings of a pilot. His suit coat was draped over the maroon bag he was wheeling behind him. David cocked his head and squinted. *Could it be?* The pilot paused in front of the row of monitors near the door to scan the information. David stepped left to get a better look at him. The man turned and began walking toward David.

It *was* him!

A sense of relief and astonishment washed over David. Not only had the messages led him here, but here was *Bill,* the man from the convenience store-- and he was a *pilot!* There was no way his mind could have orchestrated *this.* Clearly something greater was guiding things. Maybe it was stress, or perhaps just the lack of sleep, but David gave in to the emotion welling up inside him, and began to cry. Something deep within him was stirred to know that the author of the messages could do this! That he could truly be in contact with God was overwhelming.

Bill slowed as he approached, then stopped. His bushy white mustache rose and the wrinkles around his friendly eyes deepened. "I know you." He pointed. "From the convenience store, right? I never did get your name."

"David. David Chance." He sniffed and held out his hand.

Bill took it. "Are you alright?"

"Yeah. I just got a little overwhelmed when I saw you."

He looked at David sideways. "--Why?"

"Why?" David looked down at the tiled floor. Good question. What could he say to that? Was he going to tell him everything, lay it all on the line? Time was running out. Whatever it was, he needed to say it fast. "There's so little time. I don't know where to begin."

"Just take it one sentence at a time, son."

David took a breath. "You remember how I won that money on the lottery ticket?"

"Well yah! I'll never forget it." Bill laughed.

"Well it wasn't luck. I *knew* that ticket was going to be a winner because something supernatural is happening to me." The words came tumbling out. "I can't expect you to believe me. I can hardly believe it myself. But I *need* you to believe, because I need you to fly me to Bangor."

"Whoa, slow down, son. You need me to do what?"

"Fly me to Bangor. Because if you don't, something very bad is going to happen. When I saw you," he looked at Bill with pleading eyes, "I knew you were sent to take me."

Bill stared in stunned silence.

"I know it sounds crazy, but I'm telling you the truth. You've *got* to believe me."

"So you need *one* seat-- and you're going to *Bangor.*"

"I don't even need a seat. I'll sit on the floor."

Bill ran his hand through his graying hair. "Well I'll be."

David squinted. "So- you believe me?"

His brows rose. "Oh, I believe you alright."

David bent over and exhaled. "Oh thank *God.*"

"I had a feeling I got stuck here for a reason."

David looked up. "Huh?"

"The only reason I'm here is because last night one of the passengers on my jet got sick, and I had to make an emergency landing. But when I tried to take off again, I kept having all kinds of warning lights come on. I never saw anything like it! And now, this morning, the mechanic calls and says there's nothing wrong with the plane!"

David smiled.

"And now here you are, and you need to get Bangor."

"So-- can you do it?"

"Why not? I'm going there anyway, and I have a seat open. I gotta tell you, son, I'm amazed. You're either the luckiest man on the planet, or you're telling the truth. Either way, it'll be a heck of a story for the Mrs."

David dug in his pocket. "What do you charge for a ticket?"

"From Lewiston to Bangor, I'd say four-hundred..."

Their eyes met.

"Come on son. Let's get you to Bangor."

The message said, *bomb in pieces hangar eleven luggage cart end runway.* David replaced the magazine in the pocket of the seat in front of him. He looked out the window. Apparently Alex had to put the bomb together first. And put it on a cart to be detonated when Air Force One was at the end of the runway. It was horrible to think that Alex had come to the place where he could kill a plane full of people to achieve his goals.

His head felt numb.

The plane made a thump as the landing gear touched down, and David studied the building in the distance. For an international airport, it wasn't much larger than the one in Lewiston. They taxied around and came to a stop several yards from the gate.

Bzzz. "Thank you for flying North Blue, it has been a pleasure to serve you today. The pilot has turned off the seatbelt sign so..."

David quickly unfastened and headed to the front of the plane. "Can I see the captain?"

The thin blonde stewardess gave a red lipsticky smile and moved aside to reveal a cramped high-tech cockpit. Bill's head poked around the chair.

"I figured you'd be the first one off."

"Yeah. Hey, can you tell me where hangar eleven is?"

"Ah- I think south of the airport. Just grab a taxi, they'll get you there."

"Thanks, Bill. You have no idea how much you've

helped me out."

"Don't mention it. It's my pleasure!"

David was looking over his shoulder at the stewardess unlatching the door.

"Here." Bill held out a business card. "When this is all over, I want you to give me a call and tell me the whole story."

"Yeah, sure thing." The door opened. He was halfway across the tarmac before the second passenger exited the plane. He burst through the double doors and ran up the escalator to the security checkpoint. Just outside the gate was the main concourse, a large open room lined with stores and restaurants. He jogged by the military greeters in front of the magazine store, skidded down the escalator to the lobby, and out the sliding doors to the front of the building. A City Taxi sat at the far entrance. David ran over. "Are you waiting for someone?" He breathed hard.

"Yep. You."

David leapt in.

"Where to?"

"Hangar eleven."

"You won't be able to get neah theya tahday."

David shook his head. "Ah- yeah. Just get me as close as you can."

The cab pulled away from the curb and started a slow circuit around the parking lot. "So-- y'ever been to Bangor bafowa?"

David looked at the back of the driver's head. "Yes, sir, I have. I'm in kind of a hurry. Can you get me there quickly?"

"I c'n try, but theya's lots a traffic here tahday You know who's visitin' don't ya?"

David looked out the window at a field filled with

hundreds of parked cars and a stream of people heading
north. "Yeah, that's ah, why I'm here."

"Yessir. All them people's headed to the airbase just
north a heayah."

The taxi followed a road around the airport and passed
by the end of the runway. The driver pointed to a large metal
building next to a parking lot. Three cruisers sat in front of a
chain link fence. Another patrolled back and forth through
the lot. "That's hangah 'leven bahind that fence over theya.
You want me ta drop you at the side of the road? I doubt
them officers will let us in the lawt."

David studied the scene. "Yeah, that's good enough."

The car came to a stop just past the two entrances to the
parking lot. David paid the man and climbed out onto the
grass.

"Have a good one!" The driver waved and smiled.

David squinted at him. *Yeah.* He was about to go face
to face with his best friend who betrayed him for money, and
there were four police cruisers between him and saving the
President of the United States. There was a *pretty* good
chance he was *not* going to *have a good one.* The taxi pulled
away, and David glanced up the street. He crouched down
and pretended to tie his shoe. Casually he looked up at the
parking lot. The three cars were still bunched together. The
fourth was reaching the far end of the lot and turning back
toward him. *How would Alex get in?* There was no way he
could go through the front gate. If he was in there, he must
have found another entrance, or scaled the fence. David
starting walking up the road. There had to be a spot where he
could get through. *--I hope the fence isn't electrified.* A siren
went off behind him; he twisted around.

Lights were flashing on the patrolling car as it pulled
out of the lot with two of the other cars close behind. They

headed off toward the airport, leaving one car at the gate. David squinted. It looked like there was only one officer in the car. *Maybe the Secret Service found out about the plot and called for backup?* The door to the police car opened, David leapt behind a postal box. He gritted his teeth. *Oh YEAH! How suspicious was THAT?* He looked up at the sky. *How you chose ME for this I will NEVER understand!* He stole a quick look around the mailbox. The officer apparently hadn't noticed him and was now on the other side of the fence-- heading toward the hangar! Frantically David looked around, traffic was heavy on the road, but the parking lot was clear.

He scrambled to his feet and bolted across the lot. The cruiser was empty, and the officer had disappeared. He looked over his shoulder as he approached the padlocked gate. Casually he reached out and pulled on the lock. It came loose and the gate swung open. He grabbed it, slipped through, and replaced the lock.

Did the cop go inside? There were no windows on the front so he couldn't see in. *He could be circling around the back.* David scooted across to the building. He carefully turned the doorknob. His heart throbbed in his chest as the door swung open. *What am I supposed to do?* There was no time for second guessing. He had to make a decision. Enter or don't. He looked around, then peered into the building. Still no sign of the officer. He eased in and closed the door behind him.

It was a small lobby lit by a single florescent lamp over the entrance. The room had the appearance of a repair shop waiting room, with a sealed receptionist window across from a magazine covered coffee table and a tattered couch. On the far end in the center of a wall littered with OSHA approved literature, was a metal door, and at head level, a tiny plexiglass window. A dim light flickered in the room beyond.

Did he go in there?

David crossed the room and listened at the door; there was a faint scuffling. He quickly poked his head up and stole a glance through the small dirty window. The officer was standing beside a set of wooden boxes shining a flashlight on the side of one of them. David took a deep breath, then slowly raised his head to the window again. The officer brought the beam up and scanned the dark interior of the hangar. David ducked as the beam shined out through the plexiglass.

Where's Alex? His heart pounded. At any minute a gunshot was going to ring out from a dark corner of the hangar and the officer was going to go down. But all was silent. *Is he waiting for the officer to move on? He can't wait long.* David's heart pounded harder as he looked again through the window. The officer had laid the flashlight down and was prying one of the boxes open with a crowbar.

This is it! If Alex was watching, he would *not* allow this man to interfere. *I HAVE to warn him! I CAN'T just sit here and watch him get killed!* Frantically, David looked around the dimly lit room. Nothing spoke to him-- and there wasn't time anyway. He *had* to warn the officer. With a trembling hand, he gripped the doorknob and pulled in a deep breath. *I have to do this. God help me!* He peered through the window one last time before twisting the knob, but what he saw made him freeze in place. His hand recoiled. The cop had turned, the light was now showing clearly on his face. David stepped back from the door in horror. *Alex!* The officer *was* Alex.

He had spoken of powerful friends. They must have orchestrated everything. All the pieces were in place. He had

315

the identity, the parts to the bomb-- an abandoned hangar. The light shined again through the window; David's heart quickened. Footsteps came closer. There was a clanking sound. Was he coming out? The footsteps stopped. Scuffling. The footsteps retreated.

David popped his head up over the lip of the window. He was back at the boxes. He had left his hat, shirt, and utility belt on a metal table near the door. David eyed the belt. *If I can get to his gun without him hearing...*

Impossible! It's too quiet.

His mind raced. *Now WHAT?* He peered through the window, watching as Alex continued to work, his breath steaming up the glass. *I just need to be patient. Maybe a plane will go over, then I can open the door without him hearing.* He cocked his head. Nothing. He crouched beside the door. *What if no planes go over? What then? What if...* The muffled sound of an engine starting up seeped under the door. He stood. Alex was sitting on a tractor attached to a luggage cart. He was looking the other way.

David grabbed the doorknob, slid into the room, and crawled along the cement floor to the metal table. He reached up and grabbed the gun from its holster.

Immediately, the truck engine shut down. "You just don't give up, do you?" Alex climbed down and headed around the boxes.

David pointed the gun at his friend. "It's over." His voice shook. "I'm not going to allow you to take innocent lives."

"You really think you can shoot me?"

The pistol trembled in David's hands. "I'm not the same man I was two days ago, Alex. If you think I'm not capable, think again. I'm *not* going to let you hurt anyone."

"So, you would kill *me* to save the lives of *others?*"

"Whatever it takes to stop you."

He chuckled. "Do you see the irony here? We're no different."

"I'm nothing like you."

"Do you think the people on Air Force One are *innocent?* They're *not!* They may not go out and kill people personally, but there's still blood on their hands. *They* make decisions and people *die.* If I kill *them,* they cannot send soldiers to die in the war." He looked David in the eye. "Soldiers like *Brandon. Those* people make decisions," he said pointing out the doors, "and *good* people die!"

David's hands shook. "Two wrongs don't make a right."

Alex squinted. "I don't have time for this. Sometimes we make hard decisions for the greater good." He shook his head. "That's why I didn't let you in on this. I knew you wouldn't understand."

"Don't try to make yourself sound *noble.* You're in it for the *money."*

"Yes! I am in it for the money! You got me. I want *out* of this life. I want to have a family, settle down. I'm sick of the killing. But I'm trying to tell you something! I have spent the last fifteen years trying to make this world a better place. I've paid my dues. I've made my sacrifices. And I want *out.* I want to live the life of freedom and happiness I have been fighting for all these years."

David stood in shock. "You've been doing this-- for *years?"*

"I make the world a better place."

David's mouth hung open. "By *killing people?"*

"By *stopping* people from killing."

"You don't even *know* who's on that plane! You have no *idea* who you're killing!" He held the gun tighter.

317

"They're all responsible."

"*Who* makes that decision? Who chooses who lives and who dies?

"Thankfully, not me."

"No? You only *execute* the act. I don't care how you paint it, you're a murderer."

"I said I don't have time for this." Alex stepped toward him.

"I won't let you do this!"

"You don't have a *choice*, David! I don't *need* your consent." He waved his hand in disgust. "You know what. Forget it. Just shoot me if you want. I don't care anymore." He turned and started loading the bomb onto the luggage carts.

David emphasized his aim. "Stop, or I swear I'll put a bullet in your leg!"

"I'm done talking to you, David."

David pulled the hammer back. "Don't make me do this."

Alex ignored him.

There was no other course of action. He was backed into a corner. David aimed carefully and squeezed the trigger. The sound exploded off every metal surface in the room. But nothing came out of the barrel.

Alex jumped to his feet. "I don't believe it! You would actually shoot me!"

David looked at the smoking gun, trying to understand what had happened.

Alex strutted toward him. "Confused? That's the gun Afif used to shoot me at my house. It still has *blanks* in it." His voiced dripped with irony.

"Why would you still..."

Alex ripped the pistol from David's hands and shoved

him backwards; his eyes were fierce. "This is going to hurt you more than it'll hurt me!" He snapped a kick into David shin; the pain forced him into a hunch. Alex, anticipating the reaction, moved in and drove a knee up into David's chest, forcing him back. He tried to block, but it was useless. Alex had years of combat experience and several medals of accommodation for excellence. He controlled every move like an expert pool player setting up his next shot. Two jabs in quick succession put David's head in a spin. And he didn't see the leg sweep coming. His back slammed hard onto the concrete floor, knocking the wind out of him.

The last thing he saw was the pistol handle hovering in the air above him. Then the world went dark. Again.

It began as a low buzz, like an insect circling the room, growing steadily till the sound filled his head. And with the sound, came the pain. An enormous amount of pain. And David could not determine if the sound *was* the source of the pain. A voice spoke, but whether it came from inside or outside his body, he did not know. But he couldn't resist it; the authority could not be denied.

It spoke again. *David! Get up!*

His eyes opened to slits, the expanse of the hangar ceiling shimmered above him. Gradually the sound of the buzzing became the sound of an engine. He turned and tried to roll over. *The tractor, it's still here.* David, pushing through the pain, got to his knees, the urgency of the voice still ringing in his mind.

Alex was driving toward the open hangar bay doors.

David's heart jumped, a yelp of desperation came from his lips. "STOP!" Alex turned back with a weary expression, but the cart continued forward. "Don't do this!" Alex wasn't listening. David's eyes fell upon the pistol lying on the ground.

And he remembered.

The bullet! The one he'd picked up at the hostage house! Trembling violently, he scrambled onto his knees, picked up the pistol, and fumbled in his pocket. It was still there! Relief and dread struck him simultaneously. Relief that the bullet was still there; dread, because he was going to have to use it. He slid the bullet into a chamber, it fit perfectly. He peered back up at the tractor.

This is it. There's no turning back.

"Alex!" David stood on shaky legs. "The messages told me to pick up a live round!"

The cart came to a stop, the engine slipped into idle. Alex twisted in the seat and looked back, his face clearly displaying the bitterness he felt. "Do I need to *remind* you that I have your wife and children?"

The words stabbed at David's heart. "You wouldn't hurt them."

"*I* wouldn't be the one hurting them. *You* would!"

David tried to wrap his mind around the words.

"Your *family* is with Afif. If you kill *me,* David, and I don't return, he'll have no further use for them. Your actions *here* will determine whether they live or die. That's how it works. We make choices, and those choices go beyond the moment. If you kill one person, three could die. If I kill a plane full of people, *hundreds* could live." He turned in his seat. The engine sound filled the hangar again.

"NO!" David screamed. But the cart continued to move away. In the distance, the roar of a jet engine grew louder. He needed more time to think this through. There *had* to be something he could say to Alex to stop him. But what if he didn't stop? He gripped the gun and squeezed his eyes tightly. *I need to know-- will you protect my family? Please!* He looked around frantically. From the few sources of text in the hangar, nothing spoke to him. The words were silent. *How can you NOT answer? I've done everything! Everything you've asked!* His hands wobbled as he sighted in on Alex's shrinking form. *I can't do this! I CAN'T do this! He's my BEST FRIEND!*

In seconds he would be too far away.

MY FAMILY! He tried to focus on the moving luggage

cart. *Please don't let Alex die. Please!* He reemphasized his grip. Heart pounding. Eye blurring. There was no more time. The message said, *Stop him.* He *had* to trust the words; they had never let him down before.

CRAACK!!!

The sound reverberated through the hollow hangar.

Alex slumped over and the cart came to a stop.

David stood staring, slowly allowing the weight of the pistol to draw his arms down. The release of adrenaline had left him numb. In the enormous cavern of the hangar bay, he floated in the reverberating echo. As it diminished, he felt as though it was he who was diminishing, growing smaller with each faint pulse. The distant figure remained motionless as the roar of the jet engine came closer. Through a river of tears, through the open bay doors, Air Force One taxied into view. David sank to his knees. The pistol fell to the cement with a sharp click. It was over. He had done what the words said. He had saved the President. But at what cost? He stared at the still figure in the distance, a sharp pain pierced his heart.

He closed his eyes. *"Please speak to me,"* he whispered, chin quivering. *"Will my family be safe?"* Opening his eyes, his gaze fell on a paper lying near him on the ground, an old campaign flyer. On it were the words: Vote *YES* on Question One. A flood of tears came as the familiar feeling of confirmation washed over him. It said *YES.* His family would be safe.

God's answer had been there all along.

God, had been there, all along.

"We interrupt this program to bring you a special report."

"Hello, I'm Cindy Coulter reporting from Channel Seven News. Authorities converged this afternoon on the home of Alex Blackstone, an ex-Navy Seal who, police say, is allegedly the mastermind behind the Boston Bomb Threat. We go live now to Karen Watson on location. Hi Karen, tell us what it looks like there on the ground."

"Thank you, Cindy. This morning, in a startling turn of events, police acting on an anonymous tip raided this residential Marlboro home and took into custody Afif Al-Qadir, the man who is considered to be the financier for the terrorist cell operating in the Boston area. Also uncovered were Jerry Cook, his sister, and her two children, who were being held hostage in the basement of the home. Jerry Cook, a Harvard Chemist, and as we reported yesterday, considered to be the creator of the terrorist bomb, was exonerated today from all wrong doing. Authorities inform us that Mr. Cook had been working closely with them from the beginning of their investigation, and that he took part in the undercover sting operation which ultimately thwarted the terrorist plot. Afif Al-Qadir is believed to be the last of the Arab terrorists operating in the Boston area, but Alex Blackstone is still at large. However, authorities are working on leads and feel confident they will soon have him in custody as well."

Cindy came back on the screen. "It's certainly been a grim two days here in the greater Boston area. It's good to know Homeland Security is on the job."

"Yes, Cindy. It sure is. There is one person, however, I would like to thank personally. While authorities conducted their investigation, he was working behind the scenes, risking everything, to follow a series of mysterious prophetic messages which helped law enforcement seize the Ace Wrecking Company, and then ultimately led him to disarm the second bomb. David, if you're watching. Thank you on behalf of a grateful city. Thank you for trusting. Thank you for not giving up.

"Now back to you, Cindy."

~Author's Note~

Messages is a work of fictional allegory, that means it's not meant to be taken as fact. If you think God is sending you message through your plants, your lava lamp, or your neighbor's dog, you may want to get that checked out. That's all I'm going to say about that.

If you want to read some *non-fiction* accounts of how God interacts with us, try **Maine Miracles.** My wife and editor, Joanie Hileman, has compiled thirty-two true stories of God's miraculous intervention.

If you would like more mind-bending fiction from yours truly, you might try my first novel:
VRIN: ten mortal gods

If you would like to know when my next book is coming out, you can email me at:

johnhileman@gmail.com

or visit my blog: mystery-novel.blogspot.com

CPSIA information can be obtained at www.ICGtesting.com
Printed in the USA
LVOW07s0503150415

434580LV00002B/6/P